W9-CNA-208

Murkmere

Murkmere

by Patricia Elliott

 LITTLE, BROWN AND COMPANY

New York ᧞ Boston

Copyright © 2006 by Patricia Elliott

All rights reserved.

Little, Brown and Company

Time Warner Book Group
1271 Avenue of the Americas, New York, NY 10020
Visit our Web site at www.lb-teens.com

First U.S. Edition: February 2006
First published in Great Britain in 2004 by Hodder Children's Books

The characters and events portrayed in this book are fictitious. Any similarity to real persons, living or dead, is coincidental and not intended by the author.

The superstitions in this novel are found in British folklore.

Library of Congress Cataloging-in-Publication Data

Elliott, Patricia, 1946–
  Murkmere / by Patricia Elliott. — 1st U.S. ed.
    p. cm.
  Summary: A village girl, newly companion to the Master's ward in the days following the Ministration, challenges the motives of the religious leaders of the Divine Beings, the birds.
  ISBN 0-316-01042-1
  [1. Fantasy.] I. Title.
PZ7.E4578Mu 2005
[Fic] — dc22   2004022703

10   9   8   7   6   5   4   3   2   1
Q-FF
Printed in the United States of America

The text was set in Carre Noir, and the display type is ITC Blackadder.

For my nieces, Charlotte, Vanessa, Samantha, and Gerry, because I hope this is your sort of story, and to the memory of my mother

✌

With thanks to Chris Powling and Bob Hull for their encouragement when this novel was first conceived

*P*erhaps there is a Leah at some time in everyone's life: unpredictable, demanding, most generous best friend, cruelest enemy.

But the Leah in this story came later. When I first began thinking about *Murkmere*, it was because I had a single vivid image in my mind, and had to make sense of it. Meanwhile, I'd often driven past Murkmere Hall on the A12 in Suffolk. It hadn't become Murkmere to me then, but was a vast slab of a house set in lumpy parkland. I imagined a girl wandering beneath the dark oak trees — a girl, half-wild, shut away and bored, who was waiting for her story to begin.

The girl became Leah, and Leah's story begins when Aggie comes to Murkmere.

— *Patricia Elliott*

PART ONE

The Watchtower

I

The Rooks' Omen

louds hang low in the sky where I live. They seem to touch the flat brown fields around our village, and to shadow the broad backs of the horses pulling the plow. They drift across the wide sky like swans' feathers.

There were swans on the mere when I first went to Murkmere Hall, the first time I met Leah. There are still swans there today, but everything else has changed. All I knew then was what I saw around me: the village, the fields, and, behind its iron gates on the Wasteland road, the great shadowy expanse of the Murkmere estate. In those days I knew nothing of corruption and betrayal, and the evil of ambitious men.

But you can't wipe away the past like chalk from a slate. I can never be that innocent girl again. I am someone else now.

The year had only recently turned when I rode in Jethro's wagon to take up my new position at Murkmere Hall, and though the mist wasn't drifting in from the sea that morning, it was bitterly cold. As the wagon jerked over the frozen ruts in the road, the Wasteland on either side of us was thickly spread with a gray frost, the leafless trees glistening like sucked bones.

"Will you wish me luck, Jethro?" I said, trying to steady myself against a pile of sacks, while the bag that contained my few spare clothes rolled softly against me.

From my position high up in the wagon, I could see only the back of Jethro's curly head, and I studied it anxiously, waiting. It always took a long time for him to speak. Jethro Sim, our neighbor's son, was a boy who chose his words carefully.

Jethro didn't turn from leading Tansy, though the reins lay slack in his hands. The old mare blew warm clouds of mist around him; little puffs rose each time she placed her heavy hooves on the frozen road.

"Murkmere's no place for you, Aggie. You shouldn't be going."

"I've no choice, and you know that," I said, provoked. Who was Jethro to say what I should do? He was only a few years older than I. "It's the Master's command. Besides, my mother fared well enough at Murkmere when she was lady's maid there long ago. So shall I."

Then excitement got the better of me. I leaned forward, so I could see Jethro's profile. He was scowling.

"Aren't you pleased for me at all, Jethro?" I said, trying to coax a smile from him. "Think of all the things I'll learn, the clothes I'll wear! I'm to be a companion, not a servant."

"Aye, to the Master's ward," he retorted. "A lunatic girl. They say Mr. Tunstall hides her away deliberately."

"Oh, gossip! I've heard that too," I said. "I don't see why Murkmere should be a bad place. Why, you've never been inside the gates!"

"I have indeed. I was once late with my dues and took them in myself. I had to give them to the steward, Silas Seed. I saw . . . enough."

Words died between us. I slumped back against the sacks, clutching the sides of the wagon with numb fingers as it swayed on. Ahead, the walls of the Murkmere estate smudged the horizon.

I didn't remember my parents. Since their death from the spitting sickness when I was three, I'd lived with my Aunt Jennet. I'd always thought I'd have to spend my life at the spinning wheel as the other village girls did after leaving school. I loathed spinning with a deep and awful loathing, and knew my clumsy fingers would never support my aunt and me. Now the Master of Murkmere had offered me the opportunity to escape a spinster's life, and my wages would keep us both. All my childhood I'd longed to know more about Murkmere Hall, where my mother had worked before she'd married. I thought if I knew more about Murkmere, I'd know more about my mother.

Why, then, did I feel such dread now?

The high walls of the estate loomed on our left. Jethro halted Tansy before the gates, and came to lift me down as the mare stood blowing placidly.

"Careful, Aggie! You'll spoil your finery!"

I couldn't tell whether Jethro was teasing me or not. He always looked serious, did Jethro, but sometimes his eyes had a smile hiding in them as if he laughed secretly at me.

I knew I looked ridiculous now. Aunt Jennet had done my hair herself, in her anxiety braiding the springing copper clumps of it so tightly that it pulled my eyebrows up in surprise under my hat. Beneath my cloak, the bodice of my ancient best dress was tight as a sausage skin, and I'd so many layers on against the cold I was sure I looked as fat as one as well. I was fifteen years old and bursting out in all directions, except upward. Maybe that was why Jethro still treated me like a child, though he hadn't been grown to a man long himself, for all his new beard and solemn air.

I was sick to my belly with fear as he set me down. "Jethro," I wailed. "The birds have given me no signs. They hide away in this cold. I can't tell what's to become of me, whether it be bad or good."

My life, like the lives of everyone else, was bound by watching the signs. It was the birds that gave us the signs, the birds that showed us what was to come, for each bird had its own significance. But in the dead heart of winter few birds are active. They might have flown away entirely from the bare face of the earth, so deathly silent was the land.

Jethro set my hat straight as he might a small girl's, and his brown eyes looked into mine, bright as a robin's. "You have nothing to fear if you wear your amulet, Aggie." As he spoke he touched his own amulet, a simple bunch of dried rosemary sticking from the pocket of his old tweed jacket.

I felt feverishly round my neck for the strip of leather; the golden amber that hung from it, warm from lying against my skin, slotted smoothly into my palm like a new-laid egg. It had been my mother's once, but she had no need of protection now. It was only the living whose souls were in danger from the Birds of Night.

Jethro looked awkward. "I should go, Aggie. I've no desire to meet Silas Seed again."

Silas Seed, the steward of Murkmere, had come to the village himself a fortnight ago to search me out and give me the Master's message. I'd thought him an exceedingly handsome young man when I met him, but I thought it best not to let Jethro know this.

I nodded, biting my lip now that the moment had come to say goodbye, and drawing my thin red cloak around me. "Watch over Aunt Jennet for me, Jethro. Don't let her do too much."

"Can't stop her," he grunted, but I knew he'd milk our cow himself and carry the pail to our cottage.

The mention of my aunt nearly had me in tears. "Thank you for bringing me here," I said stiffly, turning my face away.

Jethro didn't reply, and next I heard the jingle of the harness and the clomp of Tansy's hooves on the hard ground as she began to move away. When I turned at last, the wagon had blurred with the horizon.

Beyond the gates a straight drive, as rutted as the road, ran over flat, lumpy parkland until it reached the gray stone bulk of the Hall in the distance. Among the forest of chimneys few were smoking; below them were rows of shuttered windows. Huge oaks shadowed the empty grass before the house, their bare branches scratching at the lowering sky.

A frightened homesickness caught in my throat. I thought of our two-room cottage, cramped and dark, but cozy under its thatch and furnished with Aunt Jennet's treasured possessions; and of the common nearby, busy with villagers and their animals. Now I was alone, completely alone, for the first time in my life, and the thick silence of mid-winter was all around me.

But this was my chance, and I had to take it.

There was a rusty bell hanging by one of the gateposts; a frayed rope trailed down, furled with ivy. Perhaps if I pulled it, a servant — a footman, perhaps — would come and open the gates for me. I straightened my back, plumped out my skirts, and gave a determined tug.

The jangle from the bell was unexpectedly loud and harsh in the silence, and it awoke a raucous echo: the cawing of what seemed to be hundreds of rooks. In the distance I saw an undulating black cloud rise above the cluster of beeches that must hold their nest-homes. My head full of the clamor, I sank trembling against the gatepost and clutched my amber as if my life depended on it. I knew the deadly significance of rooks. Everyone did.

"Miss Agnes, Agnes Cotter. You're welcome to Murkmere. But you look as white as bleached bed linen. Are we such ogres here?"

A man's voice roused me. It was a charming voice, the vowels musical and the tone full of concern. I'd heard it before. It was the voice of Silas Seed.

"I'm well, Sir," I moaned, my head down. "But I can't come through. The rooks have given me the sign. Death is waiting if I step inside the gates!"

Calmly, Silas Seed took off his glove and unlocked the gate with a key from his waistcoat pocket. Then he put his hand out to me. It was a white hand, very clean, the nails manicured to show the half-moons, the fingers long and elegant. My head still bent, I hid my own stubby, rough ones in my skirt. Peering under my lashes, I saw another pair of legs, this one clad in darned breeches, standing next to Silas's gleaming boots.

"Come now, Miss Agnes," Silas Seed said gently. "Don't you remember that rooks nesting near a house are a sign of Good Fortune?"

"Well, yes," I admitted, confused. That was a sign as well. I thought I knew the *Table of Significance* so well, yet sometimes it appeared to contradict itself.

"Come on through, then, without a care," said the steward. "The rooks here signify no ill omen. Why do you think I walk so freely?"

I dared look up at him. Silas Seed was a good head taller

than Jethro, taller than all the village boys, and taller than the keeper who stood dourly at his side, not looking at either of us.

"You've a fine amulet, Sir, that's why!" I muttered. I could see it nestling round his throat, a whole string of glowing amber stones above the silk cravat.

Silas Seed's dark eyes lit with amusement. "Then if you stay close by me, you've nothing to fear! I beg you come with me, Miss Agnes, for I'm sure you've turned to ice. You're earlier than I expected. I'd not posted anyone to watch for you at the gates. A good thing we were doing the morning rounds and saw you." He nodded to the keeper to pick up my bundle of belongings, and his hand remained outstretched. "I have asked the housekeeper to organize hot food for you in the kitchen. Come."

It seemed a long time since I'd had breakfast in the early morning darkness. And the bread had been stale again, with only boiled rosemary water to moisten it, for yesterday's milk was finished and we dared not milk our cow till daybreak for fear of the Night Birds.

I looked up again at the steward, at his finely drawn features and smooth-shaven jaw, his black hair glossy as a blackbird's wing beneath the three-cornered hat. I thought I caught admiration in his eyes as he looked back at me. A handsome young gentleman who did not see me as a child.

I put my hand into his at last and let him lead me through the gates.

❧

"You've never been to Murkmere before?" he said. The frosty weeds in the holes of the drive bobbed as his fur-lined cloak swept over them; puddles crackled under our boots. "Then you won't have seen the mere that gives the Hall its name. Look — there."

I saw beyond a stretch of frozen sedge, the pale sheen of ice. My first sight of the mere. I knew it immediately as a fearful, desolate place.

"Is the water deep beneath the ice, Sir?" I asked timidly.

"Some say it's bottomless, that the water turns black a little way down." He paused, and added somberly, "A maid drowned in it a year back. When she was brought out by one of the keepers, her body was full bloated with black water."

I was struck dumb. It was then that I saw someone standing motionless on the far shore, a pale figure against the dark reeds, too slight to be a man. I thought it must be the spirit of the drowned maid, and I gasped.

Silas Seed followed my gaze and frowned. "It's Miss Leah, the Master's ward, out again, alone. She shouldn't be there without her maid."

"But what's she doing?"

"We've swans on the mere. She likes to go there by herself to watch for them. A foolish thing to do when the mere's all ice. I must send a footman out to her."

He moved on quickly, the keeper tramping after him, expressionless as ever. I hesitated a moment, straining my eyes to pick out the girl's features. But even as I did so, the ghostly figure dissolved into the overgrown scrub and was gone.

In the main kitchen of Murkmere Hall a woman was standing at one side of the huge chimney, lifting her skirts to the blaze of the fire. As we came in she hastily rearranged her clothing, and the keys at her lumpen waist jangled with agitation.

"Oh, Mr. Silas. I wasn't expecting you to bring . . ." She gestured at me with a flustered hand. "I'd thought Doggett . . ."

"Doggett should be accompanying Miss Leah, Mistress Crumplin," said Silas Seed coldly, "but I see that once again Miss Leah is alone by the mere in this icy weather. I've spoken to Doggett about the danger before. It mustn't happen again, Mistress Crumplin, do you understand?"

"Yes, Mr. Silas," whined the woman. "But Miss Leah is like quicksilver. You've only to glance away and the girl is gone. Why she should want to escape outside in this weather, I don't know."

"Escape?" said Silas, and he laughed, his dark eyes on me as if we shared the joke. "You make her sound like a prisoner, Mistress Crumplin!"

I scarcely listened, still breathless from keeping up with the steward's long stride through archways, courtyards, and stable yard. I was looking at a little girl, standing almost in the hearth on the other side of the fire, who was turning a spit with great effort, her cheeks scarlet with heat. As the joint turned, the sides of the meat were glossy and brown in the firelight and the juices dripped down into a pan. I caught the dense, sweet fragrance of the meat and for a moment I thought I'd faint.

I felt Silas Seed take my arm. My vision cleared. The housekeeper was staring at me. I took in a plump, creased face, wisps of gray hair escaping beneath a cap. The steward pressed my arm, pushing me forward a little.

"Forgive me, Agnes. Let me introduce Mistress Crumplin, housekeeper to the Hall. She will oversee your requirements here."

It sounded a very grand arrangement for a village girl. I looked up at the woman and tried to smile, but the housekeeper's pasty face was stolid and cold.

"And this is Miss Agnes Cotter, Mistress Crumplin," said Silas Seed. He paused, and then added with strange emphasis, or so it seemed to me, "Her mother, Eliza, worked here many years ago. No doubt you'll remember her, Mistress Crumplin?"

The housekeeper's mouth hung loose. She gave Silas Seed a startled glance, and out of the corner of my eye I saw him nod at her, as if confirming what he'd said. "Eliza, eh?" she said slowly. "I'd not realized that Miss Leah's companion was Eliza's daughter," and she came over and peered into my face.

As I looked eagerly back at her, searching for motherliness, for kindness and welcome, all I saw was suspicion and the tiny red veins branching on her nose. "Eliza's daughter?" she said sourly, stepping back. "You have no look of her."

A pang went through me. I'd heard my mother had been a

beauty. And from the housekeeper's tone she hadn't liked her. It seemed I'd hear no fond memories from Mistress Crumplin.

"I remember your mother too," said Silas Seed unexpectedly.

I looked at him in astonishment. "You were here so long ago?"

He smiled at my expression. "My father was steward before me, so as a child I lived on the estate. Yes, I remember your mother a little."

"Oh, Sir, what do you remember?"

He shook his head. "That she was kind to me, that's all. And the Mistress loved her, so I heard."

"Eliza married a thatcher afterwards, I believe," said Mistress Crumplin. I saw disdain crinkle the corners of her mouth, and lifted my chin.

"My father was *chief* thatcher of the area before he died, Ma'am."

"Both parents dead, then," she said without sympathy. "You're all alone."

'No, Ma'am, indeed not. My mother's elder sister lives with me, my Aunt Jennet. The cottage belongs to her. She was schoolmistress in the village until recently." My voice wobbled suddenly. Aunt Jennet had turned forty and her eyesight was failing. She'd been forced to give up her beloved profession, and I knew it pained her.

Silas Seed had left the room — to find a servant to fetch Miss Leah inside, I supposed — and now I was alone, with the housekeeper staring at me again. I dropped my eyes meekly, but inside I was indignant. Why should she give herself airs when her bodice was stained with old food and the lace on her cap was frayed and gray? Then I reproached myself. I'd noticed her unhealthy color and heavy breathing. Perhaps she was ill. But I was glad when she waved me away to sit at a trestle table under one of the small, deep-set windows.

"Stop that now, and give the Miss some food, as Mr. Silas ordered," she said roughly to the child at the spit, giving her a cuff for good measure. The poor little maid brought me some soup and bread and a cup of wine, as well as several slices of the meat on a pewter plate, as if she knew I was half-starved. She looked as if she didn't get enough to eat herself: the grubby dress hung loose on her tiny frame; even her shoes were ill-fitting, and she had to shuffle to keep them on. She was too frightened to respond to my grateful smile as she set down the food.

I'd never had so much to eat: in the winter food was scarce in the village. I was almost sorry when Mr. Silas reappeared.

"If you've finished, Miss Agnes, we'll go to the library now."

I swallowed hastily and nodded.

"Have word sent to the Master that we're waiting there for him, would you please, Mistress Crumplin?" he said to the housekeeper. Although I could sense that beneath his civility his displeasure with her still lurked, he beckoned me out with an encouraging smile.

The little maid scurried to clear the plates onto a tray,

almost spilling my cup of unfinished wine. I looked back awkwardly as I left, wondering if I should thank the house-keeper for my food.

The words died on my lips. With sudden energy Mistress Crumplin had leaned toward the maid, snatched the cup of wine from the tray, and was downing the remainder in one hearty swig.

II

Wounded Eagle

I'd glimpsed the Master on his few visits to the village, but all I'd seen was a pale face peering out from a high, black coach.

His name was Gilbert Tunstall, but in the village he was known as the Master. As a member of the Ministration, the most powerful authority in the land, the Master was our landlord and ruler; but he was a kind one, and never fined us when we were late with our dues. I wasn't nervous about meeting him. I knew he'd suffered the most terrible misfortunes years ago: widowed when young, then a crippling accident. Although his sister was married to the great Lord Protector in the Capital, I'd heard that nowadays he rarely traveled there to perform his duties as Minister, but shut himself away at Murkmere.

As we left the kitchen quarters and came to a grander part of the house, I saw dark stains on the silk wallpaper and on the rugs beneath my heavy boots. The drafts couldn't blow away the sour, chill smell of damp that clung to the passages of Murkmere Hall, though they made the flames in the sconces flicker and rip. But I was used to the dankness of the Eastern Edge, the sea murk that drifted into the corners of the cottages, and thought little of it. Murkmere was vaster and more magnificent than anything I'd ever known; I did not question, then, its creeping decay.

I had clumped after Silas Seed for an age, it seemed to me, when at last he held open a door and nodded for me to enter.

I went in before him, holding my breath; I'd never been in a library before. The only books I'd read in all my fifteen years were the readers I'd had at school in the village and Aunt Jennet's textbooks in the cottage, from which she'd sometimes taught us: dull, turgid tomes, dealing with politics, social welfare, and law. I was certain that at Murkmere I'd find thrilling stories about the past, vivid descriptions of seers' dreams, or even narratives that were entirely invented.

Though the library was filled with the harsh light of winter, it was an elegant room, paneled in the stippled gold of walnut. At the long bay windows hung thick curtains of green velvet, drawn back by silken loops to show curving window seats padded in the same velvet. A coal fire burned brightly in the grate and there were candles in ornate candelabra on the marble mantel. I scarcely noticed that the silver candelabra were dull, the rugs under my boots faded and dirty. All I took in was that the shelves that lined the room from floor to ceiling were completely empty.

"But, Sir, where are the books?"

"Mr. Tunstall had all his books removed some while ago," Silas Seed said absently. He traced a finger over the surface of a small bureau and looked at it, pursing his lips.

"But why, Sir?"

It must have burst out as a wail. He turned and considered me in silence for a moment, his dark head cocked, so that his hair fell forward in a gleaming curve. "You like books, Miss Agnes?"

"Oh, yes, Sir!" I couldn't help adding, "I'm the best reader in the village." Aunt Jennet had seen to that.

"Quite the scholar, then." I feared he made fun of me, but his expression was serious. "You know the Divine Questions and the Responses?"

"Of course, Sir. We're taught them in school."

"Name for me the Birds of Light, Agnes."

I flushed. Because I came from the village did he think me so ignorant that he had to ask the most fundamental of questions? "Robin, Wren, Swallow, Martin, Lark, Sir," I said stiffly. "They are the sacred ones, the five protectors of men, the guardians of light."

"I only ask because I like to be assured that my household is devout, Agnes," he said gently. "And the Birds of Night?"

"Crow, Raven, Jackdaw, Magpie, Owl," I whispered, and felt for my amber. "Don't ask me what they do, Sir. I can't speak it in this room. I've been well taught, you needn't fear."

His eyes watched my searching hand. "I'm sure of it, Agnes." He turned away to warm himself at the fire. "That's why I know you wouldn't like the Master's books."

My head was full of questions, but I didn't dare ask them. "Where are the books now, Sir?" I ventured at last.

"Mr. Tunstall has made a bookroom in the old watchtower outside. It suits him well enough. He tutors Miss Leah there each day now." He crooked a long finger. "Come and warm yourself, Agnes. It will take time before the Master joins us. As you've seen, the passages are long in Murkmere Hall."

I trod carefully to avoid snagging the rugs. "Could you tell me about Miss Leah, Sir?"

"You know she was a foundling, left here at the gates as a baby?"

I nodded.

"The Master took her in out of the kindness of his heart and made her his ward. A generous act, since he's childless. It means she'll have the good fortune to inherit his estate one day." His tone was oblique, so that I couldn't tell what he thought.

"I meant — what is she like, Sir?"

"A girl now, grown to much your age, I'd say." He was teasing me, his voice amused. His dark gaze slipped over me as I stood by him at the fireside. "She's taller than you but not so well formed."

I lowered my eyes, shyly. I'd never had a compliment before, and was unsure whether this was one. He was standing so close to me that I could smell the flower water he must bathe in, the dark, sweet fragrance of flowers at dusk, intensified by the warmth of the fire. I'd never smelt a man so clean, so fastidiously clean, so exotically scented.

"You have hair the same color as your mother's," he said softly. "You shouldn't be named Agnes at all, but for a bright little marigold, its petals opening with the sun."

Curling tendrils had sprung loose from my braids and I touched them wonderingly.

"Do you think you could do something for me, Agnes?" he said after a moment. "I'd like you to watch Leah and tell me anything that's strange in her behavior."

"Strange, Sir?"

At once I thought that Jethro and the village gossips must be right. The birds had flown away with Miss Leah's wits.

"I mean report anything odd that takes place. Stay with her. It will be your duty, anyway, as her companion." Silas Seed smiled ruefully. "Perhaps you'll be better at it than her maid, Doggett. If you have anything to tell me, you can find me in the steward's room. It's the Master's order, you understand, that no harm should befall his ward. After all, she'll inherit Murkmere one day."

"I understand," I said eagerly. "I'll do my best to protect her, Sir."

"Good girl." He said nothing more but gazed into the fire, frowning slightly.

I drew back, and shifted my weight from right leg to left and back again. I didn't like to ask more about Miss Leah. From his expression I thought he must be bored with having to wait about with a village girl, with only fifteen years to her, however bright her hair.

I was listening to the quiet crackle of logs in the grate and trying not to fidget, when I heard an extraordinary sound: a harsh, vibrant grinding as if every scythe on the estate were being sharpened at the same time. It was coming along the passage behind the closed door and growing louder. My hand flew to my mouth. For a moment I thought the floor, the very earth beneath it, was splitting apart.

Silas Seed went to the door and opened it, and something came rolling in.

I saw the great grinding iron wheels first, then the iron bars that caged the man inside, who stared between them like a creature confined. I saw the huge head, the massive shoulders. He'd been a big man before the accident, but now he had scarcely any legs at all. The powerful torso that sat so solidly on the seat of the wheelchair dwindled into little withered things that dangled above the floor. The shrunken feet were shod in boots a child might have worn.

In the village I'd seen bodies maimed by farming accidents and disease. I wasn't frightened of the Master's appearance. I stood quietly, caught in admiration of the way he maneuverd the chair across the room, using only the strength of his hands and arms. I heard Silas Seed say, "Miss Agnes Cotter, Mr. Tunstall," and remembered just in time to bob a curtsy.

The Master beckoned me closer.

I saw, looking down at his face, that he wasn't an old man as I'd expected, but of middle years, with a high color in his cheeks, and thick, dark hair, untouched by gray, tied back into a queue.

But there was something wounded about him that had nothing to do with his ravaged legs. His face was bitter, with a down-turned mouth, compressed and angry with the burden of pain. As I tried not to stare at the dreadful chair, I wondered why he'd allowed himself to be bound by straps of iron.

"Kneel," whispered Silas Seed. "You're at his level then."

I knelt, and the Master and I regarded each other. I felt a flush rise to my cheeks: I was unkempt, untidy, my hair awry.

But there was a lift to the Master's tight mouth. "You are as I expected, Agnes," he said. "Am I as you expected, I wonder?"

I shook my head, unsure how to answer.

"Surely they tell of the monster of Murkmere in the village?"

"I think — I think if they saw you as I do, they would pity you, Sir!" I stammered.

At that he turned his head away from me sharply, his voice full of contempt. "I don't deserve pity, Agnes Cotter."

I was appalled to have offended him. He'd surely send me away now. But after a dreadful silence during which I stared miserably at the dust in the cracks of the floorboards, he said more calmly, "Your mother had a soft heart too, Agnes. She was a loyal, brave girl, as I'm sure you are. She was very special to us — my late wife and me."

I nodded, heartily relieved but not trusting myself to speak again, though I longed to ask him more.

"It was another lifetime," he said, and his expression was sad for a moment. Then he stirred himself.

"And now Eliza's daughter is to be companion to my ward, Leah. You'll have your meals with her, walk with her, converse with her. She's your age or thereabouts, but a child still. She's lived here at Murkmere all her life. I've no children, as you know, so she's had a lonely upbringing."

He sat forward a little, against the bars of the chair, and his powerful hands tightened on the arms.

"On my death she'll inherit Murkmere and take my place in the Ministration, yet she knows nothing of ordinary life. It's high time she met a girl her own age." He studied me with a half-smile. "Daughter to Eliza and niece to a schoolmistress, eh?"

"My aunt's Chief Elder of the village as well, Sir," I said proudly, and I glanced over to see if Mr. Silas had heard.

The Master raised an eyebrow. "Indeed? Then I can't think anyone could be more suitable as my ward's companion."

"I'm happy you sent for me, Sir," I said politely, thinking I should respond.

Now the half-smile was a curl of the lip, no more. "Happy? I hope you remain so." Then he nodded curtly at the steward, who went over to the bureau and opened it, beckoning me over.

I rose to my feet, puzzled. Silas Seed took out a new-looking roll of pale cream parchment, which he spread open. Inside it was covered with black handwriting and he pointed to the only clear space, at the bottom.

"Sign here, please, Agnes."

Looking over and seeing my bewilderment, the Master said with a touch of impatience, "It's the contract of your employment. It sets out the agreement between us both. Silas will sign on my behalf." He wheeled his chair to the window and remained there, looking out at the gray afternoon, his back turned to us.

Silas Seed dipped a quill pen into the glass inkpot and offered it to me, his dark eyes steady on mine. *I would show him the fine hand I wrote in*, I thought, *prove that I really was a scholar*; and I quickly signed my name with a flourish.

Mr. Silas signed his own name, and wrote "for Gilbert Tunstall" beneath it, and then the date. He was left-handed and wrote surprisingly laboriously for a steward. He sprinkled sand over the wet signatures to blot them, and glanced quickly at the Master's back as if to reassure him it was done before lighting the little wax-burner.

I watched the tiny flame glow, then the swift movement of his fingers as he rolled the contract up again and dripped hot sealing wax on the overlap. The silver seal came down on the shining, dark red globule and the sharp outline of the Eagle appeared suddenly, wings outstretched for flight.

The Eagle was the emblem of the Ministration. With a thrill of awe, I remembered that now I'd be working for one of its members.

There was a knock at the door, and the little maid who had served me in the kitchen shuffled in hesitantly at Mr. Silas's

"Enter." She dipped a bob to the Master's back and twisted her apron. "Please, Sir, Mistress Crumplin has sent me to take Miss Agnes to her room, if your business with her is done, Sir."

Silas Seed nodded; the Master of Murkmere appeared lost in his own thoughts. We left the men silent in the empty room and set off along the shadowy passages together.

"What's your name?" I asked her cheerfully, relieved my interview was over so soon.

She looked astonished that I should want to know. I saw that her cheeks were smudged with soot and tear stains. "They call me Scuff here, Miss," she whispered. "I don't know my real name."

"You don't come from the Eastern Edge, do you?"

"Oh, no, Miss. From the Capital, like all of us at Murkmere."

I'd hoped to meet a friendly face from the village somewhere in the vastness of the house, and was disappointed. But I wouldn't let my spirits sink.

"So, how did you come to work here, Scuff?" I asked curiously, for the Capital was several days' journey south.

"He came to the Orphans' Home a while back, Mr. Silas did." I had to bend down to hear her. "He was lookin' for likely maidservants. I was cheap, bein' so small, so he bought me. We only had numbers there, no names." With a sudden burst of confidence she pulled up her sleeve and showed me the number branded on her narrow forearm: 102, now a faded scar.

Pity stirred inside me. "So you're an orphan like me," I said. Scuff looked up at me, and a surprised smile brightened her pinched face.

When we found the bedchamber at last, she insisted on lighting the fire in the small grate for me. The room was even colder than the passages, and fusty, as if no one had slept in it for a long while. Then she offered to unpack my bundle, which had been put on the bed with my cloak.

I laughed, and she looked almost shocked at the sound. "It's most kind of you, but I couldn't possibly sit by while you did it. Tell me one thing instead, Scuff."

"Yes, Miss Agnes?"

"Aggie is quite enough, but tell me — why has the Master imprisoned himself in his chair in that way?"

She looked more pinched still, and her eyes grew frightened. "I don't know, but we shouldn't speak of it, Miss Aggie!"

"Why ever not?"

But I'd lost her confidence. She looked helplessly at me, hesitated, then almost tripped over her big shoes in her haste to leave the room.

I wandered around after she'd left, gazing at the furniture: the bedside table on which sat a porcelain candleholder, the washstand and blue-patterned bowl, the pair of stuffed chairs covered with crimson-striped satin, the walnut dressing table. I caught sight of my face in the looking glass and saw my round eyes. There were yellow silk curtains at the windows, and matching curtains hanging around the bed, while under it sat the grandest chamber pot I'd ever seen, made of flowered china with a copper lid. I thought of the straw pallet I shared with my aunt back at the cottage, in the cramped room under the eaves. If only Aunt Jennet could share all this with me!

But I was alone.

I unpacked my old skirt and bodice, my two shifts, my slippers. I put them at one lonely end of the big mahogany wardrobe. I went over to the window and stood looking out without seeing. I wondered what to do next.

Without thinking, I'd pulled my amulet from my bodice. It had come down to my mother through ancestors who'd lived on the coast. As I held the amber stone, I imagined the gray seas that had shaped it before finally throwing it up onto the shingle beaches of the Eastern Edge. I'd never seen the sea, though it was only a morning's walk away. Inlanders didn't approve of the coast people; they weren't devout nowadays, so I'd heard. But the amber was good protection against the Night Birds, the very strongest.

I opened the window and leaned out. The room was at the back of the house, overlooking the stable yard; beyond the stables I could see a coach house, dairies, the old leaning walls of a kitchen garden. I was looking for the watchtower where the Master kept his books, but couldn't see it, only scrubby meadows stretching into the misty distance, their flatness broken by sheep pens and cowsheds and workers' cottages.

I was fastening the latch on the window again when the door burst open and a girl marched in.

"If you think you're to be my companion, you're mistaken," she announced. "You might as well pack up your things again and go home."

She could only be Miss Leah.

III

Forbidden

She was a tall, gawky thing, with fair, almost white hair, like cotton on a spindle, and so fine and light it blew round her head with every movement she made. Her front was as flat as a wooden board, and her skirts, for all their delicate stitching and costly material, hung round her in a sadly limp manner.

"Are you deaf? I said you could leave."

I thrust my amulet back into my bodice and raised my chin. Unfortunately, she was at least a head taller and could look down her long nose at me.

"It was the Master who engaged me," I said, gathering my wits. "Is it the Master who orders me to go now?"

"It's my own wish," she snapped, tossing her head so her hair flew. "My guardian will do as I say, you'll see. I've Doggett, my maid. I don't need anyone else."

I took a chance. "If the Master agrees with you, I'll go," I said calmly. "Shall we go to him now, Miss?"

She gave me a long, hard look. "He's resting," she said shortly. "He always rests in the afternoon. I'll ask him at dinner." She looked around, as if suddenly distracted, and wrinkled her nose. "This was where my old nurse slept. It smells of her still." She glared at me again. "I've no need of another nurse either!"

"I'm to be your companion, not your nurse," I said, standing my ground. Aunt Jennet would have been amused at the idea. In spite of myself I smiled, and Leah looked fiercer than ever. Then, suddenly turning on her heel and sticking her head out of the open door, she bellowed "Doggett? Doggett?" in a most unladylike way.

We both waited, she eyeing me sideways and tapping her foot irritably on the floor. It was a large, ungainly foot, clad though it was in a fine velvet slipper. "We'll go out for a walk when Doggett comes," she said abruptly to me. "If you're to play my companion till dinnertime, you might as well come with us, I suppose."

I said nothing, but took my cloak from the wardrobe, glad to turn my back on her. I could still feel her staring at me, her eyes boring into me with intense curiosity. After Silas Seed's remarks, I was relieved that she appeared to have full use of her mental faculties. And more than enough of them too, for there was a disconcertingly intelligent gleam in her eyes when I faced her again.

"So — a girl from the village," she said slowly. "The village I'm not allowed to visit. What's your name, village maiden?"

"Agnes Cotter, Miss," I said, lifting my chin a little, for I wasn't going to forget my father had been chief thatcher. "But you may call me Aggie, if you wish."

She burst into loud laughter. I was staring at her, bemused, when there was a knocking on the bedroom door. "Come in, Doggett!" she yelled.

The maid was a sallow-faced girl of perhaps sixteen, with a pursed, prissy mouth as if she'd bitten into a crab apple, and small black eyes like beads.

"My maid, Dog," said Leah.

No wonder the maid looks so sour-faced, I thought.

We left the house through a door in the kitchen quarters. As we trailed across the stable yard, I turned to look up. The back of Murkmere Hall was as flat and featureless as the front, a slab of gray stone broken by long windows, mostly shuttered and dark. I'd noticed the creeper that covered the front. On this side too it clung to the cracks in the stone and spread leafless black tendrils in all directions; it even grew across a few of the upper windows.

The house that was now my home was imprisoned in a truss of dead, black bonds.

Leah set off across the parkland under the overcast sky, with the maid and me tagging behind, our breath puffing white.

"Where do you usually walk with the mistress?" I asked, keeping my voice low so Leah shouldn't hear.

Doggett shrugged, her face surly. "Nowhere particular. She walks for a bit all meek and mild, then she tries to give me the slip."

"What do you mean?"

"I mean, if she can, she'll go to the mere. She knows I won't follow her there."

"Why not?"

She shuddered. "It's bottomless, the mere, dug out of a marsh pool long ago. You'd drown if you fell in. She goes to see the swans aren't trapped in the ice. That's what she says."

"But swans have no need of our care," I said, puzzled. "Nor does any bird."

"Try that on the mistress! She don't give a fig for holy things."

"In the mornings when she has her lessons, do you walk with her to the watchtower?"

Doggett shook her head vehemently. "She goes with the Master. I'll not go near that blasphemous place."

I stared at her. But she'd quickened her pace to catch up with Leah, as if she didn't want to say anything more, and I had to hurry after them. It wasn't easy to walk fast: the grass was winter brown and the ground hard and lumpy with rock-like clods of mud.

Leah ignored me until she suddenly pointed with her gloved hand. "Look, there! Do you see it?"

"You mean the door in the wall, Miss Leah?"

We had reached the boundary of the Murkmere estate. A high stone wall ran as far as the eye could see, and in front of us, set into it, was a stout wooden door with iron keyholes top and bottom.

"It's locked. So are all the other doors and gates round the walls of Murkmere. And do you know why?"

"To keep out vagabonds from the Wasteland?"

Leah shook her head, and her pale hair under the black silk hat floated out like floss. "To keep me in. I'm a prisoner here!"

"Surely not, Miss."

At once she went over to the door and began to push and kick it, as if to prove to me that it was locked.

I looked at Doggett. Her little eyes slid to her mistress, then she drew me away, out of Leah's hearing, as if she were going to tell me something. The next moment we heard the sound of running feet on the hard ground, and in the distance the cawing of startled rooks.

We stared at each other and whirled round simultaneously. In the fading light, Leah was flitting away like a shadow.

"Quick!" I gasped. "We must run after her! Mr. Silas said not to let her alone!"

But Doggett stood there as if frozen, her face pasty with cold. "But she'll have gone to the mere again." She wrung her hands together. She wore no gloves, like me, and her dirty nails were bitten to the quick. "Oh, what'll I do? They'll skin me in the house if they find out!"

"I'll come to the mere with you," I said. "Between us we'll find her."

Doggett's face set stubbornly. "It's marsh all round and rushes sharp as spears. She knows the safe paths. Other folk could sink to their death in that mire."

"We must go and call her name at least," I said impatiently. "We can't abandon her! It'll be night before long, and she won't dare linger. Does she have her amulet with her?"

"Amulet?" said Dog. "She wears none." Her mouth twisted. "One day she'll pay for it, and good riddance, I say!"

I was alarmed. No wonder Leah required watching. There was no time to ask why she did such a dangerous thing as to walk unprotected.

"Then at least show me the way to the mere," I said. "I'll look for her myself."

Doggett's face was glazed and moony in the gathering dusk, but at last she turned sullenly.

It was starting to freeze. I was glad to be moving. But the sight of the mere, thickly lidded with ice, and the dense fringe of black rushes that grew up from the mud around it, chilled me further. There was a tiny island in the middle, a tangle of dark boughs hanging low. A profound silence hung over the water, as if every living creature had abandoned it to night.

Leah was nowhere to be seen.

"Miss Leah!" I shouted. "Miss Leah! Where are you?" My voice was tiny, sucked at once into the darkening clouds above us.

Dog touched my arm and made me start. "It's no good, Aggie. She'll be hiding somewhere. We'll never find her."

I stared across the lake, straining my eyes to see Leah's ghostly figure. Out on the ice the thin shadow of a bird, a heron, stood motionless against the sky.

I wasn't frightened, though I knew a heron's significance and touched my amber at once. There was a dignity about the heron as it stood alone in the dusk, an almost human quality. It looked like a gaunt old man waiting patiently for death.

Dog was agitated by my sudden distraction, anxious to leave the place. She stared at the heron in fear, and fingered the amulet of red wool around her neck. "Come, it'll be dark soon," she said, and pulled at me.

We made our way toward the house, across grass that had become powdery and soft with frost. The cold bit at our cheeks.

"You won't tell, will you?" she said. "I never tell."

"Tell what?" I said, startled out of my thoughts. In my mind, the sadness of the lonely heron and the memory of my aunt at our cottage doorway as she waved goodbye this morning had become mingled together. I felt a deep longing for home that made my heart ache.

"That we lost the mistress again," said Dog impatiently.

"But if she's not returned, we must say something," I said.

We had reached the stable yard, deserted and unlit by any lantern, silent but for the night sounds of the horses in the straw. I was making for the back entrance when Dog grasped my arm to stop me and my cloak fell back. I thought of her filthy chewed nails, which were digging into my flesh. I tried to thrust her away, but she hung on like a leech.

"Listen," she hissed. "If you want to stay, you'd do best to listen to me. Say nothing of Miss Leah's escape. If we slip upstairs unnoticed, no doubt we'll find her back already, pleased as punch with herself. That's the way it always is."

"But Mr. Silas —" I began.

She gripped me harder. "Mr. Silas will whip me if he knows what's happened."

"Surely not," I protested. "Mr. Silas is gentle and kind."

Her breath was sour in my face. "You think so? Promise me you'll stay silent?"

"I can't," I said, and thrust her away.

I hadn't meant to use such force, but my arms were strong from lugging milk pails from the common to our cottage each morning. She fell against the mounting block and must have bruised herself. When she got up, her look was malevolent.

"You know what a heron signifies, don't you?" she hissed. "The Comin' of a Stranger Who Brings Ill. The heron arrived today, and so did you!"

I said nothing, for I knew the *Table of Significance* as well as she, and what she said about the heron's meaning was true. And I realized I'd made an enemy in Doggett, something I hadn't intended and might well regret later.

We went in without speaking, and I followed her to Leah's bedchamber, which was in the same passage as my own.

Dog had been right: Leah was already there. Her fire was lit and the room bright with candlelight. She was pacing restlessly around as if it were a prison, her face stormy.

"Oh, Miss, where have you been?" cried Dog.

Leah paid her no attention. "My guardian wants to see you," she said abruptly to me. "He's staying in his bed for the rest of the day. I've just visited him."

"Is it another turn, Miss?" said Dog, all sweet solicitude. "I believe I know the cause." She stared at me spitefully.

"The cold's at his bones, that's all," Leah muttered. "He'll be warmer in bed."

"Should I go and see him now, Miss?" I said.

I knew from her manner that the Master and she must have disagreed about my staying, and that the Master had won the argument. But I felt no gladness, especially when she glared back at me and said with a kind of cold triumph, "Yes, go! If you're to stay as my companion, you'll suffer as I do — you'll be a prisoner too!"

Both girls were looking at me with identical expressions of dislike as I left. I had never felt so alone.

I found the Master's room by accident. I knew the room must be on the ground floor, but the passages were shadowy and deserted, though my boots echoed on the stone as if invisible people followed me.

Then I saw the iron chair.

It was standing beside a door, which I guessed must lead to the Master's room. Though the chair was empty, it still seemed to hold his presence. Each bar was locked to the framework of the chair and had its own keyhole. I felt a shudder go through me as I came up to it.

"What do you want here?" a voice said roughly.

My heart lurched. I hadn't seen him: a footman standing in the darkness, his face lugubrious.

"The M-Master wishes to see me," I stammered.

He knocked on the door. A woman's voice called, "Enter." The footman nodded at me, and I opened the door myself and went through.

The room seemed enormous to me, and very bright and warm and comfortable after the shadowy chill of the passage. There were armchairs covered in velvet and brocade set invitingly before the leaping fire, and rugs in jewel colors over the oak floor. On the walls, framed miniatures were hung together in a diamond pattern. Every polished surface displayed the pale luster of porcelain or the rich shine of lacquer.

A room in which to enjoy one's leisure, I thought, at first.

Then I saw the physic bottles ranged along the shelves of a mahogany medicine cabinet near me: enough to stock an apothecary's shop. Beyond the cabinet was a table on which a cluster of glass measures held the twinkle and gleam of silver medicine spoons.

It was an invalid's room, I realized, and smelled as much: the air was heavy with burning herbs and the bitterness of vinegar. But I'd not thought the Master was ill; I remembered his ruddy cheeks that morning.

I turned in bewilderment and saw the bed, a great oak four-poster, with curtains of crimson damask drawn back. With a shock I saw that the Master lay in it, his face as white as the pillows' frills, his eyes half-closed. I wasn't sure he was awake; indeed, he might well be dead. Frightened, I tried to tiptoe out again, cursing my boots.

"Miss Cotter?" said a brisk voice, making me jump. "Mr. Tunstall's been asking for you." An elderly woman, gray hair scraped beneath a starched white cap, was standing by the door to an antechamber and giving me a very inquisitive look.

Suddenly the Master's eyes opened and gleamed at me. "You can't escape so easily, Agnes Cotter. I'm infernally bored. Come and talk to me. You may leave us, Mistress."

The nurse gave a little bob and went into the other room, pulling the door behind her. I could see she hadn't quite closed it, though: there was a crack a finger's width. I went to the bedside and stood nervously, looking not at the Master but at the shining army of bottles. "I'm sorry you're feeling poorly, Sir."

"They fuss too much, all of them, forever pouring tinctures down my throat. Now tell me, how are you getting on with my ward?"

I hesitated, and saw a smile crinkle the corners of his tired mouth.

"Miss Leah wants me gone, Sir."

"But I don't wish you to go, Agnes. I believe you'll be just the thing for her."

"To protect her, Sir?"

His eyes narrowed. "I meant you would be good for her. Who's told you she needs protection?"

"Mr. Silas, Sir."

He relaxed back against the pillows. "Indeed, he's right. You must be her shadow, Agnes. I could give her a bodyguard, but she'd hate that. It's better that she has a young girl, a friend, her own age. You must counter her willfulness with good sense."

Aunt Jennet had never thought I had much of that. I nodded solemnly, nevertheless.

"She's my ward and heir to Murkmere, and there are those who'd be pleased to have her in their power."

I was startled. "What do you mean, Sir?"

He lowered his voice, glanced at the door. "I'm talking about kidnapping."

"Kidnapping?" I whispered. I thought of the soldiers of the Militia, who took young girls for their pleasure. But the Master hadn't meant soldiers, surely, but those who plotted against the Ministration.

"What about her moral danger, Sir? You know she doesn't wear an amulet?"

Something glinted in his eyes. "I'm concerned with her welfare here on Earth, Agnes. Morality is not much good to her if she's dead."

He seemed angry, and I was confused. Beneath my eyelashes I swiftly scanned the Master's form and saw no protection at neck or wrist, no amulet. What did that mean?

Perhaps he saw my distress, for he stretched up his arm and put his hand on mine as if to reassure me. I found it difficult not to recoil. His fingers were as cold as the grave, as if the Birds of Night already sucked at his soul.

"The contract binds you to be Leah's companion, Agnes, but friendship is a hundred times more valuable than the heavy words of contracts. Above all, I'd like you to be a friend to Leah."

"Yes, Sir," I said doubtfully.

He took his hand away. Though I was relieved to be free of its clammy pressure, I thought I'd disappointed him.

"You must tell Mistress Crumplin if there's anything you need," he said, sounding weary. "She'll explain everything, and provide you with clothes. You'll collect your wages weekly, like the servants, from the steward's room. Is there anything else you want to ask me before you go?"

The lines around his mouth were more marked this evening. But I had one urgent question.

"Can I return home for Devotion, Sir?"

"Devotion?" His eyes opened fully and stared at me. "My good steward is guardian of my servants' souls and takes a prayer meeting every evening. That will surely be enough devotion for you."

The Almighty was the guardian of men's souls, no other. But the Master's lip was curling: he'd meant it as a joke.

A lump of disappointment came into my throat. Soon I was due to read aloud from the Divine Book in the village Devotion Hall for the very first time. Now I would miss the honor and Aunt Jennet the reflected glory.

"But if I'm not to go to Devotion in the village, when may I see my aunt, Sir?"

"You must arrange that with Mr. Silas. He'll arrange for a man to ride with you along the Wasteland road."

At least I was not to be a prisoner as Leah had said. "But, Sir, I walk it alone always!"

"But now you work at Murkmere," he said patiently. "There are secrets, things men would like to know that they could learn from a companion to the Master's ward. We wouldn't want you to disappear suddenly, and then to find your body in a bog days later. I'm a Minister, Agnes, and have many enemies."

I stared at him in dismay. I'd begun to be contaminated by a dark world of which I knew nothing.

The anteroom door inched open again. "You'll have your free time when Leah takes her lessons," the Master remarked louder, watching it. "I hope you'll find enough to do."

For a moment I thought I'd not heard him correctly. "But won't I stay with Miss Leah while she's in the tower, Sir? Can't I sit with her in the bookroom?"

"So you've heard about the bookroom already, have you? But you'd be a distraction to her. Besides, I allow no one into the tower but the two footmen whose help I need to reach it, and Mr. Silas, who sometimes brings me the accounts there."

"You mean I won't be able to read the books?"

He frowned. "The books wouldn't interest you. They're old, some of them ancient."

"I'd take great care of them, Sir!"

A little color came into his face. "What is this? None of my staff has ever shown the slightest inclination to read them before. They consider them blasphemous."

"But books aren't blasphemous, Sir!"

He laughed shortly. "Not the ones you've read, you poor goose."

I was too upset to speak. Did he think me foolish?

His voice was stern. "I repeat: you're not to go to the watchtower. It's a forbidden place, you understand?"

"Yes, Sir," I managed, dejectedly.

He wagged his head at me as if I were a young child with a whim. "Come now, be cheerful. You've the whole of Murkmere in which to roam! Why should you want to go to the tower?"

IV

The Battle of the Birds

*I*f you're staying," Leah said, "you'd better make yourself useful."

Scuff had found me as I came out of the Master's room, to tell me that Leah wanted me in her parlor. I found her writing at a little bureau, scratching furiously away at the parchment sheets and cursing every time a nib broke. There was an open book beside her at which she sometimes glanced for reference.

"You can cut more quills for me; I'm running out. Sit over there." Without looking at me, she nodded brusquely at a hard, upright chair. Beside it was a table on which lay a silver tray piled with feathers.

No one would dare commit sacrilege by killing birds, but it was permitted to collect the precious feathers they dropped. You were allowed to use the feathers in the making of quill pens, and I'd heard that bunches of feathers sold by specialist vendors in the cities fetched high prices.

I knew how to make and cure pens; Aunt Jennet had showed me how to do it with the occasional feather she'd pick up from the fields or common. But I'd always hated the stiff, lifeless feeling of feathers between my fingers. It made me uneasy, frightened even, to touch them.

Without speaking, I went to sit down by the table. I wondered fearfully if a feather from a Bird of Night might not be among the bunch lying on the tray, and I'd be damned without even knowing it. I felt for my amber on its leather strap and took it up over my head, laying it carefully down close to the feathers on the tray. I should be safe enough now.

Leah looked up as amber clicked against silver. Quickly, and trying to control a shiver, I took up a long brown-dappled feather, and in my right hand the small penknife, which had a blade sharp enough to slice through stone.

She means me to cut myself! I thought. The candlelight shone on Leah's silver-fair hair and fiercely pursed mouth as she went back to her work, and the feather gleamed between my shrinking fingers.

I pulled myself together, and soon the concentration it took calmed me. I worked quietly and carefully, stripping some of the lower barbs away, then making a sloping cut at one end of the shaft's point. If a quill has a good hollow and is cut and cleaned well, it holds the ink for longer.

"What is that jewel?" said Leah suddenly. I looked up with

a start to see her looking over at me again. How long she had been watching me I couldn't tell.

By the tray, my amulet glowed golden in the candlelight. "It's amber, Miss," I said.

She rose and came over, gazing at it in fascination. "Fossil resin, but pretty, nonetheless. I've seen the same around the neck of Silas Seed." To my horror she picked it up to examine it closer. "Do you understand its properties? I believe that if you rub it for long enough, it gives off sparks of light."

"Oh, please, don't do such a thing, Miss Leah," I begged. "It's my amulet, and you might rub it away!" I stood up, with my hand outstretched, waiting for her to give it back.

Leah stood regarding me, with the strap dangling from her hand and the amber swinging to and fro like a golden heart. "I like it," she said slowly. "Perhaps I'll keep it for myself."

"Give it back, please, Miss," I said desperately. "It keeps me safe. You should wear an amulet of your own."

"A village girl lecturing me on religion!" she said. But she didn't look angry, more amused. "What do you think will happen to you without this, Aggie? Shall we wait and see?" She scissored the fingers of her free hand at me like a beak. "Will you be pecked to death in the night?" Then she began to back away, dangling the amber on its strap, a smile still playing around her lips.

Too frightened to be left by the tray of feathers without protection, I took a step after her, and then another. My heart began to thud with distress and frustration. She was goading me to make a grab for it, and then I would be dismissed for assaulting my mistress. Now she was standing on her chair so that she was taller than ever. She spluttered with laughter as I reached up uselessly.

It was a game to her, I realized suddenly. She didn't want the amber at all, but at the same time she was not going to give it back easily. She wanted me to jump up and make a grab for it, and I was sorely tempted.

I stood still and looked up at her smirking face. "The amber was my mother's. She wanted me to have it, none other. Please give it back."

Her hand paused. "It was your mother's?"

"Yes, and it's precious to me."

The smile had left her face, I was pleased to see. "Where's your mother now?"

"She is dead, Miss," I said, in a choked voice.

We gazed at each other for a heartbeat, then Leah climbed off the chair. Somehow the amber was back in my hand. "Tell me about your mother," she said urgently. "Tell me everything about her, every little thing you can remember. I want to know about mothers."

She sat down, arranged her skirts, clasped her hands on her lap, and looked up at me expectantly, suddenly docile.

"I don't remember my mother at all," I said, bewildered and upset. "I was too young when she died."

Leah stared at me in silence, as if testing the truth of what I'd said. I put the leather strap back over my head, slipping the amber down safely beneath my bodice. Slowly I calmed myself.

I didn't meet her gaze. I'd already seen the hunger and disappointment in her eyes.

I'd scarcely recovered from this episode and only cut a few quills when a bell sounded in the passage outside. Its doleful clanging made me start; the blade of the knife almost slipped against the flesh of my fingertip. The bell tolled on, heavy and gloomy, echoing back, then fading gradually.

"Is it suppertime, Miss?"

"Devotion," Leah said, not looking up. "A gong sounds for meals, the bell summons souls. Our worthy steward thinks it's more appropriate that way."

"May I go, then, Miss?"

She frowned, as if irritated at being interrupted again, and the quill paused. "You wish to go to Devotion?" she said, as if it were the oddest request on earth.

"Oh, yes, Miss, I must." *So should you*, I thought, *if you've any care for your own soul!*

She stopped writing at last and looked at me scornfully, as if she had guessed what I was thinking. "The Master has employed a prig for my companion," she said. "And a pious prig to boot!"

Silently, I collected the feathers I'd worked on and laid them back on the tray. My hands were trembling. I didn't want her to see how much she'd hurt me.

But that night I hated her.

Devotion was held in the servants' dining hall, close to the kitchen quarters: a long room with stone walls and small, bare windows, darkened by the night outside.

All the long tables except one had been pushed back, and the candles in pewter holders set on them sent a flickering light round the room. The remaining table was at the far end, the chairs placed in rows before it. When I went in everyone had taken their seats, and some were already kneeling on the stone-flagged floor. A pair of kitchen maids peeked at me curiously between their fingers.

There was no spare chair. I'd have to stand at the back.

Dog's greasy head turned toward me, and she prodded her neighbor and whispered something. The other girl turned to stare, and whispered back. I saw them both cover their sniggers with their hands.

Heat rose in my cheeks. I was conscious that I looked different. I wasn't wearing a cap and apron, my hair had come loose from its bindings and sprung around my shoulders, and my much-patched best dress was too tight around the waist. But I stared grimly back and the girl's gaze fell.

The low murmuring in the hall died abruptly. Everyone rose as Mr. Silas swept in, a great leather book under his arm. He went to stand behind the top table, putting the book down before him. In the silence I could hear the quick breathing of the maid in front of me.

He looked up. "Sit down, please."

There was a shuffling of feet and scraping of chairs. I had no choice but to remain standing, with a table digging into my back. I couldn't even shrink into the shadows against the wall. But they had forgotten me, those squint-eyed, sniggering girls. Their whole attention was on Mr. Silas. Everyone in the hall waited.

Mr. Silas paused, opened the book slowly, and then his beautiful voice began.

"In the distant beginning of the world man walked in the rain and shared the greening land with cat and cow, donkey and rat. Bird was god, for he flew in the air and could see all there was to be seen. The greatest bird of all was Eagle. He had laid the egg that was the world."

The familiar words of the Preliminary had been read. Now the Responses began. My lips repeated them automatically, but my eyes admired the soft glow on the steward's face from the candles on the table.

A thick golden haze quivered in the hall. From time to time he looked up and his dark eyes swept us like a flame.

"The Great Eagle lays the egg of the world . . ."

"But the Crow tries to steal it from him," we answered together.

"The Great Eagle tells the Robin and Wren it is their inheritance . . ."

"But they heed Him not."

"While they play and dally, Crow seizes his chance and summons the Birds of Night."

"They fight for possession of the egg that is the world; they fight the Birds of Light."

I thought of the Birds of Night. It's written in the Divine Book how in the skies they fought the Birds of Light, tearing out their throats for possession of the world, while far above them the Great Eagle watched in solitary majesty.

Mr. Silas held out both hands to us, and the ruffles at his wrists dissolved like foam into the sleeves of his velvet jacket. His voice was earnest and passionate. *"Then let us remember that that Battle is not yet done. Let us remember that the Battle will be won by the Light, in righteousness and truth. For what can the Birds of Night do if we so allow them?"*

"They can steal our souls," we muttered together, and a shudder ran through us.

"What must we do to protect ourselves?"

"We must follow the path of righteousness and humility."

And we must wear our amulets, I thought to myself, *as double insurance.*

The Responses were at an end; it was the time for the evening sermon. Mr. Silas closed the book and looked up with a smile. I thought he'd caught my eye, was smiling at me, and I smiled back.

"We all know the old story of the avia, those men, back in the greening time, who dared desire wings so they might fly like the Gods. We all know their punishment. They were trapped between two forms for eternity, forever half-bird, half-human. That must be a warning to us, a reminder. We must be content with our humanity and accept our frailty."

Like everyone else, I knew the story of the avia. At the beginning of the world a group of men and women weren't content with the skills they'd been given, but wanted to fly like the Birds. They had grumbled together, and Crow overheard them and told Eagle.

When I was small, it had frightened me to think of the Great God plummeting like a thunderbolt to Earth to deal with the small band of humans who'd dared rebel against their lot, who'd wanted the freedom of flight. I imagined their guilt and fear as they looked on the vast feathered wings that could touch distant galaxies. I could hear their moans as He turned the cruel, unforgiving side of His Eagle face toward them. Like them, I could see His bill sharp as death, His eyes empty. In my mind's eye, I saw the men, women, and children draw closer together, like nestlings in the great shadow of the Eagle's wing, their wails like the cheeping of birds.

"You were not happy with what you were given," He said. "You were created men, to labor on Earth, yet you envied the wings of the gods. For this each of you must be punished — you and your children, and your children's children — through all eternity. Your human soul will be trapped within the shape of a bird, but you will be neither the one thing nor the other. You will never be content."

The story of the avia had always sent a chill through me. It was the last thing I wanted to hear my first night at Murkmere.

Mr. Silas had finished speaking. The girls in front of me gave a little sigh together and looked at each other with dazzled eyes. The rows of servants stood as he took one of the candlesticks from the table and passed down between them. The men — footmen and stablehands, keepers and estate farmers — stood with bowed heads as he greeted them. He came to the female staff standing together and patted a maid's head, made a soft remark to another girl, smiled at yet another, seeming to share out his favors equally among them. If he was aware of their simpers and blushes, he didn't show it.

I longed for him to pick me out, smile at me, say something. But he didn't speak to me, stuck on my own at the back. He left without noticing me at all.

The Master didn't join us for supper. Leah and I sat alone in the small dining room next to her parlor. Though I was hungry again, I've no idea what we ate that night: the food stuck like warm wool in my mouth. Leah didn't bother to make conversation, but I'd catch her staring at me, with unblinking gray eyes that looked black as night.

Afterward she went into her parlor to read; she didn't bid me goodnight. I was standing hesitantly in the dining room, watching the footman clear our dishes and wondering if it was part of my job to help, when Scuff shuffled through in her big shoes. "Please, Miss Aggie, you're to follow me. Mistress Crumplin has some clothes for you."

She took me to the laundry rooms by the kitchen, where Mistress Crumplin, a tipping tankard of ale clasped in one hand and grumbling all the while, managed to find me two nightgowns and some dresses and shawls in the depths of a vast airing cupboard.

"They're not much, but a deal better than what you're wearing," she remarked thickly, eyeing my dress.

I clutched my skirt, worried she'd wrest it from me: one of my few reminders of home. "But shouldn't I wear a cap and apron?" I asked, wanting to be like the other girls.

"Gracious, no! You're the mistress's companion, not a maid." She gave me an odd look. "Your mother Eliza was only a maid, you know, for all the airs she gave herself."

"Please, Mistress, what do you remember about my mother?" I said, thinking she was in her cups and might open up to me.

At once she looked shifty. "Nothing, girl. Too long ago." She paused. "One thing, though."

"Yes?" I said eagerly.

She breathed damply into my face and her lips shone with the ale I could smell on her breath. "Greatly favored by Master and My Lady, was Eliza. Mystery why she ran away."

"Ran away?"

"Aye, didn't give notice, just upped and was off." She leaned closer still, so that I drew back involuntarily. "She was frightened, that's my opinion. Something at Murkmere got her running."

It was strange and lonely in my bedchamber when at last I found it. Before I climbed into bed I opened the window wide for a moment to let the frosty air blow away the staleness. The fire, which I'd poked back into life, spluttered and died in the bitter draft.

I lay in the darkness like a corpse in the long nightgown, between linen sheets that smelled of damp. I wondered what my mother's first night had been like. She would have slept with the other maids. What had her work been, her daily routine? Why had she run away?

Aunt Jennet had said little about my mother's time at Murkmere, but she'd looked troubled when I received the Master's summons. "I never rested easy while Eliza was at Murkmere," she'd said. "And shan't do so with you there." I hadn't asked her for any explanation. I was too set on escaping the monotonous drudgery of spinning, and thought she fussed needlessly.

But now I felt again the fear in her grip as she'd put her thin arms around me and hugged me as if she didn't want to let me go.

A tear slipped down my cheek, then another. I longed for her arms again. I wept for my aunt; and I wept for my mother, who was lost to me.

Then a sound came to me in the silence of the night, outside somewhere, far away. At first I thought it was moaning on the wind, but there was no wind over the frost-gripped land outside.

The moaning came closer. It wasn't far from the house. As the unearthly sound came closer it rose to a bloodcurdling pitch.

My tears froze on my cheeks. My eyes stared wide into the dark. I knew what it was now. It was the baying of dogs, a great pack of hunting dogs. I could hear them panting and gasping, their paws pounding the hard ground.

They were coming closer. Soon they'd be beneath my window; they would scent me. Then they would leap into my bedchamber, jaws wide, teeth white in the moonlight, saliva dripping on the floorboards.

Beneath their howling, I could hear my own whimpering, faint with terror, hopeless. I was trembling like a rabbit. My amber was under my pillow. I must touch it, hold it in my palm. That was all it would take to keep me safe: one little movement of my arm and hand.

But I couldn't move.

I heard the hounds prepare themselves to leap. They were ready for the kill. I saw their black lips roll back.

But the sounds were fading. The dogs had gone; the monstrous pack had moved on. The baying died away. I lay numb with shock, and around me the night folded into a deathly silence.

V

Speaking to Mr. Silas

Each night I heard the midnight baying beyond my window. In time I learned from Scuff that what I heard were the guard dogs of Murkmere, let loose from their kennels at night to roam the grounds, but during that first week I was most horribly frightened. Morning and night I gazed down from my window, longing to see my aunt materialize miraculously in the stable yard, to take me home.

At least I saw little of Leah during the day. She had lessons with the Master all morning and after luncheon at noon, for a further hour before he rested. Then she'd wander the grounds in the bitter weather until dusk fell, Dog and I trailing along silently behind her, until, invariably, she managed to slip from us and flee to the mere.

"She's your responsibility now," said Dog, with hateful satisfaction. "Go, find her yourself — if you can!"

And she'd retreat to the warmth of the kitchen quarters

while I traipsed off in pursuit of Leah, scouring the edges of the muddy wastes and frozen reeds for a sight of that flying silvery hair and lanky frame.

I didn't see the heron again. Nor did I ever glimpse the swans as I stared out over the ice to the dark little island. Sometimes I wondered if it were only Leah herself who could see those mysterious birds.

She never spoke to me at mealtimes, but pointedly brought in a book to read, as if I weren't there at all. Usually we were waited on by the taciturn footman, Jukes, whom I'd seen outside the Master's rooms, but one time Scuff came to serve us, her face intent and anxious as she waded over with the dishes.

Leah looked up from her book. "Your apron is disgustingly stained, Scuff! You should be ashamed."

"She's only young, Miss Leah," I dared protest as the poor child crept out with our dirty plates, her head hanging.

"That's why she'll take notice of me," snapped Leah. "The other servants care nothing for my wishes. Haven't you noticed how ill-kept the house is, how disordered? My guardian doesn't notice, he's too much in his rooms, he doesn't see his housekeeper's a sot. Outside we're short of keepers and the estate runs to weed." She stared somberly at her fingers for a moment, then glared across at me. "Wait until I'm Mistress here, I'll change things! I'll get rid of the lot of them!"

I was so amazed that she'd actually spoken to me, I couldn't think of a thing to say.

❧

The Master spent a couple of days in his bed, but in the middle of the week he was pushed into the dining room by Silas as we were finishing luncheon. He looked pale, his great hands twisted together in his lap, their strength sapped. Leah leaped to her feet, leaving her stewed apple uneaten; her face was transformed with joy. She knelt next to the chair and stroked the Master's grooved cheeks.

"I'll look after the Master now," she said to Silas. "You may leave us." She put her smooth young cheek close to the Master's and said gently, "I shall take you to oversee your property, Sir."

And then she began to wheel him from room to room.

I saw what an effort it was for her to push the heavy chair, how her arms bent like celery stalks; yet she persisted. I didn't know what to do with myself. I hovered miserably behind, jealous of their private jokes, of the affectionate way the Master rumbled back at Leah's whispers.

When he was well enough to tutor her again, I went after the little group as it started off on its expedition to the watchtower. The tower stuck up like a finger from a copse of silver birch on top of a grassy rise to one side of the Hall. From a distance it looked similar to the one near our village: a plain square structure built of the local dark red stone. Once, watchtowers had been built all over the Eastern Edge to guard against invasion from the sea; now they were mostly used in the summer months to look out for bands of marauders.

When I'd asked Scuff how the Master managed to reach the top room to tutor Leah, her eyes grew wide. "He's raised up by a magical contraption, Aggie — a 'lift,' he calls it. I've seen them before in the Capital, but this is his own design. You'll see!"

And of course I was determined to do so, if I could.

A bitter wind was gusting from the north as Leah pushed the chair up a well-worn track, with the Master bundled up in rugs, bumping from side to side. Jukes the footman followed behind with a basket of medicine bottles covered by a blowing white cloth; I followed Jukes at a discreet distance.

Leah's face was strained and pale, and her black-gloved fingers were clenched on the bar of the chair. "Let Jukes take over, my dear," said the Master as he struggled to keep his balance on the seat. "It will be easier for us both."

Leah looked more determined than ever. "I don't need help," she said furiously. "It is only that the ground has become so hard and cracked." As she stopped pushing to catch her breath, she caught sight of me. "Why have you come? Go back!"

In dismay I came closer to explain. "I only wanted to see the lift, Miss."

The Master, gray-faced with cold and convalescence, peered around at me. "And see it you shall, Agnes. I'm always happy to show off its working."

"Then let's hope it does so," muttered Leah, giving me a resentful look.

"Come and walk beside me, Agnes," said the Master, thumping the arm of his chair with enthusiasm. "Let me explain the mechanics of it."

It went over my head, the Master's description of pulleys

and weights and wheels; but he took unbounded pleasure in it. His cheeks took color and he waved his hands about, his voice loud to emphasize the finer points of the lift's workings. When I glanced over at Leah, I surprised a smile on her face before she had time to hide it.

At last we came to a sizeable tussock, frozen solid in the middle of the track, and there was no going around it, for we were into the birch copse now and surrounded by gorse and scrub. Leah struggled in vain for some moments, Jukes looking on in concern, yet not daring to help her. At last, I said tentatively, "Perhaps if we do it together? If I press on the lower bar, it will lever up the front of the chair so you and Mr. Jukes can lift it over."

Leah knew she had no alternative but to agree. She nodded curtly at the footman to put down his basket, and then the three of us managed the maneuver with little difficulty. As we started off again, my bare hands were still on the push bar. I could see Leah looking down at them as she took hold of the bar again herself, but she did not protest at my help. Side by side and in silence, she and I pushed the chair the remaining distance together.

To my delight the lift turned out to be a tiny house with a gilded roof and chimney. It sat beneath a pulley system that ran to a window at the top of the watchtower. Supports ran up the side of the tower to keep the house steady on its journey through the air, and I stared at these with incredulity as I rubbed my numb hands together. *I'd never dare trust my life to machinery*, I thought, and wished I'd listened better to the Master's explanations.

A footman was waiting for us by an enormous winch, his sleeves already rolled up for action in spite of the freezing wind. He gave me a suspicious look as I peered through one of the arched windows of the little house. Inside I could see rich fabric on the walls, even candelabra for night journeys; a small brazier was lit against the chill.

"Everything's ready for the Master, just as it should be," the footman growled to no one in particular.

"Miss Agnes is merely satisfying her curiosity, Pegg," said the Master, with a smile. "She has never seen a lift before."

"Well, if she is satisfied enough, Sir," Pegg grunted, "we'll be getting on pushing you inside it."

Jukes secured the wheels of the chair by iron grips to the floor and closed the door. "Take it up, Mr. Pegg."

As we watched, the squat but burly Pegg began to crank the handle of the winch, his muscles bulging beneath his jacket. I thought he'd find it impossible, because of all the weights attached to the chains. To my astonishment, the little house began to rise slowly up the side of the tower.

"Come, Jukes," Leah said, moving away. "He'll be at the top in a minute."

Jukes followed her to a door in the base of the tower, which closed behind them. Soon I heard the window at the top opening, and then the lift had reached it, hanging in space against its supports.

I looked in alarm at Pegg as he took his hands from the

winch, but the lift remained steady. "Be gone now, Miss Cotter," he said roughly, "there's nothing for you here."

I took a last look up at the tower, at the window behind which must surely be the forbidden bookroom: even now I thought the Master, who'd been so kind to me, might change his mind. Then defeated, watched by the disapproving Pegg, I left, winding my way back disconsolately through the blown gorse.

Somehow I lived through my first week at Murkmere. I helped Leah wheel the Master to the tower each day, but was never invited inside. Back in the house, I'd wander its dark, icy passages until I knew them by heart, or stay in my bed-chamber, staring at the damp-patterned ceiling. I thought I might die from boredom.

So far I'd nothing to tell Mr. Silas, for every time I'd followed Leah, I'd lost her. On the whole she ignored me: she certainly never told me where she was going.

One evening at Devotion, toward the end of that week, Mr. Silas favored me with a smile. Perhaps he was wondering why I hadn't been to see him. Perhaps I'd do so the very next day. At least I could ask him for permission to visit Aunt Jennet.

After luncheon, when Leah had returned to the tower for her afternoon tuition, I approached the steward's door and knocked. Now that the moment had come to see him alone, I felt slightly sick. If it hadn't been for my longing to see my aunt, I might have run away.

There was a rowdy noise coming from the kitchen quarters and it was hard to hear if Mr. Silas had said anything, so after a minute I lifted the latch and went in.

He was sitting at a desk with papers spread in front of him and a quill pen in his left hand. There were gold coins neatly arranged in glinting columns on the dark wood — more money than I'd ever seen in my life, a miser's dream — and I stared at these as I came in. I could feel my eyes widen. Then I looked at him.

He was wearing spectacles that changed him into someone I didn't know. I thought I saw a frown between his smooth brows as he looked up; his eyes were magnified and glaring. Then he removed the spectacles and was smiling after all, smiling as he opened drawers in the desk and slid the money in deftly, as if he knew without looking where it should go.

He locked the drawers and put the keys in his breast pocket. "You surprised me, Agnes. I didn't hear your knock."

He motioned me to a chair in front of the desk and I sat down, feeling more nervous than ever. He was tidying away his papers now with quick, neat movements, and I, not wanting to stare, fixed my gaze on the mahogany cupboard behind him where a huge Eagle carved in black wood glared down at me, wings raised ready for the kill. It was intended to convey the Almighty's sacred form, but it was the ugliest thing I'd ever seen.

At last he looked up. "You've come to talk about your mistress?" he said gently, leaning a little toward me, his dark eyes on my face, his elbows in finest tweed resting on the cleared desk.

I nodded, clutching my hands together.

"How do you find her, Agnes? Is she very different from other girls her age?"

I began to talk, haltingly at first, but then faster, encouraged by his sympathetic questioning. I forgot I'd been anxious about seeing him. It all poured out: Leah, her unfriendliness, the impossibility of tracking her to the mere. At the end he stood up, came over to me, and laid a hand on my shoulder reassuringly.

"You've done well, Agnes. I know how hard it must be for you to come from your home to a place like this, to such a demanding position. I fear Miss Leah's soul has been lost already, whatever you try to do for her."

I stared up at him. "You don't mean the Night Birds have taken it?"

His hand gripped my shoulder with a warm pressure through the gray serge of my dress. "Not yet. But she wears no amulet."

"It's not only her soul, Sir. What about the danger from kidnappers?"

To my astonishment I saw him smile slightly. "I don't believe there's any real risk. Murkmere's not a rich estate. Mr. Tunstall doesn't even attend Council — he hasn't done for years — he's privy to no state secrets worth possessing. No, we must concern ourselves with Leah's spiritual welfare, you and I. Watch her behavior, see if your good influence can save her, Agnes. I see you at Devotion. I know your soul is safe."

His fingers touched the skin of my neck. He moved on to the leather thong that threaded my amber. He pulled the stone from my bodice and held it in his palm, close to me, as if examining it. Beyond his head I could see the black Eagle on the cupboard, with its cruel, curved beak.

"Your amber," he whispered, "keeps you safe from harm, doesn't it, little marigold? Yours is an unblemished soul — a sweet, pure delicacy of a soul — and we must keep it that way, mustn't we?"

"Yes, S-Sir," I stammered. His eyes were intent, unblinking as he gazed down into mine. They were so dark, the pupil merged with the iris. I couldn't look away but had to stare back, my own eyes wide, my heart beating fast. I could smell the dusky flower water he used; he must have dabbed it on his wrists, his fingers. Then he blinked suddenly and dropped the amber so that it fell back against my skin.

"I should return to my work, alas," he said. "But come again, Agnes. I want to know if anything worries you, any little change in Leah's behavior. All the souls in Murkmere concern me, but Leah's particularly, of course. The estate will be hers one day, and she must be fit to run it."

He fell silent, and when I looked up at him again, he was gazing at nothing, almost as if he'd forgotten me, the little frown back between his brows.

He worries for her, I thought, *he truly worries.* I was hesitant about interrupting such worthy thoughts, but I had to seize my chance, else it would be gone.

"Please, when may I see my aunt, Sir?"

He focused on me with a start. "Why, Agnes, you've arrived only recently! Don't you have enough time off as it is?"

"I long to see her, Sir," I said in a small voice. I clenched my hands together. "I worry for her all alone. If she should fall sick, or if the Militia should come to question the village . . ."

He looked startled. "Who told you the Militia was coming?" His voice was strange and harsh, his eyes narrowed to cat's slits as he stared down at me.

I looked up in alarm, thinking that somehow I'd angered him. "No one, Sir. I don't know why I said it."

I seemed to convince him. He went back to his desk and relaxed into the chair, stretching out and saying idly, "The Militia is quick enough to sniff out traitors, it's true. I hear there are some pockets of unrest in the Eastern Edge, but I don't believe there's any ill feeling here in the village."

"Oh, no, Sir," I said, since he'd made it sound like a question. "But we heard about the rebellion in the south last summer. The packman told us. The Militia killed the rebels, every last man." It still sickened me to think of it.

He studied my face. "What would you have felt if the rebels had been successful? Would you have thought it a good thing?"

I shook my head so energetically that my braided hair loosened. "Oh, no, Sir! To have the country ruled by a rabble, no one to care for our welfare as the Lord Protector does. None of us in the village wanted that."

"All loyal subjects, then," he said. "That's good to know."

There was another silence. I cleared my throat. "Sir, my aunt?"

Then we both heard it, the soft rustling at the window, the brushing of feathers against the glass.

He waved a hand at it, his mood changed to lightness. "There's your answer, Agnes," he said. "You can't see your aunt while the snow lies, but neither will she be plagued by unwelcome visitors!"

His hand was ready to open the desk drawers as soon as I'd gone. "Come again soon, Agnes," he said, and smiled. "But next time knock a little louder. A steward's work is not for all eyes."

I smiled weakly back, and stood up, surprised to find that my legs felt wobbly, as if I'd escaped some danger. On my way out I passed a chair by the door. He'd left his three-cornered hat hanging over the corner of the back, and on the brocade seat lay a black-handled riding whip. It was both elegant and vicious.

For an instant I thought of Dog, of her desperation when we lost Leah my first afternoon — and, fleetingly, I wondered.

VI

The Tower

The snow fell all that afternoon and evening. Surrounded by glimmering curtains of flakes, Murkmere Hall was shut away in its own world.

Leah looked white and furious. Jukes the footman had locked the main doors on orders from Mr. Silas, who said it was the Master's wish. It was too dangerous for her to go to the mere, with snow hiding the ice. I passed the Master's door on my way to the kitchens and heard her arguing inside: her voice raised and angry, the Master's deep rumble patiently pacifying her for a second until she began again.

For the rest of the afternoon, while the daylight lasted, she paced from window to window, as if the next she came to might show her that it had stopped snowing at last.

When darkness had fallen, we went to her parlor to pass the time until she had to change for supper. Leah began to play Solo, slapping the cards down and muttering to herself.

I took up the mending; my stitches weren't as neat as Doggett's, but it was something to do. The evening stretched before us, as bleak and boring as every other at Murkmere Hall.

The prospect finally drove me to look up from my needle and venture, "It might be more entertaining for you, Miss, if we played a game together."

Leah paused. "You play cards?" she said in surprise.

"Aunt Jennet taught me."

"Your schoolmistress aunt?" Leah looked disappointed. "Then I suppose she taught you improving games, like Calepin."

"We didn't spend much time on Calepin." I studied my stitches modestly. "Aunt Jennet considered my vocabulary sufficiently good without it. Indeed, we both thought Calepin profoundly dull."

I could feel Leah staring at me, as if a whole world of new possibilities were suddenly unveiling itself before her. "You know Palabra?" she demanded, in growing excitement. "Six Pairs? Niello?"

I nodded to each, and she sprang up. "I've a special pack for Niello!"

"Niello is over so quickly," I said, for I knew she'd win it. I never won at Niello, even with ordinary cards. "And there's not much skill in it, to my mind."

Leah was taken aback. "What do you propose then?"

"Do you know Commotion?" I said slyly, for I knew she would not. Aunt Jennet had once invented it to take my mind off a toothache. It was the most amusing, rambunctious game I knew. And there was no skill in it at all.

Leah's face lit up, like a small child's when offered a treat. "Commotion? No, I don't know Commotion. Teach it to me."

We laughed and laughed, sprawling on the floor, our legs in all directions, skirts crushed, cards scattered. Leah's fine hair hung down around her face and her cheeks were pink. By the end of the game I was giggling so much I could scarcely speak.

Jukes had to cough several times before we realized he was there, his long face reproachful. "Please forgive the interruption, Miss Leah. I wanted to tell Agnes Cotter that the bell has gone."

"The bell?" I said stupidly, the giggles still bursting inside me.

He nodded solemnly. "Mr. Silas thought you'd like to know, since you always come to Devotion."

"If Mr. Silas calls, then you must go. Mr. Silas runs this house." The laughter on Leah's face vanished so fast I might have dreamt that I'd ever seen her so happy and uninhibited. A moment ago I'd believed we'd become friends, as if the card game had wrought some alchemy between us. But now I saw that I was quite mistaken.

By the following morning, the sky was clear and filled with bright white light, but it was evident the Master would not be able to ride through the soft deepnesses of snow to reach his books. The path to the watchtower was completely covered. It was decided that Leah's lessons would take place in the Master's rooms.

But what about me? I thought. *Am I to be a prisoner all day, shut inside like his ward, forever walking up and down these stone passages to pass the time?*

And a secret defiance began to smolder inside me. I had to get outside, into that white glistening world under the open sky.

I waited, biding my time. It seemed an age while Leah ate her breakfast and collected her work. I followed at a distance as she made her way to the Master's rooms, and I heard Jukes announce her. There was the sound of the door closing.

Upstairs in my room, I threw on my cloak and fastened my boots with hasty fingers. It would be no use going to any of the main doors. They might be locked. But the back doors in the kitchen quarters would be open to allow for the coming and going of servants into the yard.

By now I knew Murkmere's labyrinth of passages and wove swiftly through them unnoticed, to a door near the pantry that led out to the vegetable garden. I was lifting the latch when Mistress Crumplin came jangling her way round the corner from the kitchen. She stopped when she saw me, the keys jumping at her waist, and eyed me suspiciously.

"If you wish to walk, Miss Agnes, you should have someone with you — Doggett perhaps. I'll call her."

"I'll be perfectly safe, Mistress Crumplin," I said. "I've been walking in the grounds before today without company. I've my amulet with me and won't be in danger by daylight, I'm sure."

But to my dismay Mistress Crumplin and her keys had already swung around. She was on her way back to the kitchens, shouting "Doggett, Doggett," in her loud, flat voice; in a minute my chance of escape would be gone and the moon-faced Dog would be at my side.

As she turned the corner, I slipped stealthily through the door and was outside, shutting it behind me with the tiniest click of the latch falling back into place.

The new snow was soft but firm, with a slight stickiness that held my steps steady. I began walking away from the house as fast as I could, conscious of my lone, dark figure in the white landscape and, in the utter silence, the faint squeaking of the snow under my boots. I was frightened they'd send a footman after me or that I'd hear Dog herself wailing my name on the glittering air; but no one came.

The snow lay in perfect folds, as clean and fresh and new as bride's linen. It was piled up against the wall of the kitchen gardens, against the trunks of the oak trees beyond; the bushes looked as if they had been hung with tablecloths.

I went through the door in the garden wall and skirted around the back of the stable block. I could hear the ostlers shoveling the snow away in the yard, but the buildings hid me. Then I saw the tower beyond the stables. The rise was smooth and glistening with untrodden snow, the trees a dark crest at the top.

There'll be no one there, I thought, *no keepers working round it, no one outside or in.*

My heart began to thump. I didn't think anything more than that, I didn't put my real desire into words, but I began to climb the rise, drawing in deep breaths of the sharp air to calm myself.

At the top I stood for a moment in the soft blue-gray shadow the tower cast on the snow. Nothing moved in the copse behind me. Far off I could hear the scrape of the ostlers' spades on the stable cobbles, but round the tower the silence was frozen, as if I'd entered a magic world.

I began to walk round the square walls, my boots crushing snow-matted weeds. The bricks glowed a deep blood red above the snow, but in the sunlight I could see where the salt winds were starting to eat them away. The huge winch and the chains that ran up to the top window were outlined with a delicate tracery of ice, the little house half-hidden under a crown of snow.

Then I came to the door that Leah and Jukes had used.

A brass latch, weathered and green, was set in the oak. No bolts, no keyhole, no iron bars or chain. I put my hand out and the brass was cold under my fingers. It lifted easily, as I knew it would. The tower wasn't locked: the Master trusted his servants to obey him. Anyway, none of them dared venture so close to such a blasphemous place.

The door opened under my hand, into darkness, scraping over a stone floor.

At first I couldn't make out anything after the brightness of the snow, but then I saw a vast, empty room, narrow wooden stairs at the far side rising under a brick arch. Some light came down from a small window high up; tiny dust motes danced in the beam. The air was musty, smelling of raw wood.

I wanted to go in. I wanted to find the books, to touch them, to look at them. The words came into my head by themselves: *I'll be so quick, no one will know.*

I think I hesitated a minute, no more. In that minute the snowy air I'd drawn through my lungs seemed to fizz through my blood, filling me with boldness. I lifted my skirts, stepped in, and pulled the door behind me.

If I'd thought of the consequences of being discovered, everything would have been very different.

Silence closed round me, a different silence from outside, expectant, as if the tower were waiting to see what I would do.

I looked at the stairs rising up through the dusty light from the window, and swiftly crossed the stone floor toward them before I could change my mind. The unstained oak boards were marked darkly by feet: Leah's and Jukes's, and Mr. Silas's, perhaps.

I put my own feet in their marks as if I too had a right to be there, and I began to climb, clutching the handrail and peering down at the shadowy rafters and supports that crossed the empty well. I was out of breath, and the sweat of fear was beginning to prickle beneath my clothes by the time I came up into the wide landing that ran round the top.

To my left was an open space containing lift machinery. Through the far window I could see the chains that carried the lift up to this level each day, the iron supports that held it in place while the Master's wheelchair was brought in over runners laid across the landing.

Before me a door was half-open, light blazing through the gap. I stepped from the last stair, across the landing, and went through into the bookroom.

The light was coming from what I took to be a huge door of glass, long and broad, reaching down to the floor in the outside wall of the room. It looked as if you could step straight out into pearly sky over the snowy trees of the estate; I could see the boundary wall, even the Wasteland beyond. It was like a picture in a frame, except that the clouds moved.

But I was a child of darkness, brought up in the greasy gleam of tallow. I'd never seen so much light and space. I didn't dare go near the window in case I fell out. I scarcely saw what was in the room itself: the cabinets of polished wood, with glass lids that reflected the clouds.

Then I grew braver. I told myself that the window was shut firm until it was opened; that there was strong glass between me and the sky. Curiosity overcame me, and I began to investigate the cabinets.

The nearest was filled with neat stacks of books. The largest were at the bottom, piled up to the smallest at the top, each carefully indexed with labels stuck to the underside of the lid, and handwritten. I read some of the titles: *Visions of*

Other Worlds, The Fight for the Future, The Free Soul, Journeys in Uncharted Seas. I felt my eyes grow bigger and bigger, like a hungry man at a feast.

But the lid was locked.

I tried all the cabinets in turn, flying from one to another, forgetting my fear of the window. They were filled with books, but they were all locked.

Sick with disappointment, I stared down. The faded leather covers were curling and ragged at the edges, the gold tooling of the titles almost worn away. They couldn't have been more different from the readers I'd had in school, with their bindings of bright linen and the new white paper inside on which the black ink stood out boldly. Even now I could smell the sweet vanilla scent of that paper, so enticing until you realized the dullness of the words printed on it.

But these were proper books at last.

I looked around as if I might suddenly see a bunch of keys lying somewhere, on the mantel over the empty grate or on the seat of one of the chairs. Even the drawers of the desk were locked. I should have realized that the Master wouldn't leave his possessions freely available for intruders.

There were covered braziers around the room to protect the books from damp. I thought suddenly that someone must light them each day. I should go before I was discovered.

But as I turned to leave, my eyes fell on the pair of double doors set in one of the inside walls. I'd been too distracted by the cabinets to pay them attention. They must lead to another room, somewhere else the keys might be hidden.

I tried the right handle; it turned easily, and I stood on the threshold of a dark, windowless room that smelled stiflingly of dust. It was too dark to see where the room ended, but it seemed surprisingly large and something was filling all the space. I opened the door wider behind me to let in light.

And then I saw the vast bird that floated beneath the ceiling.

It wasn't moving. It was dead, and had been dead a long time. Its body had decayed away into nothing. Only its giant skeleton was left suspended in the air, bare bones gleaming in the half-light, knobbed head reaching out for the kill. Even the feathers had crumbled from the huge papery wings. It was greater in size than any bird I had ever seen and, even as my mouth opened in a silent scream, I knew what it must be.

Somehow I got out, closed the door, and stumbled out of the bookroom, my hand at my amber, my heart thudding, my hair coming down around my ears.

Then far below me I heard the door open.

VII

Crow

In panic I turned back to the bookroom, my boots thudding over the floorboards. One of the double doors to the inner room was still open, and I closed it. My hands were shaking so much it was hard to turn the knob.

The only place to hide was behind the armchair on the far side of the fireplace. I darted over and crouched down behind its high, upholstered back, clutching my amber to me, thankful that the chair's embroidered skirts hid my boots.

Thoughts beat like frightened birds in my brain.

I'd seen what no human eye should see. I'd discovered the real reason the tower was forbidden to the servants, the secret in the inner room. What would they do to me? Would they have me taken to the Capital? Would they simply dispose of me, in case I told what I'd seen? Who'd ever miss Aggie Cotter but her Aunt Jennet, and what could she do against the power of the Ministration?

I could hear voices now, rising up the tower stairs: a man's voice and a light, high one, a girl's. Then the voices stopped and all I could hear was the soft swishing of a cloak over the boards outside.

"She'll be in here. There's nowhere else."

"I'll find her for you, Sir."

I recognized the voices of Mr. Silas and Dog. I had a sudden vivid picture of my dark footprints in the smooth white snow, and I knew how they had found me. Dog must have betrayed me; she'd followed my footprints and then returned to report to Mistress Crumplin, or even direct to Mr. Silas.

At first I felt relief. Mr. Silas liked me; he wouldn't report me to the Master. But then I thought, *He's a good, devout man; it's his duty to report sinners.*

My eyes were fixed on the gold and green pattern of the chair cover. It blurred before me; I wouldn't have been able to describe it though it was so close. My hands were damp with sweat, but I had to use both to balance me now, I was so stiff with kneeling. A whimper rose in my throat.

They had come into the room.

I heard Dog scurry around, heard her exclaim at the cabinets, at the great window-door. She'd never been here before; she'd never trespassed like me.

Then her head came over the top of the armchair. She saw me at once. Her little eyes gleamed with triumph, and she opened that prissy mouth of hers to tell. I shook my head violently, pleadingly; put my finger to my lips. My eyes, agonized, stared up into hers.

"She's here, Sir," called Dog. "She's over here."

I tucked my amber away and stood up.

Dog's face was full of spite, the steward's expressionless. I couldn't tell if he was angry or indifferent that I was there, in a forbidden place.

"You may go, Doggett," he said. "I'll deal with this."

"Did I do well to tell you, Sir?" smirked Dog.

"Very well. But leave us now."

She tripped out, all smug, twinkling smiles; I heard her hobnailed boots slow on the stairs, then clang merrily across the stone of the ground floor as she went on her way to tell the other servants.

I spread my hands out to Mr. Silas. "I wanted to read the books, Sir; I wanted to see them for myself."

"And what did you find?"

The changing light moved over his face. Even in that strong light he was handsome. He wore no hat, as if he'd left in haste, and his dark hair fell free and unpowdered across his brow in its glossy black curve, so like a blackbird's wing.

"I found the books were locked away," I said, shamefaced.

He came nearer, his cloak sweeping over the floor behind him; the fur at the hem was draggled with snow. He looked down at me gravely; he didn't seem so very angry. "And why do you think that is?"

"They're old and fragile, Sir."

"Because they are dangerous, Agnes. You don't know how close you came to sullying your soul."

I was bewildered, and frightened too. Why should books be dangerous? I smelled the scent of his flower water, faint but growing stronger now he was near.

"B-but the Master reads them. So does Miss Leah," I stammered.

"These books contain blasphemies, they tell of a time before this land was civilized by the Ministration, when men walked the night unprotected, exposed to evil. They describe the old, bad time, Agnes; they make wicked conjecture in the fields of theology and philosophy."

I gazed at him, shocked.

"I've tried to persuade the Master to destroy them." Silas Seed shook his head. "He becomes angry and I worry he'll have another seizure, so I say nothing more. But in time this place will destroy itself, anyway." He gestured toward the stairwell, visible through the open door. "The bricks are soft, the supports half-rotten with damp. One day the tower will simply collapse inward, and the books will be buried beneath the rubble."

He spoke calmly, without feeling. Then he looked down at his hands in the light, studying their clean, white tips, turning them this way and that. "Did you discover anything else up here?" he asked softly, at last.

I began to tremble again.

In the same gentle voice, he said: "You can tell me, you know, little marigold. It won't go further."

I relaxed a little. Aunt Jennet had taught me that only cowards lie to save their skins. "Yes, Sir, I did."

Softer still, he said, "And what was that?"

I brought my hands to my face. "It was the skeleton of a great bird, Sir."

He was silent for so long I knew I'd done a truly terrible thing. There was only one bird whose skeleton would be so supernaturally vast. The hairs rose on my neck.

He was very still, then he looked at me at last, his fine dark eyes full of sadness and reproach. "I'm disappointed in you, Agnes. You've committed a sin, you understand that?"

"But I didn't mean to," I whispered. "Oh, please, Sir, forgive me."

He shook his head, wearily it seemed to me. "It's not my forgiveness that matters, but forgiveness from above. You've an inquisitive, impulsive nature. I'd not realized that before. I believed you could set an example for Miss Leah. I thought I could rely on you."

I was filled with remorse at the sound of his sigh. "Oh, Sir, please, you can still do so! What should I do? Pray for forgiveness?"

"Yes, indeed." I waited, yearning to be back in his favor. Then he said, "Your aunt's a God-fearing woman, I know. She's Chief Elder in the village?"

"Yes, Sir."

"It wouldn't be right for her to hear of this."

"No, Sir."

"And no one else must know — no one here or in the village."

"I swear I won't tell a soul!"

"Then we'll ask forgiveness for what you've done, pray together. Give me your hand."

I let him take my hand in his long, pale fingers; his grip was cool and strong. He began leading me toward the double doors. I shrank back.

"Please, Sir! Not in there, I beg you!"

"Here, then." His voice had changed strangely. It was rough, thick, choked with emotion. "Come to me, you child of sin."

He dragged me back toward him. I was completely unprepared, still overcome by the thought of how I'd sinned. I lost my balance and fell against him as he pulled. His face was very close, looming above me. In the white cloud-light of that room his mouth was cruel, his hair no longer immaculate in its glossy blackbird arc: it hung, disheveled, over his face, untidy as the feathers of a carrion crow. Mixed with the flower perfume, now overpowering, was a sweet-sour smell as he breathed heavily into my face.

He fumbled at the folds of my cloak, seeking a way to reach my bodice. "Take your amulet out. You must hold it while you pray. Here, let me do it for you."

I struggled to free my amber. But his hands were there already, like claws, ripping at the stuff of my bodice, tearing the lace.

"Let go of her! Let go of her at once, do you hear?"

It was Leah, straight and tall as a cold, white flame in her cloak. She had slipped silently through the doorway in her soft kid boots and now looked him up and down with a contemptuous fury.

Mr. Silas had freed me as soon as he heard her voice, and I, gasping with shock, struggled to cover myself. He stood back, smoothing his hair into place and straightening the fur collar of his cloak. It was as if he'd straightened his face back into place as well: it was once more the charming, courteous face I knew.

"You surprise us, Miss Leah. We thought we were alone."

"And this is how you behave when you're alone with a maid?"

"I endeavor to save all souls, whether they be those of maids or not, Miss Leah."

"I warn you, Silas."

"Of what do you warn me, Miss Leah?" he said smoothly, and he dusted his fingers together as if touching me had dirtied them.

She paused, then turned away angrily and pointed at the doorway. "Get out! Leave us, go!"

"As you wish, Miss Leah." He bowed to her, but his eyes rested on me — with an expression of sorrow, I thought, though whether feigned or genuine, I wasn't sure. A shiver ran down my back. Did he think me damned for what I'd seen?

"Good day to you, and to your companion, Miss Leah."

Then with a swirl of his cloak he was gone, the wet hem leaving a dark, glistening trail on the wood floor.

Leah said nothing until we both heard the door thud shut at the base of the tower. Then she rounded on me. "Fool!" she spat out. "How could you?"

I was still trembling. I shook my head dumbly. I couldn't

understand how she could know that I'd opened the doors to the inner room, but I couldn't understand anything, least of all how my noble Mr. Silas had turned into a monster.

"You were lucky to escape," Leah said grimly. "Last year Silas forced a kitchen maid. It was to save her soul, you understand. When she found she was with child and he wouldn't acknowledge it — he was even going to cast her out from the estate in shame — she drowned herself in the mere."

I stared at her. Her words didn't make sense; I couldn't take them in. "Mr. Silas?"

"*Mister* Silas," she mocked. "None other. The little maid, Scuff, saw him with her — what he did. No one but I believed her, poor child."

"He told me himself how the servant's body was found," I said in a low voice.

"You would have been the next one, Aggie," she said grimly. "Don't you see that?"

I sank down in the green-gold chair. I saw the pattern clearly now: the birds with bright wings that flew so joyously through the lush foliage. *Silas, my handsome, elegant gentleman, who'd said such beautiful things to me, called me his marigold* — I buried my face in my hands to shut out the light, and sat motionless.

Leah left me to recover, and then it seemed even her hard, scornful heart was touched. She came over to me and said, gently for her, "Don't take on so, Aggie. Maids have been taken in by his looks before. But he's a dangerous man, and a clever one."

I was close to tears. "But his soul is pure, it must be! He takes Devotion, he wants to save our souls!"

"Have you never heard of hypocrites, Aggie? He's all high religious talk — it's easy to be deceived — but if you were to uncover his soul, you'd be looking at a nasty little black thing, shriveled as a dead leaf. Stay away from him."

I raised my head and brushed a hand across my eyes. "I'm never going near him again, Miss Leah."

"What? Even on payday?"

She smiled. To my astonishment I realized she was trying to cheer me, she who'd been so unkind. She curled her long limbs gracelessly into the chair opposite mine and regarded me with curiosity. "Did he ask you to meet him here?"

I shook my head. "Dog must have told him I was here." I glanced at her enquiring face and decided to tell the truth, or part of it. "I'd come to read the books." I thought, *If she asks me about the inner room, I'll confess. I don't care what happens to me now.*

But she didn't; she looked astounded. "You risked coming here so you could read the books? Don't you have books in the village?"

"Not like these, Miss," I said, surprised out of my misery. Did she know so little? "The books my aunt taught us from are dull things, the reading approved by the Council. No folk have books in our village. Most children leave school before they can read properly. People are too poor to lose their children to school, they need them to work."

I was reluctant to talk, but she kept asking questions, as if all the curiosity she'd kept inside since my arrival were finally bursting free. My misery lifted a little. I couldn't believe that this was my cold, disdainful mistress.

"I wanted to find out what real books were like." I hesitated. "Mr. Silas says they are blasphemous."

"Fiddlesticks!" said Leah. "We should be free to discuss all sorts of different ideas from our book reading, not have them approved first by a Council, let alone a steward!"

"But the Master's library can't be kept secret from the Lord Protector," I said. "What will happen when he finds out?"

She raised her eyes heavenward. "Don't you know anything, ninny? Years ago, when the Protector married the Master's sister, certain books were banned. But that was only the beginning. The Protector wanted the Master's books out of the Hall, but he gave him special permission to have his books up here, providing they were locked up." She gave a wicked smile. "Of course, the Protector doesn't know I read them now."

"The Master gives you the freedom of the cabinets?" I said wistfully.

"I keep the key for him. The Master's rooms are never private; he can't have any secrets there." She reached into the pocket in her cloak and took out a small brass key, which sparkled in the light as she held it up to me. "He asked me about a book yesterday. That's why I came just now — to look for it. I keep the key in my room, in an old pot. It had chamomile face cream in it once. Even if Dog found the key and guessed what it was for, she'd never dare unlock the cabinets."

"I won't say anything to her, Miss."

"A companion should know her mistress's secrets; that's why I'm telling you. But if you tell anyone else, like your precious Mr. Silas, I'll cut your throat, do you understand?" Her eyes blazed suddenly and I reeled back. "I'll know if you do, and I keep a knife under my pillow. Remember that."

"I won't say anything, Miss Leah," I repeated faintly. I'd no doubt she'd carry out her threat.

She looked bleakly toward the long window where the clouds were darkening, sending shadows into the room. "If only the Master would rid himself of Silas."

For a moment I felt his white hands on my bodice, and shivered. "You saved me, Miss. I should thank you."

She went on as if I hadn't spoken. "Silas's father was steward to Mr. Tunstall's father in the grand days of Murkmere, you know; that's why Mr. Tunstall won't get rid of Silas now. The old Master even paid for Silas to go to school in the Capital. He came back changed, they say. I was a tiny child wanting to play and he'd set butterflies on fire to tease me."

She was silent awhile, her face bitter. My own heart was bitter too. I wondered if it would ever recover.

"That's when I bit him!" said Leah suddenly. "On the right hand, it was. You notice he writes with his left now?" Her voice was gleeful. "The wound went septic. It took so long to heal he had to learn to write all over again, with his left hand." She leaned closer and made a face at me. "He tasted of the dung heap!"

I shuddered; I couldn't speak for a while, looking at her chuckle to herself. "He asked me to watch you, Miss Leah," I said at last. "It was spying he wanted, in truth."

She snorted. "Do you think I don't know? At least you're honest."

"But isn't it your guardian's wish? Isn't that why Mr. Silas wants it?"

"Gilbert Tunstall worries about my safety because he loves me. Silas Seed loathes me. I've no idea why he spies on me."

She began to stride around with her mouth turned down, touching her neck restlessly and easing the collar of her cloak as if it choked her. Finally she flung round to stare at the window. "I hate this aerie of my guardian's, though I've never told him. There's all that sky outside, but it's shut away. I can't breathe."

"A strange place for a library," I said. I could tell from the sharp glance Leah gave me that she knew exactly what I was thinking.

"The Master wanted to be near the clouds. When I was small he'd come alone and watch them for hours." She sucked her cheeks in. "I know it's impractical, mad. The cost of strengthening this floor, then constructing the lift, nearly bankrupted the estate. All the pieces of the pulley system are welded separately. He cut down some of the Murkmere oaks to build the stairs." She sighed. "But he was determined to do it. He has a strong will."

I watched the clouds beyond the glass piling on each other, thick as curdled cream. What strange compulsion would draw a man to watch them alone, suspended between heaven and Earth, day after day?

When I looked back at her, Leah was studying me with her piercing gray eyes, an odd expression on her face.

"There's another reason my guardian used to come. There's something he keeps here. And I think you know what it is."

VIII

Great Bird

She pointed to the floorboards by the double doors, where there was a muddle of dirty footprints, now dry, left by the melting snow from my boots. I felt my cheeks go hot.

She was grinning at me, pleased with her keen eyesight. I couldn't tell if she was angry yet or not; it was like that with Leah. Sometimes her rage boiled slowly.

"It's no secret," she said. "Silas knows what's in that room, and so do the footmen, Jukes and Pegg, but none of the other servants come here alone. They're forbidden, but anyway they wouldn't come. They think the tower's damned because of the books, and they've probably heard what else is up here."

"I'll be damned, Mr. Silas says," I whispered. "Oh, Miss, I'm sorry. I wish I'd never seen it."

She looked at me blankly. "Damned? What on Earth are you talking about?"

Frightened again, I pointed dolefully at the doors. "The image of the Almighty."

She let out a howl of laughter. "You poor goose."

She caught hold of my hand, dragging me with her, ignoring my terrified protests. She leaned her weight against the doors of the inner room and they burst open.

"Now, look," she commanded, and gripped my hand so fiercely I couldn't run. At that moment I was almost more frightened of her contempt if I did so than of the thing that floated in the air above us.

"It was never alive," said Leah. She looked at me, pitying yet amused. "It's made of wood."

In the light that came through the doors I could see that it was suspended by thin cords, inside a frame that was almost invisible. "Touch it, go on," urged Leah.

I felt a smooth-grained texture that was warm under my fingers. It swung slightly from its taut cords as I touched it, the pale wood gleaming in the light. The outstretched wings were covered with linen, not skin after all; the frame was made from thin bands of the same wood.

"But what is it, Miss?"

"It's a flying machine," she said, with a sort of triumph.

"You mean — a man could *fly* in it?"

"That's the whole point of it, silly," she said impatiently. "My guardian had it constructed before his last illness, from diagrams in an old book. The carpenters were frightened to make it at first, because of the blasphemy, but he paid them well." She turned to me and her breath came faster. "This contraption can glide on air, Aggie, it can take its pilot soaring through the sky. Isn't it our dream to fly like the birds?"

I felt cold. "But that's what happened to the avia, Miss. They had dreams, then were imprisoned in them forever."

"But wouldn't you want to fly if you had the chance, to fly out of this little life? Who knows what currents of air might take you to other worlds, maybe better ones?"

"That's blasphemy, indeed, Miss," I whispered.

Leah slapped her skirts in disgust, and the sudden movement made dust rise like smoke from the linen wings of the flying machine.

"Blasphemy! Does everything always have to be sin and punishment? You sound like Silas. He said the Great Eagle would swoop down on my guardian one day for building this. He'd suffer the same punishment as the avia." She let out a sudden wild laugh. "What sort of bird do you think my guardian would be?"

I shook my head, and her laughter died abruptly. We stood together in the shadow of the great wingspan.

Slowly my horror seeped away. It was hard to believe that the delicate contraption hanging above us was evil; it seemed to grow more strangely beautiful as I looked at it. But it was too frail, too inadequate for what it would encounter in the teeming sky. Even the padded body brace that hung from its wooden ribs was light as a puff of thistledown.

"How does it work?"

Leah roused herself. "I don't know. It's heavier than it looks. You can wheel the whole structure out into the other room in its frame, but it takes two men. It can be launched from the window once it's released from its cords. Then the wings unfurl to their full breadth. There's not room for that inside. My guardian could sail straight out into the clouds, only now that his health is bad he can't try it out. It stays in here, getting dustier and dustier."

I knew the contraption was made of wood, yet it seemed alive. I felt its melancholy overwhelm me as she spoke; I sensed how its bones longed for freedom while remaining motionless, impotent, earthbound. I looked at Leah, suddenly apprehensive that she who longed for freedom would be tempted to escape in it herself one day.

But as if she knew what was in my mind, she shook her head. "I haven't the courage, Aggie. What would make it stay up? I don't trust it not to crash into the treetops, let alone to reach the clouds. Its journeys are dreams inside the Master's head. I'm thankful he's too weak to try it out. When I leave Murkmere, I'll go in my own way."

We left it alone with its sorrow at last, in the close darkness of the inner room, swaying forlornly in the draft as we shut the doors: a dusty, silvery bird, with clipped wings.

The outer room was ominously dark. Outside the clouds had turned hard-edged as iron. "It's going to snow again," Leah said. "We must leave."

I turned toward the doorway obediently, but she had rushed to a cabinet. "The book! I forgot the Master's book!"

She unlocked the cabinet and took one out, looked at its spine, and tucked it beneath her cloak. Then she glanced at

me and reached in again. Suddenly a book was thrust at me, leather-bound, smooth and soft, like a small animal. "You can borrow it. Hide it away safely."

The first flakes were falling as we left the tower.

"We'll head for the boundary wall," said Leah. "We can cut across when we see the icehouse. There's a sheltered walkway that runs from it to the house."

We stumbled across the snowy hollows behind the tower to a level area, broken by pine and silver birch. Snowflakes were already beginning to fly into my eyes and mouth, whirling in all directions like feathers at a cockfight, but it was easier to see among the trees, and the boughs gave us some shelter.

I noticed a set of dark footprints — man's prints — in the snow in front of me, and beginning to fill with new flakes as I slithered along, clutching my precious burden — my book — under my cloak. The fresh snow was slippery, and my feet seemed too cold and clumsy to support me.

A keeper must have been this way earlier, I thought as I followed the two trails: the keeper's prints and Leah's long, narrow ones.

Her cloaked figure was still a little way ahead, almost at the wall, when suddenly I heard her give a cry. When I caught up with her she was speechless, white-faced, snow matting her hair where it trailed out under her bonnet and lying on the rabbit-fur collar of her cloak. My own hair was stiff with it and my cheeks felt pinched and bloodless.

We stared at each other like two wraiths; then she pointed.

There was a man sprawled facedown among a confused mess of footprints not far away. As soon as I approached him I knew instinctively and absolutely that he was dead, frozen to death as he lay in the cold. The outflung limbs were rigid, the heavy cape bunched up over the still body.

Death is commonplace in the village: folk die from sickness every winter; the women go in childbirth. I'd been familiar with death all my fifteen years; my own elder sister had gone when I was five. I wasn't afraid. I approached the body with scarcely a qualm, except of pity.

"It must be a keeper, Miss Leah," I called back.

When she saw me so bold, she too came closer, not to be outdone, her pale jaw set. "Is he dead?" she asked nervously.

"I think so, Miss Leah."

"He's murdered, then."

I stared at her. It was as if she stated a fact. "Murdered?"

She gestured at the footprints all trodden together around the dead man's body. "There's been a struggle. See?" She looked a little closer, putting her hand to her mouth. But there was no stench yet; the coldness of the air prevented it.

"We must get back quickly, Miss." I looked through the snowy trees, half-expecting to see a dark figure emerge and threaten us. But nothing moved except the falling snow, and the sifting of the flakes was the only sound.

Leah was peering at the body, as if fascinated. "He's not one of our men. Not one of the keepers here. None of them has a cape that color. He must be a trespasser. That's why they've killed him."

"Who've killed him?" I said, appalled.

"The keepers, of course. One with a knife, maybe another to bring him down first. There'll be blood, but it hasn't seeped through." She spoke carelessly, squatting down and brushing snow from the man's cape. It was dark with moisture and pitted with snow, but it would be green when dry, a forest green that might have hidden a trespasser in summer but was all too obvious in winter.

"Leave him, Miss!" I cried. Next she would be lifting the cape to examine the mark of death.

"I want to see what he looks like."

She was struggling to turn the man over. There was nothing I could do but help her, though my gorge rose as I touched the cold, dead shoulders. He was heavy and it took both of us.

Then with a soft thump into the new snow the man was staring up at the sky. His jacket was caked with the frozen snow he'd lain on.

"A handsome man, not old," said Leah.

I stared down at the untouched face.

"I know who he is," I said.

IX

Matt Humble

You know him?" Leah whispered.

My face felt frozen into a mask; I could hardly move my lips to speak. "He's a packman called Matt Humble."

Spring, summer, autumn, Matt had come to our village with his wares. One morning you'd see his sturdy figure come tramping out of the early mist, all hung about with pots and pans, his pack full to bursting on his back. He'd stay a night, tell his stories, then next morning be on his way again. Only last autumn, when I'd turned fifteen, Jethro had bought me a blue-green ribbon from his pack to bind my hair. Matt had told us it was the color of the sea.

Snowflakes were falling into Matt's open eyes. My own hand felt as cold as death, but with a clumsy finger I tried to close the lids, to shut away that dreadful stony stare and bring him peace. It was no use; by now his eyelids were as stiff as vellum.

Leah seemed transfixed by the body. I could hear her panting. Her mouth was open, and she trembled with cold and a febrile excitement that made her eyes burn in her bloodless face. "He must have been trespassing," she said. "We don't allow packmen here."

"That's no reason to murder him!" I said, not caring that I spoke so sharply to my mistress.

She was surprised enough to drag her eyes away and look at me. "My guardian imagines danger for me everywhere. The keepers act on his orders. Anyone caught trespassing is questioned and then, if the keepers aren't satisfied . . ."

She didn't finish. Nor did she need to.

"If they'd questioned him, they'd have discovered he was only a packman going about his work," I said, appalled. "They must have killed him in cold blood."

She shrugged carelessly. "He'd no pack with him."

It was true. I stared at Matt's body in bewilderment, as if I could make it give up its secrets, my knees turning numb through my skirts as I knelt in the trampled snow. *What had he been doing here? He must have known the danger that would face him if he dared climb the wall into the Murkmere estate. And it was early in the year for him to be traveling.*

Leah put out the tip of her tongue and licked the crusted snow round her mouth, regarding the body with a hard, bright gaze that held no trace of pity. "We must say nothing about this," she said, as if she relished the thrill of such a secret. "It's safest to keep silent at Murkmere."

"What will happen to the body, though?" I said, my voice trembling. "Will the keepers come for it?"

She turned away as if suddenly bored, beating her mittened hands together like a dirge. "They'll move it soon enough when the thaw comes — what hasn't been eaten by the night dogs."

I think a fit of the horrors seized me then.

I scrambled to my feet and forced my numb legs to move as quickly as they could from that forsaken spot. Leah was making for the gray dome of the icehouse between the trees, and I followed her into the covered walkway that led from it. There was a paved surface beneath our boots, thinly powdered with drifting snow. Beyond the stone arches that supported the roof, the flakes still whirled relentlessly, but under its shelter it seemed unnaturally calm, so that her voice, loud in my ear, made me start.

"I'm sure I recognized that packman's face too. Strange, isn't it?"

"You said no packmen came to Murkmere, Miss," I said, in disbelief.

"But I think I saw him once, in the house. I remember his healthy, outdoor look. I thought he must be a new keeper."

"One face looks like another in death," I said shortly. "The flesh shrinks to the skull."

"Certainly you couldn't call him healthy now," said Leah, with a grimace, and she fingered the bones of her cheeks thoughtfully.

I thought Leah would take her book straight to the Master when we returned. He'd be alone in his room waiting for her, his iron cage wheeled to the window so he could stare out at the falling snow.

But Leah didn't turn down the passage to his room. Instead, she gathered her skirts together and dashed at her usual pace up the dark back stairs, the servants' staircase, as if she wanted to talk more about the murder. I'd no choice but to follow her all the way to her bedchamber.

As we went in, Dog looked up, startled. She was at the table by Leah's bed, setting down a silver tray on which stood a steaming goblet. The smirk that still hung round her lips began to fade as she saw us together: her mistress in high good humor with the disgraced companion.

"Oh, Miss Leah," she gabbled, avoiding my eyes but all little smiles and bobs to Leah. "The Master told me you'd gone out in this dreadful weather! I ordered Scuff to make you a hot posset —"

She didn't get any further, for Leah flew at her like a madwoman, knocking off her cap and sending the goblet bouncing onto the polished floor so that the posset spilled out in a rich golden froth. Dog began to squeal, clutching the silver tray to her bosom like a shield, while Leah danced around her in a frenzy, belaboring her with her mittens and yelling insults.

"Sneaktongue! Malicemonger! Crudspreader!"

"Not me, Miss!" shrieked Dog. She pointed at me with a

shaking finger and the silver tray clattered to the floor to join the goblet. "It was her, Miss! Her who done wrong!"

"It was you who reported it, fool!" cried Leah, and she swooped on her again.

With her long arms beating around the unfortunate Dog's head and the mittens flapping, she reminded me so much of a scrawny mother hen defending its chick that I felt bubbles of hysterical laughter burst from me. I ran forward and restrained my mistress as respectfully as I could, and Doggett staggered back still shielding her face. I received only a sullen glare for trying to rescue her.

"To tell Silas!" Leah hissed at Dog. "Silas of all people!"

Dog shook her greasy head wildly. "Mr. Silas asked me, Miss. I had to tell him."

"Indeed?" said Leah, looming over the maid. "And what was Silas doing outside alone? I believe you both left the Hall together."

"No, Miss!" Dog began to gabble as if the speed of her story might persuade her mistress of its truth. "Mistress Crumplin asked me to go after Aggie, to walk with her. Then I saw her was headin' for the tower and I knew it was forbidden. I was goin' to warn her, honest, but Mr. Silas and a keeper came out of the trees at the top of the tower rise. Mr. Silas questioned me. He said we'd go and find Aggie together. He took my arm so firm I couldn't do nothin' but go with him, Miss."

There was a long silence only broken by the occasional aggrieved sniff from Dog, while her little beady eyes darted appraisingly from one to the other of us. But I couldn't speak. I knew what Leah was thinking, for I was thinking it too.

Silas and the keeper together — had they both been responsible for Matt's murder? How long had they been in that part of the grounds? Had Silas given orders, or done the deed himself?

I couldn't believe it and I didn't want to, for a piece of my heart held to him still. I remembered the way he had stared at his hands in the tower, those beautiful white hands, so very clean. There had been no bloodstain on them then.

But a fatal knife-thrust can go so deep that the wound bleeds little externally, especially in cold weather.

As the evening deepened, the snow stopped, and it seemed to become a little warmer. I didn't attend Devotion: I couldn't face Silas before I'd recovered myself, nor could I bear listening to him lead the servants' prayers. But tomorrow was payday, and I'd have to face him then.

With evening, Leah's mood changed again and she became withdrawn and restless. She said nothing more to me about Matt's murder; she scarcely spoke.

At supper, the dining room, with the two of us sitting at opposite ends of the long table, seemed full of her fidgets. She scowled at the elderly footman as he crept with painful slowness from door to table, the plates in his trembling hands clattering together like two gossips in the marketplace.

"Where's Jukes?"

The old man jumped as she snapped the question, and

the plates of boiled mutton jumped with him. "He's sick, Miss Leah."

"Sick?" Leah said the word as if no one at Murkmere should have the temerity to be in such a state.

"He has the feverish ague. Many of the servants are afflicted, Miss."

"Is that why the onion sauce is gray?" she demanded, staring at the sauceboat in disgust. "The cook's sauce-maker is sick too, I suppose. Take it away!"

The footman took the offending sauceboat and shuffled off. Leah pushed the mutton away angrily and pecked at her vegetables, while I couldn't help brooding. My throat closed on my food and my eyes watered. If Leah noticed she gave no sign.

She didn't speak to me until we were in her parlor.

"Shall I get the cards out, Miss?" I asked, making an effort to carry out my duties.

She was slumped down among the cushions on the tapestry daybed. She didn't answer but jumped up, went over to the window, and drew back the heavy silk curtains. "That's better," she said with a great sigh, and stared out into the dark.

In the evenings Leah's parlor was cozy, with its crackling fire beneath a pretty, painted mantel, its wall coverings of faded blue silk and curtains embroidered with forget-me-nots. It was only in the cold, gray daylight that you noticed the walls were speckled with damp. But now, with the curtains drawn back, the night outside seemed to threaten the little room.

"Come away to the fire, Miss," I said uneasily. "It's drafty by the window."

Leah touched her neck in the restless movement I was beginning to know. "To be out there, free," she whispered to herself. The moon had sailed clear of the clouds and was silvering the soft plains of snow beneath it.

"They'll break the ice on the mere tomorrow," she said, turning to me. "It's made me anxious all evening. There's a thaw in the air. Those clouds will bring rain, not snow. They'll want to break the ice while it's still hard."

She saw my baffled expression and a sudden torrent of explanation poured from her. "For the icehouse. Every winter they must break new ice to be layered in straw and keep our food stores fresh. They take sled-loads of it. The grooms and ostlers help the keepers. They alarm the swans with their din." Her lips twisted. "It's foolish to bait a swan in its territory. Last time a youth had his arm broken."

"Will you watch the ice breaking, Miss?"

"I'll go there when they've all gone." She looked at me with a half-smile, as if testing me. She knew about my fruitless searches for her by the mere. How I must have amused her, day after day, as I trailed after her in the mud and bitter cold.

But something had hardened inside me since the morning. I wouldn't let her humiliate me any longer with her cruel games. I looked back at her steadily. "The mere's a dangerous place alone, Miss. I'll come with you tomorrow. It's my duty as your companion."

She stared back at me, then to my amazement dropped her

gaze and flung herself down on the daybed. "Oh, very well. Come with me if you must."

As the howling of the night dogs passed my window that night, I lay and shuddered, thinking of Matt's body being torn limb from limb, his blood dark on the snow. Matt, who had visited the village all the years of my growing; who'd go there no longer. What had possessed him to come to Murkmere?

And what had possessed me too?

Tomorrow I'd give in my notice when I collected my wages from Silas. I'd tell him I needed to return to my aunt and take care of her. He'd know my true reason for leaving, of course, but I wouldn't let him stop me.

I promised myself that soon I'd lie on my own pallet next to my aunt; and with that thought I was comforted. Soon I'd be away from this dreadful place, where servant girls were driven to drown themselves and innocent men were murdered. No wonder my poor mother had run away.

And what of Leah, with her heathen ways and doomed soul?

I didn't care what became of her. Not a jot.

But I didn't sleep well. Next morning, I looked out of my window as I wearily fastened my bodice, and saw that drizzle had pitted the snow with tiny holes as if mice had supped on it. Leah had been right about the thaw.

Her mood hadn't improved. At breakfast, she almost threw

the oatmeal at the old footman, complaining that it tasted bitter and had black pieces stuck through it. All the time we ate we could hear the unruly clamor from the stable block as the men made themselves ready for the ice breaking.

I didn't see her again that morning, but I knew she'd be with the Master at her books. They'd hear the tumult of the ice breaking from his rooms: even indoors it seemed impossible to escape the distant chipping and thudding, the crack as the ice broke, the roar from the men as the shards were successfully netted from the water.

I'd seen the stable hands troop out earlier, trailing the long wooden handles of the nets behind them, their dark figures silhouetted against the snow that was tinged yellow under the overcast sky. There was much joshing and guffawing as they met the keepers, who were standing ready with their sledges and mallets. Then they set off together, a small militia set on destruction.

Our luncheon was late, but Leah seemed relieved now that the rowdiness of the ice breaking was over, and merely grumbled to herself when a strangely black suet pudding was put on the table before us.

"You needn't walk with us today," she told Dog when we were upstairs later, and Dog had helped her fasten her boots. "There's my mending for you to do instead."

As Dog passed me at the chamber door, she shot out her hand and pinched me. "Them swans nip harder than that," she hissed. "You'll see!"

X

Swanskin

Leah and I followed the black lines the net handles had made as they were dragged along earlier; the snow crumbled under my boots like stale cake as I struggled to keep pace with her long legs.

"Have you read the book I gave you yet, Aggie?"

Is it possible she's making conversation? I thought, amazed. "I began it this morning, Miss, while you were studying."

"What do you think of it?" She looked eager for discussion, yet I knew I'd only disappoint her with my answer.

"It seems rather — blasphemous."

She gave her mocking smile. "How fond you are of that word! A great thinker wrote that book long before I was born. Nobody's heard of him nowadays. His books are banned."

"Then isn't it wrong to read it, Miss?"

"I'm going to give you far worse books than that!" she said wickedly.

I hugged myself, shivering a little with cold and the boldness with which she spoke. I could feel my amber digging into me. All that morning as I read the book, I'd imagined the eye of the Almighty boring through the ceiling above me. But I knew I had to finish it, and read more.

"Do you understand the author's argument: that events happen by chance and are not predetermined?" Leah asked.

I hesitated, for I'd only learned the meaning of the last word that very morning. "But we've been taught that the Almighty has decided the future of the world, and there's nothing mortal man can do to change His will."

"And you believe that? That men don't have the freedom to choose their fates?"

My head whirled. "I think so."

She looked at me pityingly. "Read the rest of the book, then. It's a history. You'll find things were different once." She paused, and rubbed her neck absently. "Sometime later we took a wrong turning. I often wonder if there's a world where things didn't turn out this way, where they do things differently. The Master thinks there may be lots of universes, you know, each one only a little different from the others."

"But where would they be, Miss?" I said, puzzled, but respectful of the Master's great intellect. "In the sky? There wouldn't be enough room for them."

"Perhaps they all fit inside each other." Leah made circles with her hands. "I had a set of dolls when I was small. One doll fitted inside another doll, and another inside that doll, and so on."

"But how does the Master think the Great Eagle would fly around all these universes?" I asked faintly.

Leah laughed, and shivers ran all over me. "He doesn't think about *that* at all, Aggie! Surely you realize he's not a believer? The Master thinks that scientific information should dictate man's path, not religion." She went on passionately, careless of the horror her words caused me, "Imagine, Aggie, perhaps there's another universe somewhere with a world almost exactly like ours, but without the Ministration. Without the Lord Protector. Of course there would have to be some other system of rule in their place. But a tolerant one that allowed people to think for themselves and be represented in government, just as we used to be."

"Hush, Miss, that's treason!" I looked around nervously, but we were alone in the snowy landscape: not a keeper to be seen, not even a seagull flying through the leaden skies — for which I was glad, since seagulls are the Souls of the Drowned and can listen. "Surely Lord Grouted, the Protector, is kind? What he does is for our good. And he married the Master's own sister! You must hear about him from her."

Leah stopped and faced me, her face bleak. "Mr. Tunstall's sister? Sophia's dead. She caught the plague one summer in the Capital. Some say the plague is carried in the canals of the city. She'd given Lord Grouted a son, which was all the Protector cared about — someone to take over from him one day. I believe he's in the Militia now, in training." She shuddered, then went on. "Perhaps it was for the best that Sophia died."

I stared at her. "What do you mean?"

"I don't remember meeting Lord Grouted, I was too small. But I've heard stories about him from the servants."

"So your guardian lost his sister as well as his wife and baby?" I understood the bitterness in the Master's face.

"He has me," Leah said fiercely.

And, of course, there was nothing I could say to that.

"But these stories about the Lord Protector . . ." I prompted after we had trudged on in silence for a while, our breath steaming in the dank air.

Leah shrugged. "You'll be able to judge him yourself soon enough. My guardian's to hold a ball here at Murkmere for my sixteenth birthday. Lord Grouted and members of the Ministration will be invited."

"Then the Master must think he's a good man!"

She picked up a handful of snow and threw it at an ancient oak. "You're such a simpleton, Aggie. Can't you understand that Mr. Tunstall only invites them because it's a chance to show he's still Master here, that he can still manage his estate? Do you think he'd allow them beyond his door otherwise? It's been years since his quarrel with the Lord Protector, and neither's forgotten it."

I gasped, and my throat stung with the cold. "He dared to quarrel with the Lord Protector? Was it about his sister?"

"Sophia was in good health then; they'd come to stay. I was too small to understand what the quarrel was about. Mr. Tunstall's never mentioned it to me, I only know what the servants have told me."

She was staring ahead at the frozen mere, biting her lip. I didn't think she'd confide more, but then she sighed and the words came haltingly.

"My guardian was in his wheelchair, as usual, when they began arguing. After using words to no avail, he attacked Lord Grouted with his bare hands, so the story goes. You've seen how strong his hands and arms are? It was after that he asked for iron bands to be put around his chair, so that if he did lose his temper again, others would be safe."

She gazed at me, her eyes shadowed. "You see, he'd almost strangled the Lord Protector."

The men had cleared the ice in a broad band round the rim of the mere, and the pewter gray water lay exposed and motionless. The black mud of the shore had been trodden clear of snow and was firm under our boots. Farther along, the way to the water was blocked by a growth of dark rushes slicing up through the surface and a thicket of shrubs that spread right round the mere.

"This way," said Leah. She went down almost to the water, making the moorhens skitter away in fright.

I followed hesitantly, and suddenly she had parted the tangled bushes and disappeared.

I began to push frantically through in the direction I thought she'd taken, scratching my hands and dislodging clumps of wet snow. The mud was soft between the bushes, and I was sinking.

"Here," said Leah's impatient voice, and she hauled me up

beside her, onto a causeway of small stones. "It's the remains of an old path."

I grasped a handful of her cloak, frightened of losing her again. Mud had splashed right up my cloak and I was thankful I'd had the sense to wear my old one. My hat, though, was my new black felt, and I pulled it down firmly so it wouldn't be knocked off by the overhanging branches and twigs that spiked out at all angles; its brim was already drooping in the damp air.

"Quiet," hissed Leah. "You'll scare the swans."

But I was being quiet, I thought indignantly, as quiet as you could be when squeezing through a prickly jungle of vegetation surrounded by mud and water. I was making a heroic effort not to cry out at the creatures I thought I saw out of the corner of my eye: eels rising and slithering over the mud, voles slipping into dark places, the scurry of rats among the reeds.

I don't know how long we'd been struggling along when we came to a muddy beach and, at the water's edge, a boathouse built of planks that were rotting and green. On the far side of the beach the path was blocked by a great fall of earth that had crumbled away from the bank to expose twisted roots and gaping holes, half full of snow.

Leah scrambled up the rickety wooden steps to the door of the boathouse, and disappeared without a word. Not wanting to be left alone again, I climbed up after her.

In the dim green light inside she was standing on a jetty that ran around the three walls. There was a smell of soaked wood that reminded me painfully of Aunt Jennet's cottage on rainy days. A single boat floated like a shadow on the scummy water below our feet.

"In the old days guests would go boating on the mere," Leah said, her voice sounding hollow in the enclosed space. "But no one's cleared the weeds for years. Besides, the swans nest in the reed beds by the island. They'd attack anyone who approached at the wrong time."

I wished I could stay there, protected by three walls, rotten or not. But as I turned back after her into the daylight, I heard her say, "I can see the swans!"

Next, she had pulled me impatiently down the steps, and I knew I wasn't safe anymore.

There were swans on the marshy pools on the Wasteland, but I'd never seen them. Travelers sometimes thought them ghost birds when they saw them drifting in the murk. Now, as I saw those pale shapes emerge from the darkness of the reed beds near the island and skim languidly through the gray water, I understood why. Each swan glowed against the dullness of the mere, like a candle into which the lighted wick has fallen. Their necks were slender and elegant, and they carried their heads so proudly it seemed each one wore a crown.

Leah was counting. "They're all safe. Those men are such monsters with their mallets and noise. When the ice is thin enough the swans break it themselves, you know. I've seen them slit it with their bills and make a narrow channel to swim along."

I watched the swans weave between each other on the water, like dancers in a dream. "There are so many!"

Leah smiled complacently, as if, like a trickster at a fair, she had produced them herself from inside her cloak. "They're the descendants of a pair that came from the pleasure gardens of the Capital. They were given as a wedding present to my guardian."

So that was why she cared about them so much. She was protecting them for the Master's sake.

"You know the language of birds, Aggie. What do swans signify?"

"But you don't believe such things!" And I was quite sure that a copy of the *Table of Significance* wasn't among the books in the watchtower.

"All the same, tell me."

"True Love and Happiness in Marriage, Miss," I said, thinking she'd laugh at me.

But her face was sad. "In that case it was an excellent present. My guardian loved his wife deeply. Did you know that a group of swans together are called a 'lamentation,' Aggie? The swans still mourn for her, just as he does."

She shot me a sly glance, her mood changing suddenly. "Do you have a sweetheart?"

The question surprised me, and I was put out to find myself blushing. I'd immediately thought of Jethro Sim, for no good reason at all. "Swans are thought of as messengers too," I said quickly.

"The Murkmere swans aren't messengers," she said, sad again. "The keepers clip their wings to keep them here."

The swans were gliding toward our part of the shore as if

they had made the decision together. As Leah went closer to the water's edge, they suddenly rose out of the water with a tremendous splashing and rearing of necks and bills.

I didn't know what to do; I was frightened they'd attack her. Now they were advancing up the beach toward her, waddling in an ungainly way, looking enormous against her frailty. She was suddenly surrounded by a cloud of dazzling plumage.

She stood motionless, making a strange clicking sound with her tongue. The swans responded in the same way, varying their clicks with soft snorts. Then, very gently, they began to rub their heads against her black cloak. They ruffled her fine silvery hair and twined their necks round her gawky frame, up, down, while she ran her hands slowly over their feathers.

Her face was rapt; she'd forgotten me. For her, nothing else existed at that moment but the circling swans, and she stood like a queen among them.

I felt a chill run through me, as if I looked on something unearthly.

I drew back, my gaze still fixed on her. The next moment I had slipped, clawing at the bank behind me, feeling a great root give under my hand, and sending clods of wet earth and snow thudding over the hard mud of the shore.

The swans turned, and hissed furiously as they saw me, their necks rising and curving back as if they were preparing to strike. They began to move ponderously toward me, raising their wings with a sound like wet linen flapping in the wind. I could feel the vibration of their coming through my boots.

"Go back!" shrieked Leah. She pointed at the bushes. "They can't follow!"

I scrambled back in, my heart beating fast, not caring whether my new hat was ripped to shreds.

Leah was making soft, soothing noises. Gradually, the hissing died away and I heard the swans start to click and snort again. There was splashing, then silence.

"You can come out," Leah called. "They've gone."

The stretch of gray water was deserted. Leah took in my disheveled appearance without sympathy. "I should never have brought you here. They were trying to protect me." Her eyes were bright; her cheeks had lost their pallor.

"You look happy enough, Miss!" I blurted out resentfully.

Her face softened and was suddenly vulnerable. "I discovered the swans when I was a small child. They've been my companions always, my only friends. I've had no one else to talk to."

Pity tugged at me. "I know what it's like, Miss. My sister died when I was little."

She'd been gazing at the empty water but now she turned to me, her interest caught. "Didn't you have friends, though?"

"None of the other girls wanted to be friends with me," I said, with an effort. "I was the schoolmistress's niece. I was privileged, you see."

She smiled at me, as if she suddenly saw me properly for

the first time. "Then we're the same, you and I. We know what it is to be alone."

And I was so touched that I smiled foolishly back at her.

As we turned to go I almost fell again. The globe of white root that nearly tripped me as it lay on the mud was the very same one I'd pulled out in my fall earlier.

Leah steadied me, screeching with laughter at my disgruntled face, and then she saw the hole that the root had left behind in the bank.

"Wait. There's something in here."

The hole was nearer her eye level than mine. She flung back her cloak and rolled up the sleeve of her wool dress as if to plunge her bare white arm into the oozy darkness.

"Don't, Miss Leah!" I cried in disgust, thinking of what might be hiding in there: water snakes, coiled slippery and cold, and the crawling things with lidless eyes and sharp teeth that dwell in the dark.

But she didn't listen. She felt about and brought her arm out at last, mud-smeared to the elbow; she was clutching what I thought was the filthy, rotted carcass of some animal.

I drew back in revulsion, but instead of dropping it at once, she examined it curiously. "It's a sack, Aggie, and there's something inside!"

"Leave it, Miss!"

But as I spoke, the wrapping shredded from her hand, leaving her holding a spongy bundle.

"It's a dead bird," I said, and clutched my amber for protection. "Lay it down so its soul can go free."

"But there aren't any bones," said Leah.

I tugged at her arm, but she held on. "Drop it!" I screamed.

Maybe my scream brought her to her senses, for at last she loosened her grip and the wet mass of dirty feathers slapped down onto the mud.

But she didn't speak to me all the way back to the house.

Perhaps it was just as well that Leah was such an unpredictable, contrary creature, I thought. At least I wouldn't regret leaving her.

All day I'd pushed away the thought of seeing Silas that afternoon when the servants' wages were given out. Somehow I had to find the courage to give in my notice, and so far I hadn't even planned what I was going to say.

As I went into my bedchamber, I looked with dread at the mechanical clock. In the time I'd spent at Murkmere I'd learned to read clocks like this, though I still preferred the old sand-timer at home. *A little after four: I must hurry.* I threw my cloak on the bed, smoothed my unruly hair, and rushed downstairs.

There were servants in an untidy line down the passageway outside the steward's room. They stopped their coughing and snuffling to eye me up and down.

Dog was the last one there, and I went to stand behind her, sticking my chin up and avoiding their gaze. I knew by now that none of the servants came from the Eastern Edge;

they'd all come from the Capital, like Dog. I could hear it in their clipped, nasal voices and see it in their offhand manner. Among them, only Scuff ever spoke to me.

The line shuffled on, each servant going in alone through the open door. Dog ignored me and made a great show of chattering to the girl in front of her. When at last she went in and I was left outside in the empty passage, I heard Silas's voice.

"You let them go together?"

Dog murmured something, then she cried out, "No, Sir, please no!"

Then the voices went quiet. I was astonished when she came out at last, looking pleased with herself and clutching coins in both hands. She brushed by me and went off with her head in the air.

"Next," called Silas.

He must have known I was the only one left. I moistened my dry lips and went in.

XI

Wet Feathers

Silas was sitting at his desk beneath the carved eagle. Dusk was drawing in and there were more candles lit than there had been the other morning, yet still the room seemed shadowy. There was a closed iron box on the desk and what appeared to be an open ledger; and I saw, with a jump of my heart, his black-handled riding crop lying across the corner.

As I stood before him, Silas marked something with a tick in the ledger and then looked up at me through his spectacles. "I'm sorry to hear what Doggett says," he said, chiding me like a father with a disobedient child.

I cleared my throat. "What does she say, Sir?"

"That you went with Miss Leah to the mere this afternoon."

I understood now the reason for Dog's triumphant look. "You wanted me to stay with her, Sir."

"But are you going to tell me what took place there?"

I bit my lip. "I can't spy for you, Sir, I'm sorry."

I thought he'd be angry. But he merely laid down his pen and put the tips of his fingers together. His voice was very gentle.

"I've told you her soul's in danger. She'll lead you into wicked ways if you let her influence you. Indeed, I believe that may be the explanation for your behavior in the tower yesterday." He took off his spectacles and his eyes were clouded with concern, his fine features softly gilded by the candlelight. He wanted me to repent, and if I did, I knew I'd be his marigold again and bask in the pleasure of his approval.

But I couldn't forget the beast that lurked inside the quilted silk of his waistcoat. I saw him suddenly as I had yesterday, his smooth dark hair wild as a crow's wing, his open mouth loose and wet. Had he so conveniently forgotten his own behavior? And Matt's murder?

I stayed silent, hoping to appear cool and unmoved.

"Such sullen looks, Agnes?"

"You let me believe I'd seen the Almighty Himself," I muttered.

He held up a hand, chiding me. "Hush, you mustn't speak His name so lightly." He turned and looked up at the carved Eagle behind him as if they were in secret collusion. "But He's everywhere, Agnes. You know that, don't you? Besides, the tower is forbidden to the servants. It was right you did penance." He lowered his voice and gazed back at me steadily, his eyes fathomless. "But in trying to persuade you to repent,

I frightened you. I regret that deeply. I've done penance my-self for it, believe me."

I stared at him in amazement, hearing the honesty in his voice.

"As for Leah," he added gravely, "heed my warning. I know more than you about your mistress. I've observed her since she was a strange, willful little child."

I held myself stiffly, my heartbeats thumping in my ears. "I'm afraid I must ask you to find another companion for her, Sir. Someone else must watch her for you, better than I can. I want to give in my notice. I must return to my aunt. I worry about her, all alone. I never should have accepted this position."

His eyebrows rose. "But you did, Agnes. You signed your agreement to stay on unconditionally — with your own hand you did so."

I was speechless. He turned to the rolls of parchment on the shelves behind him. His hand hovered; he picked one and, facing me again, smoothed it out on the desk. I recognized it as the contract I had signed so carelessly on my first afternoon.

"There it is, Agnes, your signature at the bottom, above my own for the Master. And there's the clause, look, that binds you to stay until Leah's coming of age this summer." He sounded regretful. "You see, it's always wise to read such things through first."

He looked at me, a smile lurking in his lustrous eyes. He knew he'd won.

"But what about my time off?" I cried desperately. "May I at least go and visit my aunt?"

"You've plenty of free time here in the mornings. It wouldn't be fair on the other staff if I were to give you extra. Besides, I can't spare an ostler to ride with you on the Wasteland road. It would mean a wasted day for them."

He sounded so reasonable, I knew I was defeated. I turned miserably toward the door, then remembered. In a small, choked voice I said, "May I have my wages, then, please, Sir?"

He opened the iron box and I saw it was full of money: brass coins, not the gold I had seen on his desk before. His fingers hovered, then he took a single coin and gave it to me. It was a half-revere. Surely not a fitting wage for a mistress's companion?

"When you do your duty properly," he said, "then you'll receive proper wages, Agnes Cotter."

I put the coin beneath my pillow and tried to blink back my tears. I'd never be able to go back to Aunt Jennet with my baggage chinking, and pour out gold coins with a flourish at her feet. I'd never receive more than a half-revere a week, for I'd never do my duty properly in Silas's eyes. I knew what he wanted. Yet if I went straight to the Master himself and complained, he too would tell me that he wanted me to watch Leah. Worst of all was the thought that now I had to stay at Murkmere until Leah's birthday. How was I to bear it?

I gazed at my tragic eyes in the mirror. *I must bear it*, I thought. My mother had been here for years, whereas I'd only months to face alone.

I wiped my eyes, put on one of my new wool dresses, and went along to Leah's room to see if she needed anything before supper. She didn't answer, so I turned the door handle and went in, expecting to find Dog in there, helping her dress. But she was alone.

She had her back to me, so absorbed in what she was doing she didn't hear me cross the room. Though she was fully dressed and still in her mud-splattered serge, she was standing at her washstand, rubbing at something in the basin.

"Miss Leah . . ."

She jumped and turned, dripping water over the floorboards. Her eyes glittered as if she had a fever. "Look!" She hauled a sopping, gray bundle from the basin.

"What is it, Miss?"

"It's what we found this afternoon."

I stared at her, horrified. "You shouldn't have brought it into the house! Heaven knows what you've done!"

"Oh, superstition!" she snapped.

"You went back to the mere alone, in the dark?"

"It was still twilight," she said irritably. She spoke very fast and each cheek had a bright spot of color. "I'm going to wear it at my ball. It will make an excellent wrap."

She brought the disgusting thing closer still, so that it was almost under my nose and I could see the wet feathers all stuck together. There was one feather glued to the side of her mouth as if she'd brought the bundle to her lips.

"Don't you see what it is?" she said. "It's a swanskin."

I recoiled. "You'd wear a dead swan on your own back? You know that's sacrilege. You must be mad!"

There was a terrible silence. I'd gone too far. Then she darted toward me, the outstretched fingers of her free hand, pallid and wrinkled from the cold water, poking at my face, and her teeth bared in a hideous grimace. "Mad? Perhaps I am!"

I backed away, frightened, a hand to my open mouth, shaking my head at her feebly, until I reached the door.

And all the way to my room I was followed by the peals of her delighted laughter.

XII

Planning Escape

I lay huddled on my bed, trying to get warm, filled with dread that through the crack in the door I'd hear Leah summoning me; but everything was silent, except for the tearing of the candle flame in the draft. I kept seeing her urgent hands raise the filthy bundle from the washing-bowl and plunge it back into the water, rinsing, rinsing.

Leah would risk the anger of the Gods if she wore the swanskin. She'd be punished. And what would happen to me, her companion? Would I too face punishment? What was I to do?

It was so simple, I realized at last. I wouldn't stay at Murkmere. If Silas wouldn't accept my notice, I'd leave anyway, escape. *Escape!* The word had such a brave and joyful ring. It was what my mother had done, and I'd do it too. I'd stay with our relatives inland until enough time had passed for them to forget me at Murkmere.

I'd lay my plans carefully. I didn't know what they were yet, but I'd think of something. After all, I had plenty of time on my hands. Meanwhile, I'd act the demure companion, carry out my duties, attend Devotion. *No one must suspect, least of all Silas.*

I swung my legs off the bed, pulled on my wool dress, fastened my hair up, and by the time the gong sounded for supper I was ready, standing with folded hands by Leah's door.

"So quiet and abashed, Aggie?" she greeted me teasingly. "This isn't like you. What can be the matter?"

I bit my lip, but said nothing. I'd decided not to mention the swanskin again.

Leah's cheeks still burned feverishly, though her neck and thin chest in the low-cut gown were startlingly white. Without either my own or Doggett's help, she hadn't bothered to do up all the tiny silk-covered buttons at her back, and her shoulder blades jutted through the gaps.

"Stop fussing me!" she said, when I tried to do the buttons up myself. "It doesn't matter what I look like. Who's to see me in this dreary place?" She grabbed up her silk skirts with both hands so that the delicate lace was crushed, and darted down the stairs. "Come on. I'm starving!"

The doddering old footman who had served us at luncheon was not in the dining room. Instead, Scuff was there to wait on us, looking even more anxious than usual, though she had been given new slippers for the occasion. "The Master will be joining you tonight, Miss Leah," she whispered.

Leah whirled toward me, her eyes shining. "Hear that, Aggie? He must be feeling better. Now, how shall we sit ourselves, I wonder?"

And she fretted around the long table, rearranging the heavy silver cutlery to her satisfaction: a solitary place at one end and two places laid close together at the other. I could see that I wasn't going to be allowed to usurp any of the Master's attention.

When the clanking of the iron chair was heard along the stone floor outside, she flew to the door and flung it wide. I saw her bend and hug the Master, and his great thick arms, the velvet sleeves falling back to show the strong wrists emerging from a froth of lace, came up and enveloped her scrawny back. I thought how those fingers could crack her spine like a string of nuts.

The two held each other for a long minute without saying anything, and then Leah straightened. Her feverish color had gone and she was suddenly calm.

"Take that chair away from the table, Aggie," she said, and she pushed the Master toward the empty space, placing his wheelchair so that it would be easy for him to reach his food. "This is an occasion, indeed," she murmured, stroking his thick hair. "Why, you've not eaten with me this fortnight past."

He smiled at me. "I'm sorry I've not been able to watch your progress at Murkmere, Agnes. You've been finding my ward a tolerable mistress, I hope? And how has it been to have a companion your own age at last, Leah?"

"Tolerable," muttered Leah. She shot me a glance.

His eyes sparked with amusement. "I'm glad you have the measure of each other. Now, where's my supper?"

Scuff scurried from the room, and I sat down in my lonely state at the end of the table. Leah kept her voice deliberately low as she talked to the Master, so that I should hear nothing.

I rose to my feet and took the claret jug from the sideboard, intending to catch their conversation while I poured the Master some wine. At once Leah snatched the glass away, so quickly I couldn't prevent some crimson drops spilling onto the mahogany. "Mr. Tunstall never drinks wine or spirits; they upset him," she hissed at me.

I stammered my apologies to him and found a napkin, with which I dried and repolished the wood. "You weren't to know," he said gently.

I'd retreated, defeated, to my place, when Scuff came back with a kitchen boy even smaller than herself. Between them they lugged a steaming tureen.

"Is there no one else to help?" asked the Master. "That looks too heavy for two children."

"No, Sir," gulped Scuff, looking frightened.

"Very well. So what is this soup we're to feast on?"

"Eel and onion, Sir," said Scuff, and she lifted the lid of the tureen with an effort.

The recipes of Gossop the cook were his own and always good, in spite of the state of the kitchens. But tonight, when Scuff ladled out the soup, it looked as if our bowls had been filled with muddy puddles. I wasn't hungry, anyway, but Leah stared at her soup as if it were a personal affront.

"What's this foul mess?"

"Eel and —," began poor Scuff again.

"Take it away before I throw it at you! Where's Gossop? Go and fetch him. The Master can't eat this!"

The Master shook his head mildly and raised a spoonful to his lips. "I daresay it's not as bad as it looks."

Leah knocked the spoon from his hand so that soup spilled on the table. "Don't drink, Sir! You'll poison yourself! Perhaps that's what they're trying to do — poison us!"

She looked wild-eyed at Scuff, who cowered back and gasped out, "Please, Miss, Mr. Gossop is took to his bed. No one else can cook like him."

"But if the Master doesn't eat, he will die!" Leah hissed at her, then suddenly turned to the Master aghast, as if in her mind's eye this event had already happened.

He laid a hand on hers. "Hush, my dear. Let Agnes go and sort this out. There's sickness among the servants, I know. I've sent my own doctor to do what he can. Now stay and keep me company."

Leah subsided back into her chair, glowering at me as I stood up and took one of the candlesticks from the sideboard. I was flattered by the Master's confidence in me, but apprehensive: I'd avoided the kitchens since my first day at Murkmere, for I knew Mistress Crumplin disliked me.

But there were no servants in the main kitchen. An elderly mastiff, too gentle-natured for the night's running and now too stiff, was stretched out on the hearth, while Mistress Crumplin herself was snoring gently in front of the smoking fire, her chin in folds and an empty tankard in her hand. There weren't any candles lit and the firelight was weak.

It wasn't until I came closer with my own candle that I saw the grate was thickly furred with soot. There was a shriveled joint of beef sitting in charred grease on a plate on the table, and a dish of gritty cabbage.

I went over to the housekeeper and bellowed loud enough to make a cat spit, "Mistress Crumplin! Wake up!"

The dog opened an eye, looked at me in reproach, then shut it again. The old woman smiled foolishly in her sleep and held out her tankard as if I'd just offered her more ale. I put my hand on the stained shoulder frill of her apron and shook her, so that she dropped the tankard and opened her eyes with a start.

"Mistress Crumplin," I said loudly. "Our food's black! The Master's sent me. We can't eat it."

She tried to straighten herself, smoothing down her rumpled clothes and raising herself with an effort; but she no longer had the power to disconcert me, for all that her eyes had their old sly gleam.

"Black food?" she said slurrily, all mock-offended, her bosom swelling like a pouter pigeon's. "Why, Gossop's sick. We're miserable short-handed, 'deed we are."

I hesitated, but stood my ground. If she'd not been in her cups, I'd never have dared do so. "It might help if the chimney was swept, Mistress."

She stood there swaying for a moment, trying to stare me

down, but I returned her look, and suddenly she started wringing her hands and wailing.

I couldn't make out any words but I noticed a strange thing. She was frightened. She'd lost the flush of drink and her flabby cheeks were gray and damp as clay.

Eventually I persuaded her to sit down again in the chair, whereupon she threw the apron over her head and made little moaning sounds. The dog woke up again, rolled his eyes at us, and made for the door.

"Whatever's the matter, Mistress?" I said.

"The birds!" she cried in a voice of doom, muffled by the apron. "The birds!"

"What birds?" I said.

After a fit of coughing she took the apron away at last and fixed me with watering eyes. "There's an old nest fallen in the chumney," she spluttered. "Gossop sent a boy on the roof to see. We daren't get it out, for all it brings the soot."

"Can't you send for the sweep?" I asked. Chimney sweeps had the Protector's official pardon to remove bird nests, though our village sweep, Gammy the Soot, was a blasphemous man, who cared more for money than forgiveness. I'd never seen him pray in the Meeting Hall.

"Mr. Gammy only comes from the village three times a year," moaned the woman. "Now's not his time."

"But can't someone be sent for him?"

"The servants are too sick, and those that aren't say there's a curse on this house and the nest confirms it." Raising herself again, she hissed wetly into my face, "'Tis a *rook's* nest, Agnes Cotter!"

A chill went through me before I pulled myself together. "Rooks don't nest in chimney stacks, Mistress Crumplin." It was more likely to be a daw's nest, though that was as bad. "I know Gammy the Soot and his chimney boy. They'll come if you pay them."

She shook her head adamantly and her chins quivered above the bedraggled lace collar. "There's not a fit body here who dares go into the village. They're a dangerous lot, the folk there."

I opened my mouth to protest, then suddenly a wonderful idea came to me. "Well, Mistress Crumplin, I'll convey this to the Master," I said grandly. "We'll see what he has to say."

With that, I swept up the roast and the cabbage and left her alone with her fears and the smoking fire. And if I hadn't been laden with food, I would have run all the way back to the dining room, I was so eager to tell the Master my idea.

When I broke the news that a bird's nest blocked the chimney, Leah looked dumbfounded. "No one will remove it?" She threw her arms out, and Scuff and the kitchen boy melted back into a corner. "Do we have nitwits for servants?"

"They think it will bring disaster if they touch it," I said, not looking at her, but putting the dishes of food on the table.

"What greater disaster than to die from starvation?" retorted Leah. "You believe such stories too, don't you? Admit it!"

I was uneasy about admitting anything of the sort in front of the Master, for I'd a feeling he despised such beliefs even more than she did, though I didn't know what kind of god all his book learning had brought him. I went back to my place and sat down, watching him from under my eyelashes, waiting for the right moment to mention my idea; and slowly my hopes faded.

His expression had grown dark and withdrawn. He'd said nothing while I described the scene in the kitchen, but tapped the end of a fork on the table as if in imagination he beat it on someone's head.

Now he laid it down and put his hands on his shrunken legs, kneading them viciously. "Look at me," he growled, "grown so weak I can't even supervise affairs in my house any longer, but must trust others to do so instead."

Leah ran to his side and knelt down by the iron chair, angrily waving Scuff away when she tried to serve the Master. "Let me do what you'd do, Sir," she said urgently. "Let me rid the place of these useless servants. Why should we be surrounded by strangers from the Capital?"

"If they go, who'd come?" he said. "You'll find no villager willing to work here now. Silas told me that when he last looked for a kitchen boy he had to find one from another estate."

"Silas!" Leah burst out. "He brings in those who've worked for the Ministration! He's overrun the Hall with people from the Capital, and you let him! No wonder no villager will work here!"

"You go too far! I am a Minister myself, remember."

They glared at each other, then she hung her head. "I'm sorry, Sir."

"Silas has worked for me since he was a boy," he said wearily, his anger gone. "I trust him. He does his best for Murkmere in difficult times. I can't give his duties to you, you're still too young." He took her hand and stroked it. "The time will come, I promise."

"So you'll ask Silas to ride to the village for the sweep, I suppose?" she said, not looking at him. "There's no one else who'll go."

"Yes, there is," I said quickly, louder than I meant. "I could go."

They both stared up at me as if they had entirely forgotten I was there. Then suddenly the Master smiled, and the melancholy lifted from his face. "Why, I'd forgotten. We've someone village born and bred, after all. Our very own Agnes Cotter!"

I didn't think he was mocking me, so I smiled back at him, in relief. "I know where Gammy and his chimney boy live, Sir. Their cottage is nearest the water pumps, before you reach the lawman's dwelling. They'll come if I ask them, even if it's not their time. They'll come for emergency pay."

"I'm sure they will," said the Master dryly. "Well, yes, indeed, you may go tomorrow, and with our heartfelt thanks. I'll ask Silas to make sure a stable hand rides with you on the Wasteland road."

This wasn't part of my plan at all. How could I escape Murkmere if I was accompanied?

"But I —," I began, and then Leah interrupted me. She was still kneeling by the Master's chair, and now she gripped his arms. Her face was intense, imploring. "If Aggie goes to the village, may I go with her, Sir? I long to see it!"

My heart sank further. Now there'd be no chance of escape.

The Master's face went strangely blank and closed. "No, Leah. I can't allow that."

Her voice rose. "But why?"

He said patiently, as if he talked to a young child — perhaps, I thought, they were words he often had to repeat — "You know I can never let you beyond the boundary of the estate. You may come to harm. It wouldn't be fair on the stable hand to guard you both tomorrow."

"Send two men, then, one for each of us!"

But she knew she couldn't win the battle. The Master's lips closed in a thin line.

Leah began to fling herself about the room. Her pale hair fell down in fine strands around her face; her hands slapped at her silk skirts as if they bound her legs. "It's not fair!" she ranted. "Why should Aggie go? She's my companion and should be imprisoned here, like me! She should suffer too! It's not fair!"

Scuff and the little kitchen boy cowered against the wainscot while I, thinking to restrain Leah for her own safety, tried to hold her arm. At once she threw me off, snarling like a wild creature.

"Leah," said the Master helplessly, "Leah." He bowed his head in his hands as if he couldn't bear to watch.

Then something — the two frightened children, my own expression, the Master's despair — halted her.

She looked at me with great wounded eyes that had turned dark with emotion. A sob tore through her, then another. As the tears streamed down her face, she went on gazing at me from those drenched, dark eyes as if she implored my help. I stood uselessly, not knowing what I could do, and a lump rose in my throat. I felt my own mouth quiver.

At last, weeping noisily, she ran from the room.

In the bleak silence she left behind, I motioned the two white-faced children to leave. "Say nothing, Scuff," I said in a low voice. "The mistress isn't well tonight. I can trust you, can't I?"

She nodded, her lips pressed tightly together to show me. When we were alone, I turned back to the Master. "Shall I go after Miss Leah, Sir?"

He took his hands from his face. I saw with a shock that his eyes were full of unshed tears. "No," he said quietly. "Leave her. Nothing can be done." Then he gave a sigh that seemed dredged up from his soul. "What kind of tyrant do you think me, Agnes? My ward accuses me of imprisoning her, and it's true."

I didn't know how to answer; my heart was wrung at the sight of his tormented eyes. "You love Leah, Sir," I managed to say. "She knows that."

But I wondered if it weren't the wrong sort of love, when the desire to protect the beloved could cause so much pain to them both.

At last I persuaded him to eat a little.

Later, when I carried the used plates through to the kitchen, I found a gaggle of maids sluicing dishes from their own meal in the servants' dining room. Mistress Crumplin would still be lolling befuddled at the head of the table in there, a full tankard in front of her. Silas Seed's presence might have controlled her, but I knew he ate in his own room.

The maids were too busy with their chatter to pay me much attention. I put the remains of our food in the larder and slipped quickly away from the kitchen quarters. I was concerned about Leah, and feeling guilty too. I'd be escaping Murkmere while she remained. A silly softness made me want to see her one last time.

I expected to find her sobbing still, but there was no sound from her chamber. I lifted the latch quietly and looked in. A single candle burned by her bed and showed me her motionless figure beneath the covers, her sleeping face on the pillow, marked with tears. Even in sleep she wore her frown.

And she was clutching something.

It was the swanskin, no longer dripping but wet enough to darken the fresh, white linen.

I stood, transfixed with horror, until a sound made me start. I turned to see Dog standing in the doorway watching me, a cup of milk in her hand. "So," she said. "You're leaving."

"How do you know?" I whispered.

She smiled, and her little eyes glinted in the candlelight. She was too intent on me to notice what her mistress gripped so hard. "Everyone knows. The Master's sent word to Mr. Silas. At first light tomorrow you're to have a horse, and a stable hand to ride with you."

"I go to fetch Gammy the Soot, nothing more," I said distractedly.

She came closer to the bed and put the milk down on the table, still watching me like a cat. "Ah, we'll see," she said, not bothering to whisper in spite of her sleeping mistress.

I saw in her eyes that she knew I planned to escape and was glad I was going. And I feared that if she'd guessed the truth, Silas would as well.

The first pale light was filling the sky when I crossed the stable yard next morning. The air was crisp, but the cobbles shone in the sun where the frost had already melted. I was dressed in my old clothes again under my cloak, but without any telltale baggage; my only regret was that I was leaving my precious book unfinished. All I had to do now was to work out exactly how I'd lose the stable hand outside the walls of the estate.

But my luck wasn't to hold. As I approached the stables to tell the ostlers I was ready, a figure strode toward me from the other side of the yard.

Silas had found me out.

He was dressed in riding clothes, his crimson coat swirling around his breeches as he walked, his gleaming boots ringing on the cobbles, and his black-handled whip held lightly between the fingers of his leather gauntlets. I stood still, my heart almost stopped by fright and despair.

"Good morning, Agnes," Silas said easily. "The Master's asked me to find you a good horse." He nodded to a stable hand, who led out a small chestnut mare from one of the stables. I began to breathe again. Could Silas really be allowing me to leave?

He had come close and was standing over me, his dark eyes smiling down. I couldn't raise my eyes. He was too close; now he had taken my hand to help me onto the mounting block. I wanted to protest that I didn't need his help, but was afraid to speak.

My hand was imprisoned in his. The scent of languorous evening was suddenly in the clean air. "Good fortune for your mission, Agnes," he said softly, and his eyes slid over me, trapping me with their power.

He turned my hand over in his gloved fingers, and slowly he stroked the inside of my wrist with his riding whip. "But if you don't return, I'll know where to find you. Won't I?"

XIII

The Wind of Desolation

We rode past the surly keeper sent to unlock the gates. Above, the rooks were damning my escape. My heart beat fast; I fixed my eyes on the freedom of the road. I didn't look back at the shuttered windows of the Hall, nor at the mere in its dismal fold. Then the walls of Murkmere were behind us, and I was urging my mare on between the icy ruts as fast as I dared.

But winter was loosening its grip at last. The mare's hooves struck up small pebbles that glittered in the sunlight; on either side the snow was shrinking back over the shining marshes of the Wasteland. I was free, and in my exultation it was suddenly beautiful to me, this place I'd known all my life.

The stable hand was riding silently beside me, a stout stick for our protection across the saddle in front of him, dark green cape bundled up around him. He couldn't see the promise of spring. Then I looked at him harder.

"Where did you get that cape?" I said, my voice harsh above birdsong and the soft thud of the horses' hooves.

He stared at me as if I were the strangest creature he'd ever seen, and chewed his lip. At last he opened his mouth and growled, "Stables."

So the clothes of poor murdered Matt must be in the stables for anyone to take. There was no escape, for all the while I thought I was free, Murkmere's corrupt shadow rode beside me through the bright morning.

When we arrived at Gammy the Soot's cottage, I slid down at once from the mare. She began to graze on the rough grass while I hammered on the door. Somehow I had to lose the stable hand. But now he too had dismounted, and was following me, stick in hand.

Gammy opened the door. Gray-faced, hand clutched to his chest, he looked frightened at our sudden appearance, more shriveled still than when I'd last called on him for Aunt Jennet six months before.

"It's Aggie Cotter, Gammy. I've an urgent job for you at the Hall."

"Murkmere?" he mumbled, bewildered. "It's not our time to clean the big house." He looked at the stable hand, armed for action against the wild folk of the village, and fell back, one hand raised.

"Don't be frightened, Mr. Gammy, we mean no harm," I gabbled. "Please come with us. It's but one chimney that's been blocked by a nest."

If I can only get Gammy outside, I thought, *the stable hand might be distracted for a moment.*

"My chimney boy's at the pumps. I'm doing naught without him," said Gammy stubbornly. He shuffled over to the meager fire and sat down, scowling at us both.

"They have to cook luncheon for the Master by noon," I said desperately. "If you can clear it by then, you'll be paid extra."

There was the gleam of greed in Gammy's face. Then he shrugged. "Can't do naught without my boy, they ladders be too heavy."

Biting my lip, I looked around at the brushes and ladders hanging on the dirty walls. *Where was the handcart I always saw him out with? Perhaps he kept it out at the back.* My heart began to thump. I turned to the stable hand, skulking in the doorway in his stolen cape. "You'll help him get ready, won't you, Mister? He needs to carry the ladders out to his handcart. I'll commend you to the Master if you do."

The man turned and spat on the ground behind him as if to show his contempt, whether for me, his Master, or for Gammy, I wasn't sure, and for a moment I thought he wouldn't budge.

"Mr. Silas will be pleased with you if we return in good time," I said breathlessly, gripping my hands together.

At this he grunted, shifted himself from the door frame at last, and came into the room.

As they carried a ladder around to the back, I ran from the front of the cottage and took the mare's reins. Somehow I flung myself across her, my legs astride her glossy back, my skirts bundled up, thanking the heavens she had a calm nature and stood still for me. Then I was away, riding fast back up the track, and the wind was in my hair.

I couldn't believe how easy it was.

I heard nothing behind me, no shouts, no pursuing hooves. Perhaps the stable hand hadn't yet realized I'd gone; perhaps he was too feckless a rogue to bother to chase me.

All the same, I avoided the high road to the village where I might be seen by the lawman in his hut. Instead, I rode the mare toward the common. At this hour the milking would be done and the cows left to graze where the snow had melted.

I thought I might see someone I knew still there, and was relieved yet puzzled to find the common completely deserted: no girls lingering to gossip before going home to their spindles, no children climbing on the sheep pens. Then, as I felt the first trickle of unease, I saw the figures lolling against the wall of the cow shelter, gray uniforms almost indistinguishable from the stone, light glinting on the rifles propped against it.

The Militia! The soldiers had come while I'd been at Murkmere. The snow hadn't prevented them marching east. They must have arrived in the village before the first flake had settled on the road. Last summer they had cleared the south of any rebellion. Now they had come to "sweep" the Eastern Edge.

And my heart filled with the horror of it, for I'd heard what they did.

The soldiers billeted the best cottages, driving out the owners. They devoured precious food stocks, stole horses and cows for their own use. They dragged away the prettiest girls, forced the healthiest youths to join up. But worst was the sweeping itself. Officers suspicious of rebellion where there was none; villagers interrogated in their own homes. If suspected of disloyalty to the Lord Protector, they were taken prisoner and shackled to the wagons for the long march back to the Capital — even the elderly and sick. Those taken were never heard from again.

That's what a sweeping was.

And how would Aunt Jennet be faring?

The mare had halted, perhaps sensing my fear and indecision. It was too late for escape, anyway: the soldiers had seen me. They gestured at me to ride over. There were four of them, and one shouted something.

I guided my pony between the pens and came up to them. One of them seized my bridle. Another roughly ordered me to dismount.

I stood on the ground trembling, the mare tossing her head. The men surrounded us, hair hacked brutally short, hard-eyed, the emblem of the Eagle worked in black across the front of their sweat-stained jerkins.

"This pony yours, girl?" demanded the soldier holding the bridle. He cursed as the mare flung her head away.

"Never. Too good for a village girl," rasped another. "You've stolen it, haven't you, girl?"

I shook my head dumbly, taking quick breaths like a rabbit in a snare. The rifles still rested against the wall. I waited for the soldiers to grab them up, to jam the barrels against my breast.

"Wait," said a third. He came close to me and squinted down into my face. His breath smelled of stale wine. "We've not seen this one before. What's your name, wench?"

I opened my mouth but no sound came out.

"Dumb, eh? A sad defect for so comely a girl. Look at that hair." And he sniggered, leering at me with greedy eyes.

"Enough," said the second one, grimmer-faced than the others. He shoved the joker aside. "The Sergeant will find her tongue for her, sure enough. She's slipped the net somehow. I doubt he's cleared her yet."

I knew what that meant. Like all the villagers, I would be questioned. I faced them, trying to control my fear, as they reached out for me.

Then we all heard it, a pail clanging against wood inside the cow shelter.

Grimface jerked round. "Who's in there?" he shouted. "Come out and show yourself!"

The soldiers' hands were already on my shoulders, grasping the wool of my cloak, when a youth came clumping sheepishly round the wall. It was Jethro Sim, and his jaw dropped to see me.

All the years of my life I'd never been so glad to see my old friend. I wrenched myself free and flung myself desperately against his sturdy bulk. "Jethro! They're taking me!"

The soldiers, confused, let me cling to Jethro while they looked at Grimface for guidance.

"We don't like being spied on, boy," he said curtly to Jethro.

"Truly, S-Sir," stammered Jethro, "I wasn't spying, but bringing the feed." My heart sank a little to see how scared he looked, his face as scarlet with shock as a guilty schoolboy's.

Grimface scowled and jerked a thumb in my direction. "This girl here. She'll not give her name, though it seems she can speak, after all. Maybe you know it, boy."

Above my head I heard Jethro clear his throat. "Aye, I know it, Sir. She's Agnes Cotter."

"She was riding this pony, and stole it too, most like," said Grimface. He nodded at the other two impatiently. "What are you waiting for? Take her to the Sergeant."

As I clutched Jethro in even greater desperation, he cried out, "Aggie's never stolen in her life! Why, she works over at Murkmere. Would the Master have a thief in his employment, Sir?"

"I was given the use of the pony to ride here," I said, courage coming to me at last, and I twisted around in order to impress Grimface with my honest look. "Of course I've not stolen her. I'm companion to the Master's ward."

The mention of Murkmere and the Master appeared to work a miracle. Grimface hesitated. "Murkmere, eh?"

The other soldiers exchanged a glance, wary, impressed. An estate owner had to be a member of the Ministration. There was a long, tense moment as we stood there in the half-melted snow, then abruptly Grimface shrugged. "You may go, Agnes Cotter."

Jethro put his hand on my pony's bridle and the soldier surrendered it reluctantly. Then we made away as fast as we could. Neither of us looked back, but I knew they would be watching us. Once we were out of earshot, I tried to speak, but Jethro held his finger to his lips warningly.

The village street was deserted, the muddy snow gouged and blackened by days of marching feet. A child's pale face gazed ghostlike from a cottage window. There were soldiers with rifles standing guard outside the door; their eyes flicked to watch us as we hurried past. I knew that cottage was where Mother Dimity lived; she was a placid, simple soul, with not a rebellious bone in her, and her husband the same. Yet it seemed that no one in the village had had the courage to protest on their behalf.

In the frozen sewer ditch that ran the length of the street, the fluttering black shapes of carrion crows tore at a dead rat. I touched my amber when I saw the crows, but nothing would save the village now.

As I turned to go into our cottage, Jethro stopped me gently, and steered me toward his own, next door.

"I must see my aunt," I said urgently, pulling away.

"Wait. I must talk to you. Your aunt's well enough, don't fear."

"But I've run away from Murkmere," I whispered. "They'll be looking for me soon, Jethro."

"You'll be safe in my place a moment," he said, and something in his face stopped my protests.

We left the mare out of sight from the street, tethered to a stake at the back of the cottage. Jethro's father, white-headed and witless, was sitting by the fire in the shadowy downstairs room. I nodded to him and tried to smile as he bared his gums at me. Suddenly I was trembling again.

Jethro fussed about me, as anxious as my aunt might be, saying, "Sit down, Aggie, you're pale," and he pushed me down on the wooden settle opposite. His father gazed on at me, his lips still parted in a sweet smile.

There were shadows under Jethro's eyes from lack of sleep. He seemed tongue-tied as he hung a pan of water over the fire and threw in a handful of nettles.

"You came at the right moment," I said in a low voice.

"I thought you safe at Murkmere."

I clenched my hands together. "Safe! Murkmere's an evil place, Jethro. I'm never going back." For a moment a frozen corpse was lying in the snow at my feet. I covered my face with my hands and wailed through my fingers, "Matt Humble's dead, Jethro! They've murdered him!"

He came over and sat close, putting his arm around me, holding me while I shuddered with a horrible dry weeping. Opposite, the old man's face crumpled in sympathy.

Jethro's jacket smelled comfortingly of cows and earth and wood smoke, and I could feel the muscles of his arm beneath his sleeve. He said nothing, nor seemed shaken by my words, but when my fit was passed, I sat back and saw that he was searching for his own words in the unhurried, thoughtful way I remembered so well.

"Aye, word was brought to us here," he said quietly. "We weren't surprised."

I stared at him, gulping. He looked straight back into my eyes.

"Matt wasn't the simple packman you thought him, Aggie. He was a spy."

"A spy? But he was a good man!"

"Be careful. The soldiers are everywhere." He glanced at his father, but he was making little gurgling sounds as he rocked himself to sleep; he couldn't understand us, anyway. "You'll remember that Matt traveled from village to village, bringing news of the Capital, of the risings in the south?"

Any packman brings news, I thought, but I nodded.

"When I was elected to take my father's place two years back and became a Junior Elder, I learned something. Sometimes the news Matt brought was secret, for the Elders only. They'd pay him for it."

"My aunt would pay?" I said, amazed.

He nodded, solemn-faced, watching me.

"What kind of news?"

"What passed in the Council Chamber of the Lord Protector."

"But how would Matt Humble know?" I said in astonishment.

"The Lord Protector believed Matt was spying for him. Matt was in his employment, you see. He'd visit the Capital from time to time, stay in a room somewhere in the palace, a patch of floor in the servants' quarters, most likely. But sometimes he'd be summoned to the Protector's apartment and mingle with his court.

"Matt brought the Protector news of the villages he traveled through; he'd tell him of unrest, of potential rebellion. Only it was always information the Lord Protector had already had from his other spies. Matt never told the Protector anything he didn't already know, you must believe that. He was loyal to us."

It was a long speech for Jethro. He said no more while I stared at him, trying to take in his words, yet seeing only his honest brown eyes and his young face that was growing too old too quickly. In truth, I didn't know what to believe. Matt Humble with his old jacket, his pots and pans — in the dark, murmuring chambers of high politics?

"Even if it's true that Matt was a spy," I said at last, "Aunt Jennet is Chief Elder and I don't understand why she would want information about the Lord Protector."

Jethro looked at me, nonplussed. "The Lord Protector is not the worthy man you think him, Aggie. He has a whole network of spies working all over the country. Somebody, one of them, betrayed Matt. Matt knew the Eastern Edge was next for sweeping. He was coming to the Elders with news of the Militia's progress, and he never arrived. We knew he was going to Murkmere on his way here, to give Silas Seed a message from the Lord Protector."

Thoughts were chasing around my mind like ferrets in a basket. "You believe Silas Seed had Matt killed, don't you?" I whispered. "On the Lord Protector's orders?"

He looked at me, and it was enough.

We both fell silent a moment, looking into the fire. I was remembering Matt running ribbons through his fingers like rainbows, his blunt, dirty fingers with the shining colors streaming between.

Then the water in the cauldron began to bubble and woke the old man, who started to gabble to himself. Jethro took me over to the table where we had more privacy.

"I can't stay, Jethro," I said, as he gave me a steaming mug. "I must see my aunt."

"Drink it. It will strengthen you."

There was something else he had to tell me, I knew it. Frowning, I leaned over the table. "What's been happening here? When did the sweeping start?"

"Calm yourself, Aggie." He laid his broad palm, ingrained with the dirt of the fields, softly down on the table. "We've been sorely tried. The Militia's been here a week. We're running out of food, let alone hospitality. But now the snow's melting, the officers are impatient to move on. There's talk they leave tomorrow."

"And what about the sweeping itself?"

He smiled wryly. "They've got their suspects among us, but can't prove anything."

"There's nothing to prove, surely?" I said indignantly. "We're all loyal subjects — except you and the Elders, I think," I dared add.

He looked back at me, his bright robin's eyes friendly no longer. "Should we be loyal when people are terrified in such a way? The Militia's the rod of the Lord Protector. He beats us with it and his hand holds it."

"But the Protector gives us other things, Jethro," I said, almost pleadingly. "Free education, a livelihood guaranteed for every law-abiding man."

"The soldiers are forcing Dolly Parson and Amy Treadwell to follow them," he said, his face like a stone. "They've picked a dozen of our boys for soldiers — mere chicks, not a beard apiece. That's the next generation of farmers gone. If I hadn't stayed low, it would have been me. These are the Lord Protector's men. Is that right, do you think?"

I couldn't bear the bitterness in his voice. I rose from the table. "What am I thinking of, lingering here? I must see my aunt, and leave."

He stood up himself and put a hand on my arm. "Wait, Aggie. I must tell you — your aunt . . ."

I stared at him and saw he was searching for the right words as always, the words to tell me something dreadful. "What is it?" I shook him, my hands rigid on the rough cloth of his jacket.

"She's been taken prisoner by the Militia," he said gravely. "I'm sorry, Aggie, truly I am. There was nothing I could do to prevent it."

My hands dropped like dead things. "Why didn't you tell me before?"

"Because it was — good to see you. Because you were grieving for Matt." He spread his hands. "There's nothing you can do, Aggie."

"Have they discovered that the Elders paid Matt?"

When he shook his head, I began to wheel about the room, beating my hands against my chest. "Why did she hide so much from me? They must suspect her of something." I turned on him. "What happens in your meetings, Jethro? Tell me! What plots do you hatch against the Lord Protector? What will they do to find out? Will they torture her?"

"Since last night she's been guarded in her own cottage, nothing more fearful than that. It's not for suspicion of treachery she's kept there."

"What, then?"

"Your cottage has been used as a billet. They allowed your aunt to remain on condition she provided for them. Yesterday they found books there."

"Books?" I repeated furiously. "But she was village schoolteacher until recently. Of course we've books in the cottage, old school texts, all approved reading by the Lord Protector. What's wrong with that?"

"These aren't schoolbooks, Aggie. They were hidden away, under the thatch. She never meant them to be found."

I jutted my chin out, so he wouldn't see my shock. "So?"

"These books have the Murkmere crest inside them. She stands accused of stealing the property of the Ministration."

I let Jethro lead me from the cottage; I was too bewildered to do anything for myself, even to think calmly. He left the mare tethered where she was. There was no sign of the stable hand searching for me, and he wouldn't know where I lived without direction.

The soldiers on guard in the street eyed us but said nothing. I put my hood up to hide my face and Jethro took my arm, half-supporting me over the filthy slush. The sun had disappeared while we had been indoors, and the chill wind of desolation blew through the village, banging doors and rattling shutters, and lifting my cloak in a swirl of icy air.

There was no one on guard outside our cottage, and for a dreadful moment I thought they must have taken my aunt away already. But when Jethro rapped on the door, a young man in the gray uniform of the Militia opened it and stood blinking at us, his right hand holding his rifle clumsily, as if he had only just seized it.

His cropped hair stood up in the wind like the soft hackles of a puppy. He didn't look any older than Jethro, half-asleep, gray-faced and spotty in the morning light, his shirt unbuttoned so that a triangle of hairless chest showed above the heavy leather jerkin.

"Who are you? What d'you want?" His voice had the sharp, clipped vowels of the Capital.

I drew myself up as tall as I could. "I've come to see my aunt. Please let me through." I added "Sir" for good measure.

But he shook his head vehemently. "No, Miss. It ain't allowed, see?" He looked nervously beyond us, as if afraid of being checked on by his superior officers. "Sergeant's orders. Sorry, Miss." As if to emphasize his point, he stretched his free arm across the narrow doorway so that he barred our entry.

"Alone here, are you?" said Jethro, craning past him. "The others on duty?"

"What's it to you?" he said belligerently. "She's an old woman. Don't take more than one to guard her."

I didn't like the look of his rifle barrel. It was too long, too close, for all that its dark hole pointed at the sky. I stepped back a little. "A pity not to see my aunt," I said slowly, "when I've journeyed from Murkmere this very morning to do so."

At the mention of Murkmere the youth took his hand away from the doorway and stared at me uneasily, fingering his spots. I pressed home my advantage. "I've heard about the matter of the Master's books," I said. "It may be that I can discover the truth from my aunt more easily than your Sergeant. The Master of Murkmere would like to know it, certainly. He'll expect a report from me."

I could almost see the information working its way around his brain. He wrinkled his forehead, letting the rifle rest against the door frame. "The Master?" he said. "The Master of Murkmere has sent you here?"

"Yes, indeed," I said firmly. "You may be sure he'll be angry if I'm prevented from seeing my aunt."

Out of the corner of my eye I saw Jethro frown. I could see him thinking it wasn't a good idea to tell yet another soldier that I came from Murkmere.

But the boy was standing aside to let me pass, lifting his rifle out of my way, and I was thankful not to have its evil length pointing up my nostrils any longer. "You'll find her upstairs, Miss," he muttered. "I'm sure I beg your pardon not lettin' you in sooner."

Jethro followed me, ignoring the boy's protests. "Aggie, what are you thinking of?" he hissed.

"I have to see her before they come for me, Jethro," I whispered, half-blinded by the sudden darkness inside.

He sighed. "I'll watch for you outside somewhere, if I can." Then he was gone.

My eyes, growing used to the dimness, saw the squalor the soldiers had left behind them. There were sucked mutton bones and lumps of gristle scattering the flags that had once been so painstakingly swept by Aunt Jennet. Filthy bedding was rolled up against the wall. The air was thick and fetid with the stench of sweat, stale ale, greasy meat.

Overlaying it all was a foulness I recognized. They had used the far corner as a latrine.

My hand to my mouth, retching, I ran up the stairs. Out of the corner of my eye I could see the soldier's lanky figure outlined in the doorway below, staring out.

There was no lock on the bedroom door when I reached it, but then they didn't need one with a slight, middle-aged woman inside and a strong young guard below, armed with a rifle.

She had pulled the pallet into the darkest corner of the room, away from the tiny window in the eaves, and was crouched motionless on it, like a sparrow with a broken wing. When she heard the door creak she turned her head sharply, and I saw the shine of her eyes in the darkness.

I said nothing, but flung myself at her, gripping her small, fragile body, holding her safe.

"It's me, Aunt Jennet," I whispered into her matted hair. "I've come back."

XIV

What Happened to Eliza

I went on holding her, stroking her back with one hand, as you do to soothe a baby. An empty bowl rolled across the floor and clanged against the timbers of the wall; a cold wind was blowing through the gaps in the thatch.

She was shivering against me. I took off my cloak and wrapped it around us both. I tried to warm her with my body, the heat of my breath against her cheek, and slowly her arms came up to hold me.

We must have clung together silently for some time. I was trying not to weep at the state of her, at the whole dreadful situation. Then at last she spoke, huskily, as if she hadn't talked for a long while.

"It's good to see you, child." With her fierce brown face close to mine, she examined me with her old shrewdness, touching my cheeks gently. "Much has happened to you, I can see that."

"What about you, Aunt?" I whispered. I couldn't worry her with my own troubles, not yet. "I come back to find — this! The Militia in the village and you a prisoner!"

She didn't seem to be listening. "Silas Seed was back in the village yesterday, but they wouldn't let me ask him how you were."

"Silas was here?" I said, amazed.

She nodded. "He saw me arrested."

"He knew, but he said nothing to me!"

She twisted her hands together. "When I heard the news about Matt, I feared for you at Murkmere."

"You never told me Matt was a spy." I looked into her eyes as if I could search out their secrets. "You're in grave trouble, Aunt. What have you been plotting against the Lord Protector?"

She shook her head wearily. "I need plot nothing. Things will take their own course. The country's stirring, the south and soon the east."

"There's so much you haven't told me. Why did they find books from Murkmere here?"

She hesitated, but I stared her out. "I'm old enough for the truth, Aunt Jennet. Can't you see?"

She nodded at last. "Come close, then."

I couldn't help smiling, for there we sat on the pallet pressed together for warmth, whispering at each other. "We are close."

"Closer still. No one else must hear." She put her mouth against my ear so I felt the tickling rasp of her breath. "I'm going to tell you a story."

"A story? Now?" I hissed, half-exasperated.

"Trust me, Aggie, and listen."

I thought hunger and cold had addled her poor brains, but I couldn't bear to stop her when it might be our very last meeting.

"I never wanted you to go to Murkmere," she said grimly. "You see, I'd heard too much from your mother."

"It was my mother who stole the books, wasn't it? And then ran away?"

"Not Eliza! She couldn't read. I was the clever sister, she had the looks. Her head was always full of fancies, not facts. When she went to Murkmere as a housemaid, I think she dreamed she'd marry the Master. Gilbert Tunstall was young and handsome and athletic. It was before he lost the use of his legs." My aunt shook her head, pursing her lips. "Silly hopes that came to nothing when Mr. Tunstall found his bride."

Her voice stopped. Was that all there was?

"How did the Master meet his wife, Aunt? You said it was a story."

She frowned, huddling into herself. "It's Eliza's story, not mine, and I suspected even then that that was all it was — one of her stories."

She took a breath. And then I didn't interrupt her again as her hoarse whisper went on and on against my ear.

❧

"There was a ball at Murkmere one hot summer's night. Eliza was helping carry food in for the buffet. She noticed Mr. Tunstall leave, for a breath of air, she thought. He was gone awhile. Eliza went to fetch some jellies from the kitchen, and on the way back Mr. Tunstall came in at a side entrance with a girl.

"Eliza said she was so startled she stood stock still, with the jellies jiggling in the bowl. You see, the young lady was all wet, soaking wet; her silver ballgown was dripping. She stood in a pool of water and stared at Eliza with her large dark eyes, and there was something so wild and helpless about her that Eliza fell under her spell there and then.

"And someone else had done so as well. The Master.

"Her name was Blanche, but Mr. Tunstall never said how he'd found her. He just asked Eliza to fetch her some dry clothes.

"They were married very soon afterward, Gilbert Tunstall and Blanche. He asked Eliza if she'd continue looking after his wife, be her personal maid. Of course Eliza agreed.

"But it didn't make her happy.

"She'd say a little when she came to see me, but I was busy with my teaching. By now I was in charge of the school. She did say there was a kitchen maid who'd wanted her position, a Dorcas Crumplin. She was a spiteful bit, jealous of Eliza.

"And there was Silas Seed. He was a pretty lad of eleven or thereabouts. He'd already gone to the bad, listened at keyholes, was always where Eliza didn't expect him. She thought he even spied on her in her bedchamber. She found him in her cupboard one night when she was undressing.

"Then there was Blanche.

"Eliza loved her, but Blanche was a strange mistress. She seemed to care nothing for company, scarcely knew how to behave. A restless soul, she was, staring out of windows, never settling to embroidery or books. The hems of her dresses were always muddy and torn, and Eliza was always mending the rents. Blanche brought wildflowers and grasses from the mere into the house, and wouldn't allow them to be thrown away when they rotted. There was talk about her among the servants; the air was thick with rumor."

I broke in at last. "What sort of rumor?"

"That she was unnatural. She was always down by the mere watching the swans. The servants said she talked to them in their own language."

The wind rustled through the straw thatching above us and shook the little window. I shivered against my aunt.

"The whisper grew that Blanche Tunstall was one of the avia," she said, quieter still.

"The avia! Did the Master hear the rumor?"

"He must have. But he loved her, was besotted with her. He wouldn't stand for any criticism, and he had a temper. Eliza was too frightened to say anything to him. She knew he didn't believe the old story of the avia, anyway. I should have been more support to her, but I was married, with a baby on the way."

"A baby?" I said, startled. I'd always tried to find out my mother's story; it had never occurred to me that my aunt had one of her own.

"Only two days old when she died, my little girl. She had come early. She wouldn't suck. She was too weak to survive long."

I pressed myself against her. "I'm so sorry, Aunt."

She shook her head brusquely, dismissing my pity. "I was pregnant at the same time as Blanche. After seven years she was expecting at last. My own baby died the same night the Murkmere baby was born."

"But I thought the baby died at birth with its mother," I whispered.

"Blanche died, but the baby survived. No one knew, save the midwife and Eliza. The midwife told Eliza to find a wet nurse so the baby might live. She said that the sooner the baby was away from Murkmere the better, that the servants had believed the baby would be unnatural like its mother. If they discovered it hadn't died, they'd be out for its blood. The midwife even told Gilbert Tunstall that his baby daughter was dead."

"That was a terrible thing to do!"

Aunt Jennet shook her head. "She thought it safest. Eliza herself didn't know what to do. In the end she did what the midwife told her, she brought the baby here. She didn't know what had happened, of course — she thought I'd be able to feed the Murkmere babe with my own and save its life.

"My Tom, seeing me so distraught, had already dug a grave out the back and buried our baby when Eliza arrived. When I saw the little thing swaddled up in Eliza's arms and heard its mewl, my milk began to leak through my bindings at once. I thought she had been sent from heaven, like a miracle, to make up for what I'd lost. We pretended she was mine. In a way I thought she was. None of the villagers guessed.

"Time went by. I longed to keep her, but in my heart I knew it wasn't right. Then something happened.

"All this while the Master had been grieving at Murkmere, thinking that both his beloved wife and new baby were dead. He was ill with the despair of it. One night he must have lost his reason. He threw himself from the old watchtower."

I jerked back from my aunt in shock.

"He never walked again," she said grimly. "When we heard that he was lying half-dead in bed, we knew we had to return the baby. She might give him the will to live.

"Eliza went to Murkmere and demanded to see him alone. The servants sneered at her for thinking better of running away; they thought she'd come to beg for work again. But she told the Master our secret, and together they hatched a plan. It was the saddest day of my life, but it was the saving of him.

"I was to leave the baby at the gates of Murkmere, so she would be seen and taken in. I was in such a state, leaving her like that, but Eliza heard later that she'd been found and was safe in the head keeper's cottage. In due course the Master had her brought to his own rooms in the Hall. He told the servants that he'd adopt the foundling as his ward and heir in place of the baby he'd lost. In the village they believed that my baby had died suddenly in its sleep. No one guessed the truth, and I — I was grieving all over again."

I held her tightly a long moment.

"So Leah is the Master's daughter," I said. I found I wasn't surprised; it was as if I'd sensed it all along.

"But she is Blanche's daughter too," said Aunt Jennet. "That's why he couldn't acknowledge her. She'd have been in danger. He knew he could trust Eliza to say nothing."

"But he could acknowledge Leah now, surely?" I said. "The servants won't remember her mother; they're all from the Capital."

"What about Silas Seed? And Dorcas Crumplin is still there."

I frowned. "But the Master trusts Silas."

"Who knows why he keeps the secret? It's none of our business. But the books came from the Master, he gave them to Eliza to give to me for saving his daughter, and maybe to keep my silence down the years. Eliza knew I wouldn't want money. They were the best present I could have had, books that hadn't been approved by the Lord Protector.

"They opened my eyes, those books. Eliza was almost afraid to touch them. She married your father soon after, and forgot I had such wicked, dangerous things in the cottage." My aunt smiled. "But I found I couldn't go on teaching the approved ways when I knew they were wrong. In the end I had to give up."

"I wish you'd told me." I looked at her steadily. "I've read a book too, a proper book."

"Be very careful, Aggie."

"I will be."

There was no sound outside on the stairs or from below, only the hissing of the wind through the thatch. My aunt's face was grave. "I may be taken away from here, Aggie. If I don't come back —" I couldn't bear her to go on. I flung my arms round her and spoke into her soft, seamed neck. "They shan't take you for trial, Aunt! I'll tell the Master what's happened. He's a Minister. His word will set you free."

"But Aggie, dear child, it's been years since he gave me those books. He won't remember."

"I'll remind him!"

I stared at her sad, doubting face, trying to fix a picture of it forever in my mind. I longed to protect her, she who'd always protected me, but my heart was full of foreboding. I didn't know if I'd succeed in saving her, and she knew it too. I couldn't add to her fears by telling her everything that had happened to me over the past week, and now for her sake I had to face going back. My triumphant escape had come to nothing.

And now I feared for Leah as well.

My aunt spoke again, hesitantly. "There's something more I should tell you before you go."

"What is it?"

"You'll say nothing of what I'm about to say? No one knows this, no one."

I nodded, puzzled.

"When Eliza brought Leah here she was like a pearl, even when I first took her swaddling off, all her newborn redness gone, her little back so smooth and white. She was quite perfect in every limb. She cried and fed and slept as all babies do.

But Eliza told me something years later. I didn't know whether to believe her."

"What did she say?"

"I knew she'd helped the midwife, of course. I knew she was there at the birth." Aunt Jennet's voice faded. Her face was suddenly haggard.

"What's the matter, Aunt?"

"Eliza said she saw . . ."

"Saw what?"

"The baby looked different then. She saw it was born with wings."

XV

Return to Murkmere

*J*ethro had no skill for hiding. I knew he was skulking behind the broad oak across the road before he emerged — I could see his anxious face peering round at me. "Where's your cloak?" he said as we hurried away.

"I left it for my aunt. I must return to Murkmere, Jethro. I must speak to the Master on her behalf."

He nodded, but his face was somber. He slung his jacket around my shoulders against the wind. "Best ride through the Wasteland. You'll avoid the soldiers that way. I'll come with you, see you safe. I've seen no one from the estate searching for you yet."

"You won't," I said bitterly. "I've been a fool. Silas must have known all along that I'd have to return for my aunt's sake. No wonder he let me escape. No doubt he told the stable hand who came with me to let me go. That's why I haven't been pursued."

Jethro saddled up Tansy and untethered my mare. We had to pick our way over the Wasteland's marshy ground, which was half-hidden by patchy snow. I was in a fever of impatience. What if the Militia were already leaving, hustling my aunt away with them?

The gates were closed; no one was about in the chill wind. "Someone may hear if I pull the bell rope," I said, dismounting.

Jethro dismounted too. He put a hand on my arm. "One thing, Aggie."

"What now?" I said, as sick to my stomach with apprehension as I had been when I first arrived at Murkmere. The rooks sat in the distant treetops eyeing us, their feathers ruffled sideways.

"You always were impatient, Agnes Cotter." He sighed, and spoke carefully, not looking me in the eye. "Now that you've decided to return, I want you to meet me here at the gates as a regular thing, every fortnight, say," he cleared his throat, "so I can give you news of your aunt."

I thought of the comfort of seeing someone from home. "It's not too much trouble, Jethro?"

He had gone quite red with the wind. "Nay, but we must plan it carefully, or it will be dangerous for us both."

We had to pull the bell rope for some time before a keeper came, but he recognized me and let me in without question.

I trotted the mare up the drive and around to the stables. The ostlers helped me dismount and led her away. Suddenly I was cold to the bone, lost without the little chestnut, her kindly eye and reassuring temperament. I didn't see the stable hand, but I felt the others' eyes on me, saw the quick glances flicking one to another. They were wondering why the mistress's companion should return without her cloak. *How much did they know about my escape?*

The sweep's empty cart was by the kitchen entrance, the ladders and brushes taken, no sign of the sweep or his boy. I slipped around to the vegetable garden and entered the Hall that way, through the unlocked door, leaving the blustery open spaces behind me.

I was relieved to see that Silas's door was shut. I was hurrying along in the direction of the Master's rooms, trying to think of what to say to him, when Dog came toward me from the opposite direction. It was almost worth my return to see her mouth agape.

"So you've come back." Even her flat voice could not hide her surprise.

I forced my cold legs into a mocking curtsey. "As you see."

Her face tightened. "The Master said he wanted to see you if you returned."

"I wish to see him too," I said airily, though my heart beat faster at her words.

"You're in trouble, Miss Clever."

I ignored that, and hurried on. The iron chair wasn't outside the door; I could hear the wheels clanking inside as if the Master were moving himself restlessly about the room. I waited, shivering in the draft, until there was silence. When I knocked and his voice said, "Come in," it seemed to me that there was weariness and displeasure in it, and my legs felt almost too weak to carry me across the threshold.

His chair was by the window, with the bright white daylight falling on the hollows and lines of his face and on the branching veins on the backs of his hands.

At least he is alone, I thought. But it seemed a great distance I had to cross to reach him, and as I was halfway across the expanse of richly woven rugs and polished oak, Silas came out from the anteroom where the nurse usually sat, carrying a physic bottle and a little glass.

I glanced at him quickly with a sinking heart, but he looked unsurprised by my appearance. He was cold and composed, not a wrinkle on his cream buckskin breeches, not a hair out of place on his shining, dark head.

In a low, reproving voice he said to me, "Where have you been all this time, Agnes Cotter? If with your aunt, you didn't have the Master's permission to see her. You shouldn't have left the stable hand without a word."

I'd reached the Master's chair. I spoke directly to him. "Oh, Sir, I beg your pardon. But I had to see my aunt. She's been taken prisoner by the Militia."

The Master spoke abruptly, not even bothering to look at me. "You've returned to do your duties; that's all that matters to me."

He was angry, and my heart sank further. Then he waved me away in a distracted way, and I saw his anger wasn't with me but something else. The blood was up in his face. His mouth was compressed, his hands clenched on the armrests of the chair. He hadn't taken in what I'd said. Then with a great effort he seemed to bring himself under control. His eyes focused on me.

"Your aunt, you say? Silas told me this morning that the soldiers are in the village —"

His face flushed deeper as I interrupted him, but I couldn't help myself. "Sir, the Militia has been in the village this week past, since before the snow fell!"

His right hand slammed down on the armrest, and I drew back nervously. Silas swiftly measured out some liquid from the bottle into the glass and held it out. "Here, Sir, drink this. You shouldn't agitate yourself further. Shall I call for the nurse?"

The Master flung his hand out contemptuously, as if to knock the glass to the floor. Finding he couldn't reach it, he glared up, but Silas stood calmly, his outstretched hand steady.

"A week!" growled the Master. "It was bad enough to hear about the presence of the Militia in my village, but that it should be the girl, not my steward, who tells me this now! When the soldiers first arrived, why did you keep it from me?"

Silas hardly blinked. "You've been ill, Sir," he said reasonably, his voice like warm wax. "I didn't want to trouble you. The doctor thought it inadvisable. You were in no fit state to entertain any officers, after all. The sweeping's been of little consequence to the village. It remains loyal to the Protector and to you. No traitors have been found."

The Master thrust his face up. "I must know such things

in the future, do you understand? They're my concern as Master of Murkmere. There's nothing wrong with my mind, whatever's wrong with my legs!"

Silas didn't move back. "Of course, Sir."

"If no traitors have been found, then why has Agnes's aunt been taken?"

"She's accused of stealing, Sir. Books bearing your crest have been found in her possession." Silas's dark eyes rested on me. "If it turns out that Agnes's mother stole them when she worked here, then by law the aunt must be punished since they've been found under her roof."

"I know what the law says," said the Master irritably. He took the glass at last and drained the medicine in a gulp.

I looked at him despairingly. "Aunt Jennet isn't a thief, Sir. She came by those books honestly." I put emphasis on my words, trying to convey by my expression that he must know the truth of it himself if only he would remember. "She told me they were given to her many years back."

Silas clicked his teeth. "A lie, Sir. The aunt has other books, of course, the approved textbooks. She was a schoolteacher."

The Master held up a hand. He looked at me, not at Silas, and Silas fell silent.

For a long time the Master and I stared at each other, while his high color faded and his eyes that had been over-bright and bloodshot grew thoughtful. "I remember your aunt," he said, and a secret understanding sprang bright between us.

"Ride to the village at once," he said to Silas. "Bring the

commanding officer to me. I want to speak to him about this woman."

The composure fell from Silas's face. He looked startled, even shocked. "But, Sir, she's been concealing stolen goods!"

The Master sighed. "No, Silas, she has not. I myself gave her the books a long time ago. Such publications weren't banned in those days. At the time I believe I thought they'd be useful to her."

Silas tried once more. "But she hid them, Sir, instead of giving them up when the ban was pronounced. That's not fit behavior from a Chief Elder."

"Her village must decide that, not you," said the Master gently. "It elected her. Go and fetch the officer now. And Silas . . ."

Silas, who had turned on his heel, turned back. His eyes burned black. "Yes, Sir?"

"If by chance the soldiers have already left with her, I shall expect you to ride after them."

A starchy rustling in the nurse's room had warned me earlier of her presence, and after Silas had left she bustled out in her white apron to collect the used glass and the bottle.

When she had gone back into the anteroom the Master said to me, "I'm immeasurably glad you're back, Agnes. Leah needs you. She's not eaten since you left, and she's hardly spoken."

I was astonished.

I knelt by his chair and lowered my voice; the door of the

anteroom was still open, and I remembered the nurse was an eavesdropper. "Sir, I know the truth about Miss Leah. My aunt thought it best to tell me."

He looked startled; the color came and went in his cheeks. "The truth?" He glanced fiercely toward the anteroom. "Shut the door."

I did so, ignoring the raised eyebrows of the nurse; then I came back.

"Now," he said, frowning. "What truth do you speak of?"

I whispered, "I know about Leah's parents, Sir."

He was silent a long time. I wondered if I'd done the right thing in speaking so directly, but then he said, "You must tell no one."

"I give you my word I won't, Sir."

At length he said in a low voice, "I trust you, Agnes. You're like your mother in some ways. Don't betray my trust, or hers."

"I won't, Sir," I breathed.

"You needn't keep silent for long, a few months, that is all. I mean to tell Leah myself on her sixteenth birthday, I've always meant to do that. I'll make a formal announcement at the ball. The Protector and the Ministration won't be able to quibble any longer about Leah inheriting the estate when they learn she's my heir by blood."

Suddenly he looked at me sharply. "Did your aunt tell you the reason for the secrecy?"

"Yes, Sir."

"It was mere gossip about my wife, nothing more. Dangerous gossip." He compressed his lips, and a muscle jumped in his cheek. He turned from me to look out at the scudding clouds beyond the window; every now and then a gust of wind rattled the panes. "But now it's all in the past."

I spoke eagerly, without thinking. "Then, after her birthday, will you let Miss Leah walk freely, Sir?"

He turned back to me slowly. I thought he hadn't understood.

"I mean, let her go beyond the gates, to the village?"

He had to speak quietly, for fear of the nurse overhearing, but still some spittle landed on his chest with the force of his words. "Don't interfere in what you don't understand!"

"I'm sorry, Sir," I said, frightened. I went on kneeling there, but my time was over. He waved me away abruptly.

"Go to Leah now. She's in the watchtower."

She didn't hear my boots on the stairs. She wasn't reading, but had pressed herself tight against the long window, with her arms stretched out and her skirts flattened as if she wanted to melt through. The light pierced through her clothes and the fragile bones of her wrists and fingers. If the glass hadn't been there, she would have fallen out into the sky.

"What are you doing, Miss?"

She whirled around at my cry, and color came into her pale face. She left the window and darted toward me as if she were going to hug me, then stopped herself. Her arms fell to her sides.

"I didn't expect you'd come back," she said in a little struggling voice, most unlike herself. "I thought you'd leave while you had the chance."

I shook my head and tried to smile.

"Oh, Aggie, it's been so dull without you! I thought you wouldn't return — that I was alone again."

As I stared at her, she ducked her head abruptly so that her fine fair hair covered her face. The next moment she had flown over to the wing chair and tucked her long legs under her. She'd recovered herself, I could see that. The imperious manner was back. And then I realized that beneath it she was excited, and bursting to impart some gossip.

"I've some news, though you probably know it already."

"I know about my aunt," I said softly. "I've seen her."

"Your aunt?" she said impatiently. "I know nothing of your aunt. The soldiers are in the village! Silas told my guardian so this morning. Did you see them?"

"I did, Miss," I said. "I believe Silas wouldn't have told the Master at all if I hadn't been sent to the village for Gammy. He feared I'd tell him myself on my return."

"My guardian's sorely vexed. The village is under his authority, and they require his permission to sweep it. Silas must have known the Militia was coming, yet he kept the information to himself. He receives messengers from the Lord Protector, I've seen them." She looked at me, suddenly solemn. "When the ball takes place no visitor must guess that Mr. Tunstall is no longer in control of the estate. Everything must run smoothly and look well cared for. Will you help me when the time comes, Aggie?"

"Of course, Miss," I said, and now it didn't seem strange that she should ask me. "I'll do whatever I can."

I thought of the gaggle of careless, unruly servants and the ramshackle rooms of Murkmere Hall. But Leah sat straight-backed in her chair as if it were a throne, a determined jut to her chin and a regal gleam in her eye. In her imagination she was already giving orders to a willing, well-trained staff, and the rooms gleamed and glittered under their attention.

"You'll have to conduct yourself as a grand lady at the ball, Miss," I said, eyeing her rumpled dress and dirty boots. "What you wear must impress the guests."

"Oh, I will! The Master's already ordered a bale of the finest silk gauze to be made up into a gown for me." She leaped to her feet and began to dance round the room, holding her creased skirts out. "I'm to be clad in silver, he says."

"Silver?" I said faintly, then pulled myself together. "What about the feathers you'd thought you'd wear?"

"That mess we found yesterday? I threw it out. It was still soaking wet when I woke this morning, and no good for anything."

At suppertime the Master told me Aunt Jennet had been released on his request. Two weeks later, as we had arranged, I met Jethro at the gates as twilight was falling, and he confirmed it. We whispered to each other through the rusty bars.

"How is she, Jethro? Is she stronger?"

"Tough as bark, your aunt. She scrubbed your cottage flags thin as soon as the soldiers left, and now she's back organizing the Elders. They kept her as their Chief, of course."

A look passed between us in the damp dusk. I was wondering to what rebellion she stirred those old men and women. Jethro shook his head. "You can't stop her."

"I don't want to. I believe she may be right."

"Don't talk of it here." He glanced about him at the growing shadows. "She asks after you."

"I wish I could see her!"

"How are things with you, Aggie? Has Silas Seed been pestering you with his attentions?"

"I see almost nothing of him," I said, smiling, for he sounded almost jealous. "He's busy supervising the lambing. Jukes the footman has been dealing with our wages."

It was true that Murkmere Hall had become an altogether easier place for me after my return. Between Doggett and me there developed an uneasy truce. I let her see that I wouldn't take over any of her duties as lady's maid to Leah. I certainly didn't want to mend Leah's endlessly torn clothing myself, or struggle to dress her slippery hair.

Each afternoon I'd go to the tower at the end of Leah's lessons. I stopped being nervous of the long window; and the tower showed no sign of collapsing around us. After the

Master had been let down in the lift by Jukes and Pegg, she and I would sit together in the bookroom and she would tell me about what she had learned that day and unlock yet another case to show me the treasures inside.

The Master gave me a reading list, and slowly, laboriously, I began to read my way through it. I'd never be as quick and clever as Leah, but I had great curiosity. As I read more, I began to realize that there once had been a different way of ordering things, and that it had been a better way. Men had grumbled and complained even then, but at least they'd had the freedom to do so.

Leah and I would sit together on the floor in a pool of late-winter sunlight, with the books between us. Her skirts of ivory silk were spread around her; her vivid, fine-boned face turned toward me as she talked.

There were too many words in some of the books she showed me; I liked the mysterious illustrations best.

"Is this a man or an animal, Miss?" I cried, pointing at a creature that was covered with a thick pelt, yet stood on two legs and had a human face. "Does he take his fur off when he washes?"

"Look, he's got a tail as well," she said, pointing to a second illustration and giggling at my horrified expression. "But here's a much grander tail!" And with a flourish she showed me an illustration of a beautiful girl who appeared to be half-fish.

But the illustrations that intrigued me most were a sequence of four. They showed a night forest. In the first picture I glimpsed the pale form of a naked man slipping between the dark trees; then he began to change horribly, until in the last he had become a wolf, howling at the moon.

"Do such creatures exist, Miss Leah?" I said, uneasily.

She shrugged. "There are places far away where people have seen them, or so they say. After all, there are people in this country who believe in the avia. Who knows whether *they* ever existed, or if they're a myth, like so much else in religion."

It made me anxious for her soul when Leah talked like that. What exactly did she believe herself?

We were on our way out for our walk one afternoon, and for once we left through the Great Hall. This was a vast, dark room used for dining on the rare occasions the Master had visitors. It smelt of old candlewax and peat ash, and was hung about with ragged tapestries that illustrated the Battle of the Birds. The first time I'd seen them, I'd thought the birds were alive: I'd fallen on the floor in fear, covering my eyes. Even now I thought the Hall a haunted place. In the drafts the tapestries seemed to quiver with a secret life of their own, as if the story that they told were being played out still.

Leah slapped one of the tapestries as we passed, releasing puffs of dust. "We should take these down before the ball." She sneezed.

"But they're sacred!" I exclaimed involuntarily, and realized at once I'd annoyed her.

She stopped immediately; we were both standing before the last tapestry. "What do you see in the picture, Aggie?" she demanded.

"I-I see the Eagle," I stammered. I wanted to touch my amber, but under her censorious gaze thought better of it.

"Describe him."

But I did not dare.

Leah did it for me. "He is two-faced, half-bird, half-man. One side of his face is feathered, the other has fleshy cheek and bearded jaw. His eyes are tragic. Common to both sides of the face is a cruel beak that shows no softness, no forgiveness." She tilted her head in mock-thoughtfulness. "What does that mean for his creatures, I wonder? And what do his birds do in the shadows of the forests beneath him?"

"They destroy each other," I whispered, staring at the tapestry.

"In his name, Aggie." She turned away. "Throughout my childhood the kinder servants worried for my soul, and led me to Devotion." She was walking over to the main doors. "It's hard to believe in an unforgiving god, Aggie."

"It's not meant to be easy," I protested.

She laughed suddenly, startling the footman standing at the door. He opened it at her nod, and light seeped in over our feet. We stood at the top of the steps, the parkland spread before us in the damp afternoon, sheep grazing on the early shoots beneath the scattered oaks. "There's a power in everything," said Leah softly, looking about her. "I feel it all the time — a power in all creatures, all nature."

"But only One made that power," I said quickly, before she betrayed herself as a heretic, before He could hear.

"The Eagle, you believe?"

I nodded, and at her expression added even faster, "And you can't stop me believing what I know is right — you who believe in freedom, Miss!"

And I made her laugh a second time.

I didn't break my word — I never said anything to Leah about her parents. My worries for her future drifted away, for as we grew closer she seemed like any normal girl. She'd sometimes go to the mere, but now she'd take me with her. On the way back to the Hall she'd link her arm through mine. In the evenings we'd play Commotion, and the parlor would shake with our laughter. We'd talk about all manner of things: what I had read, what I thought of it; more important, what she thought of it.

One afternoon I found her at the desk in the tower, with pen and parchment. She seemed excited, and the parchment was covered in scrawls and blots and crossings-out.

"We made a guest list for the ball this morning, Mr. Tunstall and I," she said. "It's to take place sixteen years to the day that I was brought to Murkmere, the day he's always called my birthday, the day the first leaf of autumn falls, he always says. I've just been making a list of my own, Aggie, and you're to help me. It's all the things we've got to do to make the Hall ready."

I sat obediently on the floor and looked up at her. Her tongue stuck out of the side of her mouth as the quill scratched.

"First, we'll open up the old ballroom; we'll fling open the doors on to the terrace and air it thoroughly."

"Yes, Miss."

"We must check all the bedchambers to see they're fit for guests and have them cleaned."

"Yes, Miss."

"We must check the supplies in the icehouse and make sure there's the right quantity of livestock to be slaughtered, since I don't trust Mistress Crumplin to do it."

"Yes, Miss."

"And then . . ." She rested her sharp little chin on her hand and looked at me dreamily, her eyes shining. Leah's eyes were gray, but they always seemed strikingly dark in her pale face. "And then, there's the ball itself. We'll have flaming torches placed on the terrace so guests can stroll there."

"Yes, Miss."

"We'll have candles burning everywhere. There'll be garlands of flowers in the rooms, delicacies to eat . . ."

"Yes, Miss Leah."

She flung down her pen. "Is that all you can say? And you must stop calling me 'Miss,' now that we are sisters. Anyway, no man or woman is superior by birth to another one."

"Sisters?" I said, and a smile hung on my lips.

She got up and went restlessly to the long window, touching her neck. "Sisters, until you leave me for the village again."

"I won't leave you, not for a long time yet."

"What about your sweetheart?" She faced me, and her eyes gleamed mischievously. "Won't he want to ride away with you?"

"What sweetheart?" I said, puzzled.

"The young man you meet secretly."

I stared at her in consternation. She looked thoroughly pleased with herself. "I followed you. I saw you at the gates together yesterday evening."

When I couldn't speak for my confusion, she had the grace to look a little ashamed. "I shan't do it again, Aggie. I'll leave you alone to kiss."

"He is not my sweetheart, and we do not kiss," I snapped. Sometimes she tried me sorely. "He's a family friend, a neighbor. He brings me news of my aunt. That's why we meet."

"Oh, shame. No kisses, then," she said wistfully. "I long to know what it's like."

"What what's like?" I said, wishing an end to the conversation.

"Being in love, of course."

"You'll know soon enough, I daresay," I said briskly.

She sighed. "Not me, Aggie. I know it's not for me, don't ask me how." Then, as I was about to protest, her mood changed abruptly. "Why didn't I think of it before? You must ask this boy of yours to send us some young people from the village. A dozen at least! They can help prepare for the ball. Tell him to say it's my wish and the Master's, and that they'll be well paid. They can start once the harvest's in."

Jethro shook his head when I asked him. "They'll never come, Aggie, not even for the money. Time was when they trusted the Master, but now they think he's on the side of the Minis-tration. He didn't protect them when the Militia came."

"It wasn't his fault!" I hissed at him indignantly through the bars of the gate. "He wasn't told in time. He saved my aunt, didn't he?"

"They don't like what they hear about Murkmere, Aggie, and that's a fact."

"We can barely manage here, Jethro Sim, and that's a fact too! We've a ball to prepare and important guests coming! It's their duty to come and work here."

He put his hand through and took hold of one of my clenched fists. "Is it your duty too? What's this ball to you, then, Miss Agnes Cotter? Who are you hoping to meet, now you've grown so fancy?"

He was smiling. Unlike most youths, Jethro's teeth were nice and white and even. Tonight I was suddenly unsettled by his smile, but more so by his tone and the strength of his fingers on mine. Without saying goodbye I pretended to flounce away.

Leah wasn't daunted by my news. "We'll have to manage with the staff we've got, then," she said firmly. "I'll speak to the house servants sometime soon. We've lots of time."

"Of course we have," I said. "The ball will be a fine occa-sion, I know it."

She took my hands. "It will be the finest the Protector's ever attended, Aggie! But I can't do it without you. We'll make it so together!"

The days passed. The last rags of snow melted away in the pale new sun; the estate bloomed misty green; and blossom budded white on blackthorn and hawthorn and crab apple, and on tangles of wild strawberry, so that it looked as if a new sprinkling of snow had fallen in the night.

But the window of the bookroom, high above a foaming sea of cow parsley, showed us only the endless spaces of the sky, the clouds passing by and passing by again as if drawn by strings: the same clouds, it seemed, going round and round, as if they would do so forever.

We felt we had infinite time up there, but in truth it was sifting away like the sand in my old clock; and all the while, though we didn't know it, the clouds were changing over Murkmere Hall.

PART TWO

The Shadowskin

XVI

Marks in the Dust

Some weeks later I walked up the rise to meet Leah in the bookroom.

The watchtower was hidden from my view by the tender green stenciling of spring. In the lush grass, cows were grazing, and the path was fringed by young nettles and fragrant cow parsley chest-high, its flower heads white as new-washed lace before it yellows. I could hear birdsong; a robin hopped away at my approach and I thought suddenly of my copy of the *Table of Significance*. But though I lingered to see if Love would cross my path, the robin eyed me brightly from last autumn's leaf fall and ventured no closer.

Down by the gates the rooks had built their nests weeks ago, but rooks scarcely worried me nowadays. I'd not touched my amber for an age.

In the bookroom Leah was crouched in the wing chair. I was disturbed to see a despondent, defeated look about her.

"I've promised the servants extra wages if they work hard for the ball, but now I don't know how we'll pay them. Silas told me today that we're on the brink of bankruptcy. That's even without the cost of the ball."

"That can't be true! Why, I've seen how his drawers are filled with gold coins!"

"I wish I could see the accounts book myself," she said desperately. "I believe Silas deceives my guardian over the figures. Sometimes men come to see him — strangers, who carry money bags. I've always thought they come to trade with us, to buy wool or corn or some such, but now I wonder if the money doesn't go into Silas's personal coffers."

I tried to raise her spirits, she looked so drawn with worry, but to no avail. She waved my words aside and jumped to her feet. "It's not only that. I made a discovery just now. I noticed the doors weren't quite shut."

She went to the double doors and opened them, and I looked in over her shoulder. The flying machine still hung like a magic thing, silent and motionless in the empty room, the pale wood catching the light that came in through the doors. Leah pointed at the wood floor and I saw our own footprints from long ago still there faintly in the dust. But now there were the new, clearer marks of curving lines cutting through the smudges.

"My guardian has come in here alone," said Leah. "What does it mean, Aggie?"

"Nothing worrying, I'm sure," I said soothingly.

"You don't think he wants to fly the machine?"

"He can't move it," I pointed out. "You said yourself it took two men to push it out of here."

I persuaded her at last to shut the doors. "You'll not get answers by staring at it. Let's go for a walk. Shall we go to the mere and see the swans? We haven't been for a while."

She hesitated. "Perhaps it would be best if you didn't come with me, Aggie. There's a pen sitting now and you may frighten her."

I turned away so she couldn't see my hurt. I knew she must have gone there without me to know.

Through the spring days, Murkmere Hall slowly began to prepare itself for the ball. Like a great hibernating bear, it was awakened and dragged, blinking, from darkness into daylight.

Leah demanded that all the shutters be unlatched and the windows and doors opened so that fresh air could blow through the house. The dust billowed across the floors and fled into corners, and housemaids armed with brooms swept it out again.

As each room was opened up in turn, the daylight showed cruelly how dilapidated the old house was: the faded, peeling wallpaper, the damp patches on the ceilings, the holes in the rugs, the woodworm in doors and skirting boards. Leah's face would darken as she looked around her; then she would snap out an order at her trail of servants and be off to the next room.

The servants were doing their best for her, she had to acknowledge that. Even Mistress Crumplin had smartened herself up with clean apron and cap instead of her grubby frills, and was trying to regain the authority she'd lost so many years ago. But I could see the shine of avarice in the servants' eyes and how they were busiest when Leah was about.

"I'll spring-clean your chamber while you're out, Miss Leah," Doggett offered with unusual enthusiasm one morning, when Leah was about to go off to her lessons in the tower and I was ready to walk with her as usual.

Leah, busy collecting books together, nodded without much interest, then she paused. "Why don't you stay with Dog, Aggie, and see if there's anything of mine you could wear for the ball? She'll show you where my clothes are."

As Dog began to glower at me in her old jealous way, I said quickly to Leah, "But what about Doggett? Your personal maid should look suitably dressed too."

So it was that once Leah had left the room, the atmosphere between Dog and me was almost friendly. Dog seemed glad to have an audience for her grumbles as she began to make Leah's bed, on which the sheets and blankets had been bundled together in a mound.

"Like a nest," she said, in disgust. "What dreams Miss Leah must have to be so restless!"

She took the bedclothes off and put them by the door for laundering. Then she picked yesterday's clothes from the floor, shaking out each garment as if she wished she could shake its owner. I watched in silence as she went to the pair of heavy mahogany cupboards and flung them open.

"It's hard work keepin' her clothes respectable, I can tell

you. The way she treats them! When she comes back from the mere, they're all muddied and filthy."

It took Dog a while to sort through the gowns, the skirts and bodices, petticoats and shifts, many bearing her neat darns, though one needed sharp eyes to spot them. In the end I tried on two skirts, one of midnight taffeta, the other a grass-green silk. The bodices of Leah's gowns were too close-fitting for me, but I'd be able to let out the waistbands of the skirts.

"See," said Doggett, as I stood in the dark blue taffeta, "if I cut off this hem and the one on the green skirt, they'll be the right length for you. Miss Leah can't wear them any longer; look how the bottom edges are all frayed and dirty. You can sew fresh hems. They'll be good as new."

She brought out a pair of long-bladed scissors from her work basket and swiftly cut the ruined hem away. Now my feet peeked out, almost delicate-looking under the heavy folds. I shod them in imaginary slippers, with little silver heels. Doggett gave me a black silk shawl sewn with shining blue beads, to hide my old bodice. She found a gray silk dress for herself; the hem was much mended, but she said she'd have to take the skirt up anyway.

We paraded up and down the room in our new clothes and smiled at each other in mutual satisfaction. I saw myself at the ball, my skirts uncurling like the petals of a flower, my hair bright against the black silk shawl, and I could have hugged Dog in gratitude.

"We might be able to find you some shoes in the linen chest," she said as I climbed back into my own drab skirts at last.

The chest, which sat at the end of Leah's bed, was locked.

Dog put her hands on her hips and frowned. "I've never known Miss Leah to lock it before." I thought there might well be some papers to do with the ball in there, something she wouldn't want her lady's maid to see, a guest list perhaps. I knew a groom had taken the invitations to the mail-coach in the nearest town only recently.

"Perhaps she has private business in it," I said.

Dog snorted. "It's where I keep the shoes she doesn't wear much, like her old dancin' slippers. She'll need new ones for the ball, with those huge feet of hers."

Her little eyes flicked around. "I know where she keeps the key — I know where everything is in this room." She gave me a triumphant look. "I know what she keeps in that old jar of hers too!"

"I don't think we should open it."

"She's no secrets from me! I see her newborn naked, morning and night. Anyway, her clothes are my business." Dog marched over to Leah's bedside table and took a key out of a little checkered box. She held it up to me and winked.

Perhaps I had a premonition then, I don't know. But I felt a profound reluctance to watch Dog open that chest, a sudden fear of what it was Leah might be hiding away.

Doggett had no such qualms. With a complacent smile she fitted the key into the brass lock and turned it with difficulty.

I stepped forward. "Don't, Dog! Leave it!"

But she had already flung back the lid.

XVII

Destruction

There was a pause, long enough for her to gasp and let her breath out again in a shriek as she slammed the lid down again and staggered back, her face as pale as cheese.

I rushed to her as she staggered, and half-lugged her over to the bed, where I made her sit down. Her forehead was greasy with sweat. I thought she'd faint.

"What is it, Dog?" I asked, but I knew.

She held out the key mutely in her trembling fingers and I understood I was to lock the chest again. When it was locked up, she seemed easier.

I came and sat close to her, patting her on the back encouragingly and trying not to screw up my nose at the smell of her unwashed body. She put her bitten nails on the tatty red ribbon at her wrist, her amulet, and her breathing steadied. "It can't get out, not now."

"I know what you saw," I said. "It's not alive, Dog."

She looked at me in horror. "You know she has a bird in there?"

"It's only feathers — a skin, a pelt. She found it by the mere one day. I was with her. She told me she'd not kept it."

"It's sacrilege, ain't it, to keep such a thing? And in her chamber! No wonder she has bad dreams. My mistress is damned!" Dog put her hands to her face and began to rock herself, moaning softly.

I tried to think what to do. "Let me help you to your room. You should lie down. It's been a bad shock. I'll tidy up in here."

She began to wail. "I'll lose my position! How can I look after Miss Leah now I know what's in the chest? I daren't come in here again."

"I'll get rid of it," I said quickly. "I'll lock the chest again, afterward. If the mistress discovers it gone, I'll take the blame. But in turn I want you to do something for me."

She turned to me, her eyes stretched wide, still trembling. I wasn't sure if she was taking in what I said. "Dog, you must tell no one of this, no one at all. Do you understand? If you do, I'll tell the mistress it was you who pried, not me."

She nodded, and I had to be content. I helped her to her room, which was stuffy with her sour smell, and pulled the grubby coverlet over her once she'd fallen groaning on the bed. Strange how proudly she looked after Leah's appearance, yet didn't care about her own cleanliness.

"Will you tell Miss Leah I'm sick?" she said.

I could see her eyes gleaming over the coverlet. She wasn't

quite as faint as she pretended, I thought; and not unpleased at the opportunity to idle in bed all day.

"Miss Leah won't return till luncheon," I said. "I think by then you'll be recovered." And I left her.

Back in Leah's bedchamber I knelt down, unlocked the chest, and looked in. Inside was a large gray and white bundle that took up most of the space.

I had begun to shake. I forced myself to touch the thing, to take hold of it.

The pure white feathers melted softly against my fingers; the pearly gray skin was supple and smooth. It smelled of water and weeds, and something oily or fishy.

Averting my gaze, I pulled it out. When I looked it was hanging glistening from my fingers, each feather lying snug and smooth on the next. It was so light that if I breathed on it, it might have floated away.

I imagined Leah wearing it round her shoulders; I saw it nestling around her like a cloud, her long white neck rising from the feathers.

But as soon as she put it on she would realize her true nature; she would be transformed into the unthinkable.

And there would be no escape, because the swanskin would cling to human flesh like a second skin; it would stick so fast you'd peel your own away with it as you tore it off.

For a moment I stood, the swanskin hanging from my hand, while bile rose in my throat. I knew what I had to do.

I took it over to the fireplace, where the coals still smoldered.

With my free hand I used the poker, and a tiny flame licked them into heat.

I fed an edge of the swanskin into the golden center. I waited. Soon the flame would grow, rip along the feathers and turn them black. I half-expected the swanskin to scream out in pain.

Burn, I thought, *burn, and die.*

In a fever of agitation I waited for the feathers to shrivel up in a ball of fire. I stoked the coals up again, pushing the skin in deeper as the coals turned from golden to red.

After a while I had to give up. The coals were used and ashy and had begun to splutter weakly under the swanskin.

The feathers are still too damp, I thought desperately. *They won't burn.*

I'd have to take the skin outside and bury it so Leah would never find it again. It hardly mattered where I buried it as long as it was deep enough.

I found an old skirt that Doggett and I had rejected earlier. I was about to wrap it around the swanskin and carry the whole bundle downstairs when my feverish gaze was caught by Dog's sewing basket sitting on Leah's bedside table.

I threw back the lid, and from among the neatly ordered spools of silk arranged inside, the gleaming scissors Dog had used earlier winked at me.

Sharp enough to cut material, sharp enough to cut through skin and feathers. I'd destroy the swanskin utterly with those long, sharp blades before I buried the pieces.

❧

I crouched down on the floor and began to cut. The skin was oddly resistant, thicker than it looked; it was like cutting through great wads of gray vellum. Gripping the handles fiercely, almost blind with the horror of it, I closed the scissors hard together with both hands and the skin split at last.

Feathers rose around me; pieces of skin crackled emptily to the floor. I might have been skinning a goose for Aunt Jennet but for the quantity of feathers. The room was full of them: on the bed, the table, the chest top, drifting around the base of the wardrobe, everywhere. They were up my nostrils, in my mouth.

I couldn't breathe. There was no air left in the room, only feathers, floating. I fell back against the bed; the scissors dropped from my hand. My mouth was clotted, crammed, with them; I was choking. I tasted the dankness of the mere.

Then the door opened.

"Aggie?"

I looked up. The feathers had settled, covering the floor like snowflakes. I hadn't choked to death after all. My mouth was empty; I could breathe, and I'd destroyed the swanskin completely.

But it wasn't Dog at the door, as I'd expected.

It was Leah.

She looked at the feathers everywhere, and the blood drained from her cheeks. I could almost see her veins shrinking with shock. She stood there, a parchment girl.

She croaked out, "What have you done?"

I staggered to my feet, and the scissors rattled across the floor. We both stared at them.

"You've — cut — the swanskin," she said incredulously. "You've cut it up?"

I nodded, speechless.

She looked dazed. She put out her hand and held on to the door frame, as if she felt ill. When I made a move to support her, she shrank back. Her eyes were dull.

"You've cut away my life."

She said nothing more but knelt down on the floor and began gathering the feathers to her, cradling the bits against her chest, trying to fit the jagged strips of skin together like a jigsaw.

It was impossible. Tears began to roll down her face as she scrabbled about, and she made no effort to wipe them away. "My swanskin," she moaned to herself, over and over again, "my swanskin."

Watching her, I felt a terrible guilt begin to freeze my bones.

At last she looked up. "Why did you do it, why?"

"I did it f-for you," I stammered.

She shook her head blankly. "This? For me?"

For an age I watched her creep over the floor trying to gather the feathers to her, while the huge tears dripped silently from her eyes.

"Leah," I said, and my voice broke. "I'm sorry, so sorry."

At that moment I longed more than anything to have the swanskin back with all its power rather than see Leah like this, like a creature wounded half to death.

She looked at me, her face marked with her weeping, red channels inflaming the paper-white skin. I could see what an effort it was for her to hold her voice steady.

"Go from me. Never come to the tower again. I don't want to see you there." She turned her head away and whispered, "I thought you were my sister!"

My eyes filled. "I am, I am!"

She didn't look at me. "You can't be — to do this!"

"I only wanted to protect you."

I took a step closer, held out my arms helplessly. My throat was tight with tears. "Leah . . ."

She said nothing.

I started to cry. I couldn't help it. I crouched down sobbing and began to gather feathers blindly, trying to make amends. But as soon as she saw what I was doing, she lurched to her feet and her face twisted.

"Leave them! Didn't you hear what I said? Go!"

I stumbled over to the door and stopped. I longed to throw myself at her, to kneel at her feet and beg for her friendship back. But it would do no good. Our days of happiness together were gone, destroyed. I had done it. I'd cut our friendship into pieces. A huge sob filled my chest so I could hardly speak.

"Forgive me, Leah. Oh, please forgive me."

She was crawling round the floor again in the hopeless mess of feathers, keening to herself. Head bent, she ignored me.

I couldn't bear to watch any longer. I closed the door behind me and, with my hands against my face, wept into my fingers as if I'd never stop.

XVIII

Night

At the end of the morning I didn't go to luncheon. I woke Doggett, who was snoring on her bed, and told her that I was sick as well and that she must stir herself and go with Leah on her walk that afternoon. I did feel sick, sick to my heart.

From her pillows Doggett stared sleepily at my red eyes. I must have looked ill indeed, for she didn't question me, but at last nodded and heaved herself up. Only as I was retreating through her door did she say with melancholy satisfaction, "You destroyed the swanskin, didn't you? You shouldn't have done that."

A spark of indignation stirred in me. "I did what you were too frightened to do!"

"It's cursin' you already! Oh, Aggie, what a dreadful thing!"

"Codswallop!" I said. "It's not birds that damn us, but our own deeds."

But back in my own room my spirit died. I lay on my bed, and tears began to slip down my face again. I thought of Leah's surprise and pleasure when I'd returned from Aunt Jennet, and I wept for what I'd lost.

At last there were no tears left in me, just a dreariness at the very center of my being. I was empty, but had no appetite. I climbed off my bed and dragged myself like an invalid across to the looking glass. As I wearily brushed my hair, a stranger with raw eyes and pale cheeks stared back at me. Even my hair seemed dulled.

What was I to do with myself this long afternoon, and all the afternoons to come? Outside the sun still shone, the birds still sang. I looked with surprise at my window. There was a blackbird somewhere outside. I could hear his melody even in my room, the most beautiful of all birdsong. He sang of spring, new beginnings, hope: things that had no meaning for me. But I put on my chip hat and my wool shawl. I needed to escape the house and its heartache.

I let my feet walk, with no clear thought in my head as to where I was going. Sometime later I found myself standing by the edge of the mere, at the beginning of the path that Leah had first taken me along months before.

I hesitated, then began to squeeze along it, crushing soft new nettles under my boots. The reeds were brilliant green and the lake mirrored the blue sky. A rising fish ringed the glittering surface near me, shaking the water lilies that rose like white hands through the water.

The female swan, the pen, was sitting on her nest in a reed bed not far from the bank. I stopped at once, but she didn't move. She looked so serene, sitting on the vast, untidy mound of twigs and vegetation. Occasionally she would pull a blade of grass closer to tuck it round her. Her dark eye gazed down without expression. Her neck curved over her body so that it looked like a question mark.

I knew the question she asked me.

Were you right to destroy the swanskin?

"I did it for Leah," I whispered. "She's not of your kind, nor her mother's. She's like me, not you — she said we were sisters. Why should the Almighty punish her for something she never did?" For a long time I stood waiting, as if the swan could somehow answer me, but her dark eyes didn't flicker. At last I turned and moved stiffly away.

Although we kept up the pretence of being mistress and companion, Leah didn't speak to me. It was worse than the old days at Murkmere, for at least her taunts had been preferable to the total silence that now existed between us. She was silent at mealtimes, silent on our walks, silent in the evenings when we continued grimly to play cards after supper. Although she always won, her face remained shut and she did not look at me. We never played Commotion. She had withdrawn into herself and it was as if she no longer knew or cared about me.

When she was at her lessons in the watchtower I hid

myself away in my chamber, and read and reread the last book she had given me. At night I would lie awake, listening to the barking of the guard dogs as they roamed the grounds outside, and tears would fill my tired eyes.

Around me the servants swept and aired and dusted. The house was full of sunlight and excited whisperings about the ball. No one noticed I had fallen from favor, and if the Master suspected it, he did not refer to it at supper. But sometimes he would ask me how my reading was coming along. What book was I reading now? He'd look disappointed when I confessed it was still the same one.

Of course, Doggett knew of Leah's coldness toward me, but she avoided me, as if talking to me would infect her too. Scuff suspected something was amiss. When I'd retired to my chamber she'd bring me hot possets as if I were convalescent, and hover about me anxiously until I drank.

"You're so pale, Aggie," she said. "You look as if you come from the Capital!"

I smiled sadly, in spite of myself. "Is everyone pale in the Capital, Scuff?"

I don't think anyone else ever gave Scuff the chance to talk. The words rushed out of her. "There's no fresh air in the Capital. Too many people breathin', that's why. Even the black statues look as if they breathe. Them statues, they're everywhere, giant-sized: the Protector and his friends, lookin' down on us, makin' sure we're behavin'. And if you breathe too deep you might breathe in the Miasma."

"What's that, Scuff?"

"It carries the plague, the Miasma does. It's like an invisible wind of death."

I shivered. "That's what I feel in this house now."

Then at last it was time for my next visit from Jethro, and how I longed to see his friendly face.

As I slipped down the drive like a shadow in my cloak and hood, I noticed that the holes had been filled in, the weeds cleared away. So Silas had had a word with the keepers. *Of course*, I thought bitterly. It would reflect on his own job as steward if the Lord Protector thought the estate badly tended when he came.

The rooks called in the dark trees near the gates as they made ready for the night. Once I would have been fearful about being alone, but now I didn't care. I was only aware of the ache in my heart.

Then I saw Jethro's stocky silhouette behind the bars of the gate. He was waiting for me: solid, dependable Jethro. I wanted to run to him and throw my arms round him, and weep and weep.

He held my hand through the bars, and looked at me. "You're tired, Aggie. Have they been working you too hard?"

His tenderness undid me, and I'd intended to be so nonchalant. "Oh, Jethro," I gulped. "It's dreadful here, you can't believe."

"I'm sure I can," he said, and clenched his jaw. "Is it Silas Seed? If that rogue —"

"No, no," I said hastily. "Indeed, he's not spoken to me this whole season past." I took a deep breath and clutched his hand tighter. "I've brought it on myself, Jethro. My mistress won't speak to me now because of what I've done."

"What did you do, Aggie?"

"I can't tell you! Oh, Jethro, you must believe me! I did it for her own good, to save her!"

"I'm sure you did," he said gently.

"But now she hates me for it, Jethro." I looked down, my mouth trembling. I did so want to appear a grown woman before him and not give in to tears.

"Maybe she doesn't understand why you did it."

"I can't tell her. And now she'll never forgive me."

"But you haven't lost your position?"

I shook my head. He pressed my hand encouragingly and let it go. "Then matters aren't so very bad, are they? You've still your job and your wages."

I couldn't explain to him how bereft I felt; the right words wouldn't come. I stared at him helplessly, the tears drying on my cheeks. Then I noticed something odd.

"You're not wearing your amulet!"

He looked awkward. "Aye, I've done away with it, thrown it in the marshes."

I gasped. "You never did such a thing!"

He paused, then said steadily, "It seems to me that men won't have true freedom till we banish our fears."

I wanted to think about what he had said. "Oh, Jethro," I said hesitantly, pressing myself against the cold bars so I could see his expression better. "I'd so like to talk to you properly."

To my astonishment he looked as if he were blushing in the half-dark. Suddenly he said, "Can't you escape this place soon, ask the Master for permission to leave your position? If his ward's displeased with you . . ."

I pressed my hands together. "You don't understand. Now it's harder for me to leave than ever. I must make sure Leah is safe."

"Safe? What's to threaten her, locked up behind these bars? You've done your duty by her, as much as is called for, surely?" There was a note of exasperation in his voice.

"It's not . . . duty. I can't explain."

"So you'll stay on in this benighted place?"

I nodded.

"Then you must care for her very much."

I looked at him helplessly. He was staring at me, frowning, perplexed. "You will come again, Jethro, won't you? I couldn't do without your visits."

He caught my hand again through the bars and brought it to his lips. I felt them press roughly against my palm for a second. Then he dropped my hand and abruptly strode away into the dusk. Startled from my grief, I gazed after him.

I'd been so full of my own misery I hadn't even asked Jethro about Aunt Jennet. Suddenly I saw clearly how she'd perceive me: moping because my mistress was displeased with me. She'd tell me to pull myself together, get on with my duties. And I would. Tomorrow I'd help the maids with the cleaning of the Hall.

In the afternoon, when Leah's lessons were over, I noticed her in the doorway, watching as we polished the sideboard in the Great Hall. "Good," she said, and there was the glint of approval in her eye. But whether the remark was intended for the two housemaids or for me, I didn't know. Every day, it seemed, she would come and watch wherever I was for a little while, but still she said nothing to me.

One night I was deeply asleep when my shoulder was shaken roughly and Doggett's voice hissed, "Aggie, wake up! Aggie!"

I woke with a start, my heart beating wildly, for though I recognized her voice, the candle she was holding sent strange shadows leaping over her face and the lank braids of her hair, over her long white nightgown and shawl. Beyond her ghostly figure the chamber was dark as pitch, and cold. The wind was in the eaves and drafts scurried round my warm bed.

"What is it, Dog? Are you ill?"

The candleholder trembled in her fingers. "It's the mistress. I was comin' back from the privy . . ." She shook her head. "Come and see for yourself."

Instantly I was awake. I thrust my feet into slippers and wrapped a coverlet around my shoulders. Then, full of dread, I padded after her down the dark passage.

Cold air rippled around us, blowing our gowns against our ankles. When we reached Leah's door it was creaking to and fro, opening a little on its latch, then closing. There was candlelight in her chamber. When the door opened, the oak floorboards of the passage glowed for a brief moment.

We stood in the shadows and whispered to each other.

"She can't sleep," I said in Dog's ear, irritable at being woken up for this. "You should go in and ask her if she wants for anything."

"If you pass her chamber as I did," Dog hissed back, "you'll see what I saw."

Grumbling silently, clutching the coverlet about my cold shoulders, I walked past the door as it closed, then turned. Dog nodded urgently back at me.

Then the door opened a little on the latch.

From where I was standing I could see Leah through the gap. She was crouched with her back to me in a wavering circle of yellow light. She must have kept the feathers and the scraps of skin after my destruction. They were in a pile beside her, the feathers rising and drifting in the draft. Her head was bent, and there was something in her right hand.

I couldn't make out what she was doing until she brought her hand up and the candlelight glinted on silver.

A threaded needle.

She forced the needle into the skin, then out again. It was difficult, impossible. I'd cut the swanskin into countless pieces. She could never repair it.

For a long moment I stood watching her, rent with pity. Then her door banged shut, making both Dog and me jump.

I beckoned Dog back to my chamber. We were trembling,

with cold or fear or perhaps both. I sat on my bed and Dog sat too while the candles shook in our hands. I had to think how to reassure Dog that all was well with our mistress when plainly it was not.

"She's brought those bird feathers out again!" she whispered. "I thought you'd got rid of them."

"I destroyed the skin. It's a dead thing, Dog, nothing to be afraid of."

"She must have put all the pieces back in her chest. What's she doin'? It's the middle of the night!"

"I believe she's asleep," I said firmly, for Dog's voice was rising. "She doesn't know she's out of bed."

"What, with a lit candle and all?"

"It's possible. Why shouldn't you do things in sleep that you do when awake?" In truth, I did think that Leah might be sleepwalking, and it was reassuring to think so.

"Should we fetch someone to her?" asked Dog.

"No, no," I said quickly. "It would be dangerous to wake her in such a state. She's best left. She'll come back to herself naturally. I'll return in a while and make sure the candle flame is safely out."

Dog was still looking doubtful. I hurried her to the door, patting her shoulder. "There's no cause for worry, Dog. I believe such sleep activity is common enough. We'll keep it to ourselves and not worry the Master."

Dog nodded. "And you'll make sure she's back in her bed?" She shivered again. "Otherwise she might come walkin' in my chamber!"

"I'll do all that's necessary."

Her candle guttered away down the passage. Then in the darkness I made my way across the room to my cold bed and climbed in.

I lay waiting, my feet like stones. Later, I lit my own candle with a flint from the tinderbox and tiptoed back down the dark hole of the passageway. Though her door still swung on its latch, Leah's chamber was in darkness. I stood by the gap and listened, but heard only her steady breathing. Then I went back to bed myself, too cold, too full of dread, to sleep again.

The following night I kept the candle burning by my bed. The old house creaked in the wind; doors rattled. Finally, I left my chamber and stole down the passage, my candle flaring in the drafty darkness. As I neared her door, I saw again the light lying over the floorboards, narrowing to darkness as the door shifted shut. Fear seized me so I could scarcely move, but I forced my cold limbs forward. As the door opened again I stood still, hardly daring to breathe, and looked through the gap.

She was in the same position, sitting on the floor with her back to me. How long she had been so, there was no way to tell. But I saw something that chilled my blood to ice.

She was making progress in sewing the pieces of the swanskin together. Two little scraps had been joined together to make a larger piece. As she finished sewing it, she held the mended piece up to admire her handiwork before laying it with the greatest care beside her. Every now and then a little moan would escape from her, as if at the enormity of her task.

I didn't enter and confront her; I didn't dare. I was the one who had destroyed the swanskin. I couldn't prevent her from trying to repair it when it meant so much to her. I stood watching in a kind of fascinated horror, until my legs began to tremble.

Three nights more I found candlelight lining her door. The wind had died away with the end of the spring storms, and I had no more glimpses of her crouched and intent over her work, for the door stayed shut. I was tempted to lift the latch, but knew I could not do so quietly.

It came to the fourth night of my watching. I climbed wearily out of bed as soon as I thought the household slept. I'd forgotten to keep my candle burning, so had to fumble with the tinderbox. The darkness pressed around me in a stifling way. At last the flame was lit. I wrapped the coverlet about me and padded across the chamber.

But this night was different. I was about to close the door behind me when I heard the whispers.

I blew out my candle at once and froze where I stood. Down the far end of the passage by Leah's door there were two figures holding lighted candles.

I knew them immediately. It was Doggett and Silas Seed.

XIX

Alone

At first light I strode to Doggett's room and flung open the door. Only a greasy braid showed on the pillow. I flung the bedclothes from her huddled body and shook her violently. She gasped awake and drew away from me in terror, her rough, red hands across the front of her nightgown.

"You worm!" I hissed. "You've betrayed our mistress!"

She shook her lank head. "I never, Aggie!"

"You did! I saw you! You took Silas to her room!"

"I never! I never opened her door, I promise, only showed him the light."

I brought my face close and she shrank back, her eyes darting everywhere, looking for escape. "What did you tell him, Dog? Tell me!"

"I told him she'd a dead bird in there with her. I did it for the mistress's safety, Aggie. I thought Mr. Silas should know."

She stretched her eyes wide and virtuous. "He cares for all our souls."

Something snapped inside me, and I slapped her hard.

She stared at me, shocked, and put her bitten nails to her cheek. I was ashamed as soon as I'd done it. I stared back at her, my anger draining from me. She was a weak, foolish creature, and I should never have trusted her.

"I asked that you tell nobody, Doggett," I said quietly. "Was it such a hard thing to ask?"

She began to sob; her cheek flamed. After a moment of this doleful crying, I could bear it no longer. I put out my hand and awkwardly patted her shoulder. She looked up at me with eyes all bleary. "I never would have done it, Aggie, but he made me!"

"What do you mean?"

"I have to report to him end of each sennight. Tell him what's goin' on with the mistress, the servants and such. This time when I went and he asked me about Miss Leah . . ." Her shoulders heaved. "He knew I was hidin' something. He sees everything, does Mr. Silas, like the Almighty." She sniffed and wiped her nose on her sleeve. "He's so good it ain't fair on the rest of us."

"He isn't a good man, Dog. He doesn't behave as a believer should."

"But he does penance for it without no one tellin' him to. I've seen him on his knees all hours, prayin' in his room."

"You told him you'd found the feathers in the chest?"

She nodded.

"Did you tell him I'd cut it up?"

Her eyes slid away. "I don't remember."

I gripped her arm, and she flinched. "You must remember, Dog. I won't be angry anymore. But I must know."

"I did tell him so, and that Miss Leah had saved the lot. But he made me, he brought the words from me." She began to sob again. "Look."

She pushed my hand away from her arm and rolled up her sleeve. On the inside of her bare arm there were red and blue weals striping the delicate flesh.

I was sickened. "He did that?"

She whimpered at the memory. "He held my arm down on the desk. I couldn't pull away. Then he used his ridin' crop."

All day I thought about what I should do until my head ached. By the evening I'd made up my mind. Leah left the parlor after cards that evening, scarcely bothering to mutter a goodnight to me. I waited until I was sure she was safely upstairs. I did a token tidying as I waited, stacking the cards and putting them away in the bureau, picking up a book Leah had been reading before supper and tucking it under my arm to take to her chamber. Then I slipped from the room.

It was still daylight outside, for the evenings were growing longer, but the passages in Murkmere Hall were as shadowy as ever. When I reached the Master's door I was relieved to see that Jukes had left for the night, though the wheelchair wasn't in its usual place outside. I took this to mean that the Master had not yet gone to bed, and was raising my hand to knock when the latch was lifted on the other side and Silas came out.

He closed the door behind him and looked at me through half-closed eyes. I could smell cigars and alcohol on his breath, and he seemed relaxed, saying only mildly, "It's late to see the Master."

I showed him the book, privately asking the Almighty to forgive my lie. "He left this behind after he dined with us."

Silas took it from me and looked at its spine. "*A Theory of World Origins.*" He shook his head. "It sounds blasphemous, doesn't it, Agnes? It sounds as if it questions the Divinity. I hope you'd never look at such a book. Your soul isn't as robust as the Master's."

I hoped fervently that he wouldn't decide to return the book to the Master himself. But he handed it back to me and dusted his hands to free them of any contamination. *Those hands had wielded the riding crop*, I thought, and my eyes were drawn involuntarily to the brushing movement of the long, fastidious fingers.

When I raised my eyes again he was watching me with his old heart-melting smile. "It's a long time since we had one of our talks. The estate has been keeping me busy. I believe you're making excellent preparations for the ball."

"I do my best, Sir, of course," I said primly.

"I must start taking the Prayer Meetings again. I'll look forward to seeing you there." And with a nod he was gone, the skirts of his velvet smoking jacket fanning out behind him.

I knocked, and as soon as I heard the Master's "Enter,"

opened the door and went in hastily, worried that Silas might return.

The Master's chair was wheeled to the fireplace, where a small coal fire burned. Glasses and a decanter of brandy were set out beside him on a small table, and he was staring at the armchair opposite as if Silas still sat there, while he twirled an empty brandy glass between his fingers. On the floor beside him lay a pile of open ledgers and a magnifying glass. There was the bitter tang of nero leaf in the air; the curtains weren't yet drawn, and late evening sunlight slanted through the windows, making a soft golden haze in the room, in which tendrils of smoke still curled.

I stepped closer, and he looked surprised to see me. He must have thought it was a maid who'd knocked. He wasn't looking as well as he had at supper: his pupils dilated, the whites bloodshot. For all that Leah tried to prevent him drinking alcohol, it seemed he indulged when she wasn't there — unless Silas had persuaded him to it.

He saw me glance at the brandy glass and muttered, "Medicinal, merely. Don't tell Leah. I've these damned chest pains tonight. What is it you want, Agnes?" He gestured at the armchair on the other side of the fire, and winced. "Come, sit down."

The chair still held Silas's warmth, the cushions dented with his weight. It made me feel uncomfortable. "It's about Miss Leah, Sir."

He frowned. "What about Leah?"

I leaned forward, twisting my hands together and speaking quickly. "I wouldn't trouble you, but I'm worried about her, Sir.

She's found a swanskin by the mere. She intends to wear it to the ball, as a cape, perhaps. It could wake memories among the servants, Sir. There's the old story. Some say it's true."

I saw the color flood darkly into his face. "What story?"

I took a deep breath. "That when they become human, the avia leave their pelts behind to return to later. I think the swanskin that Leah's found is such a thing, Sir."

The stem of the brandy glass snapped like a twig between his fingers, and the bowl bounced on to the rug. There was blood on his hand, but he looked so angry I didn't dare go near him.

"I tried to destroy it," I said nervously. "But she's sewing it together at night, feather by feather."

There was a long pause. I watched him pull a silk handkerchief from the pocket of his smoking jacket and dab his fingers. At last he said, more calmly, "If she's making herself something for the ball, and wants to keep it secret, no matter. She's going to surprise us with it."

I persevered. "But you see the danger, Sir? What the servants may think? Silas Seed knows Leah works at something in her room."

He shook his head stubbornly. "Silas is no gossip; he's not even mentioned it to me."

"But you don't fear for Leah yourself, Sir?"

I was horrified to see his face blacken, his hands clench against his chest as he began to gasp. I rushed over to him.

"My medicine . . . ," he said thickly. "Over there."

There was a bottle with a little glass on a table in the corner, and next to it a crystal goblet half-filled with tiny brass keys. I seized them all up against my breast. I poured the medicine out first and gave it to him. I'd no notion whether the measurement were correct, but it was the amount I'd seen Silas give him; then I looked at the keys. They were numbered one to five, and on the bars that bound him the corresponding number was raised in the iron next to the keyhole. It was easy enough after that to match number to number and release him from his cage.

The bars were heavy. I laid them down in the grate one by one. When I turned to him the high color had gone from his face. "You've given yourself a terrible punishment with this prison, Sir," I said gently. "Can't you end it now?"

He flexed his fingers and stretched his arms. "Ah, that's better, the pain's gone. In some company I'm safest barred up, Agnes. I can't trust myself. I believe my wife's death half-turned my mind."

"But you're recovered now, Sir."

"I don't think so. The Protector and his men have kept away from me for many years. They don't think it either."

"Don't talk, Sir, don't agitate yourself."

He ignored me; I wasn't sure he saw me at all. He seemed to be meandering, murmuring to himself. "How could a young man so full of power and conviction tread the wrong path? And now he's coming back here, my brother-in-law, the very person who thought I wasn't fit to rule over my own estate, that it should be given to another Minister!" He looked at me, and I saw that after all his eyes were as alert as ever. "Should

I forgive Porter Grouted, Agnes Cotter? Or should I be barred up like an animal during the ball in case I harm him?"

I did my best. "No, Sir. You must show him you are in control."

He shook his head slowly. "But believe me, if he says that my daughter is not to inherit my land, I think I may well kill him. She must be accepted as my blood daughter now, my rightful heir. She loves this place as I do. She'll look after it when I'm gone." He bent his head. "I nearly killed Grouted once before, you know. He's head of the state and I shouldn't have raised my hand against him. I'm still a Minister, whatever I believe. I ought to respect him and his laws for the sake of the country's peace. That's hard, hard for someone who doesn't believe in the anointment rite. Do you believe in it, Agnes?"

"We're taught to in school," I said, taken aback. "Isn't the Protector a vessel for the Almighty's will?"

He gave a bitter smile. "Wait until you meet Lord Grouted, and then tell me whether that is so."

As the spring nights passed into summer, I would feel my way through the dense blackness of the passage to Leah's chamber, not daring to take a candle for fear of being seen by Silas. Sometimes there would be light beneath her door, and I knew she'd be working on the swanskin.

During the day I would trail her down to the mere and lose her in the thick undergrowth. The path we used to take was overgrown now, and the stinging nettles were shoulder-high.

The cygnets had hatched, four ugly gray creatures with bent, wormlike necks. They moved rapidly after their mother through the small yellow lilies that were scattered like bright coins at the far edge of the mere.

The lilies put me in mind of the wages I was collecting each week and storing away for Aunt Jennet in an old sack, now clinking satisfactorily when I took it from my cupboard. The last time I had been in Silas's room he had pressed an extra revere on top of the other two coins in my hand.

"I know you're watching Leah, as I asked. I've seen you."

I stiffened and tried to put the coin down on the desk but he forestalled me with his hand, wrapping it over mine. I shrank back from his touch at once, and he sighed.

"We're on the same side, Agnes. We're both trying to protect Leah. Any heir and future Minister must be protected until they come of age. That's our duty, isn't it, Agnes?" He leaned over the desk toward me. "Have you anything to tell me?"

His eyes were very bright and soft. They still had the power to make me weak, to make me believe he desired Leah's safety as I did.

"I've seen nothing," I said truthfully.

So through those long days before the ball Silas watched me, I watched Leah, and Leah watched the Master. I knew she was anxious about him by the way she hovered over him at mealtimes, more solicitous and gentle with him than ever. She was worried that he'd not be well enough to entertain guests.

But it wasn't only his health. I knew she checked the flying machine each day. I didn't dare ask her about it. She hated me now; she knew I followed her to the mere. She knew, and yet she knew nothing.

"Why are you always watching me?" she stormed. "You're just like the others — Silas and Dog — spying. What are you afraid I'm going to do? Grow wings and fly away?"

This was so close to the truth that I must have paled. She gave a contemptuous laugh and spat in my face. "You stupid dolthead, don't you know I'd never leave the Master?"

That was small comfort for me compared with the pain of her hatred. Jethro, seeing me still so pale and quiet when we met next, gripped me through the bars of the gate and wouldn't let me go.

"They'll come looking for me, Jethro!" I hissed. "I can't stay any longer. I have to play cards with Leah." *She'll play cards with me to amuse herself,* I thought sadly, *but she won't speak to me.*

"Leah!" Jethro said in disgust. "Always Leah! Don't you ever think of your aunt?"

"Of course I do!" I cried, stung. "I'm here for her sake."

"And for Leah's sake too, as you told me last time," he said bitterly. "If you think of your aunt, what about me? Do you think of me?"

I stared at him in surprise, and he stared furiously back. "Jethro, I do think about you, indeed I do. I wish I could tell you . . ."

"What?" He pulled me closer against the bars.

"You're hurting me."

"Tell me."

I looked nervously over my shoulder. After a fine day, a mist was blurring the edges of the drive. Though the keepers sometimes worked late through the light evenings, the long slopes to the house where earlier I'd watched the horses pull the roller mower were now deserted, the smooth grass silvered with an unmarked dew.

I turned back to Jethro and took a deep breath, pressing my face against the bars so close to his I could hear his breathing. "This must be our secret, Jethro."

"Yes?" His voice was eager, expectant.

"The reason I came back to Murkmere was because I learned the truth about Leah," I whispered. "She's no foundling. The Master's her father. But there's more. Her mother, Blanche, his wife, was one of the avia. I stay here because I must save Leah from that, Jethro."

There was a long silence on the other side of the gate. He let go my hands, but I stayed pressed against the bars.

"Jethro? Do you believe me?"

"Oh, aye, I believe you. My father always said there were rumors about the Master's wife."

Quickly I told him about the swanskin, how I'd destroyed it, how Leah was trying to repair it, and how frightened I was that one day she'd leave her human shape behind. "It's not right that she should suffer such terrible punishment, Jethro."

Jethro said nothing on the other side of the bars. His eyes wouldn't meet mine.

"Jethro?" I said desperately, wanting his wisdom.

"Let it be," he said, suddenly violent. His breath on my cheek was hot. "Don't interfere."

"What are you saying?"

His gaze shifted past me suddenly. "Hush," he hissed, "someone comes."

I was still staring at him like a loon, his face so close I could see the soft shininess of each hair of his beard and the smoothness of his tanned cheeks above. Before I could turn to look behind me or say a word more, he was gone, running swift as a hare for the Wasteland. By the time the keeper arrived at the gates, he had vanished.

It was that evening I noticed Leah's hands.

I'd hurried back to play cards, but she was in no mood for them. She was in a temper, moving restlessly about the parlor, ranting and stamping her foot.

"I can't do anything for the ball without Silas there ahead of me. He's taken it on himself to give the servants their orders already, no word to my guardian or me. He usurps my guardian's position all the time, and I can't stop him!" She whirled round on me as if I were to blame and flung out her hands.

I said nothing.

I sat stupefied with shock amongst the cushions on the settle, staring at the needle wounds in her flesh, the pocks of dried blood, the red, ripped cuticles. Her long, slender hands that had known no hardship, that had worn gloves against chapping winds and been smoothed nightly with chamomile cream, were now disfigured and raw, as if eaten by disease.

It was then I knew how painful her labor must be, night after night, as she struggled to pierce the thickness of the swanskin.

I wanted to weep for her, to stop it all. Yet still I sat dumb on the settle, fearful of letting out the truth.

My face must have shown my concern, for she snapped at me, "Don't pity me! How dare you? I'm the Master's ward, and one day I'll be Mistress here! Then it'll be my orders they listen to!"

She gesticulated again with her ruined hands as she launched back into her tirade.

"Silas has picked the oxen to be killed and roasted. He's filled the icehouse and the larders without word from me. There's hare and venison hanging up, have you seen? I've not even discussed the menu for the banquet with Mistress Crumplin and Gossop, but I find he has spoken to them and it's all planned. He's even arranged which guests are to sleep in which bedchambers! When I complain to the Master, he tells me how lucky we are to be able to depend on him!"

She sounded so desperate, I felt compelled to comfort her. "It's better this way. What if he'd persuaded the servants to stop idle and no preparation had been done?"

"We could have done it, you and I."

"All of it? Without help from the servants?"

"They were working for me," she said defiantly, "at the be-ginning."

"Because of the money promised them. They wouldn't have continued."

She flashed me a furious look, though it was the truth and she knew it.

But she didn't speak to me again that evening, retiring to bed with her temper and a book, so that as the candles burned down I sat alone in the darkening parlor, with the painful knowledge that I'd let a chance for reconciliation between us slip away.

Jethro didn't come to the gates again.

When the time for our next meeting came, I went down to the gates as usual, though this time I was more watchful. I didn't want to be surprised by the keeper again. While the rooks cawed mockingly over my head, I defied them and didn't touch my amber.

I waited and waited, all through the long, golden green summer evening, but Jethro didn't come. At last in the fragrant twilight, sick with disappointment, I slunk back to the house.

It wasn't like Jethro to be scared off by a keeper. It was something else. It was what I'd told him about Leah. I never should have mentioned the avia, for the old horror was still alive, passed down through the generations.

Jethro's father — what had he told the small boy who wanted a bedtime story?

❧

Two more weeks passed, golden days of sunshine for reaping the harvest. The keepers' faces burned mahogany and were polished with sweat.

But Silas, aloft on his horse, remained pale and elegant, his hands in soft leather gloves quiet on the reins, his face shadowed by the rim of his hat. Only the dark hole of his mouth moved as he gave his orders.

Aunt Jennet would have enough bread to eat at last. The villagers' hunger would be over, their stores replenished. It was the first harvest I'd missed. I'd hear of the feasting from Jethro, the next time he came.

"Let him come, I need him," I whispered.

Leah was becoming more fractious and ill-tempered as the ball came closer. The weather grew humid, the air heavy with the threat of thunder that never came. Though I'd removed my quilted overskirt long ago, I prickled inside my dress as I endlessly followed her, anxious about losing her for a moment.

Then, one oppressive evening while the storm clouds gathered overhead, it was time for Jethro to come again.

There was no figure waiting for me at the gates. I'd half-expected it, but a bitter lump rose in my throat all the same. It was a month since I'd seen him, a month since I'd last had news of my aunt. With Leah so cold to me, I was lonely in the extreme.

But he might come still.

I clutched the bars as if his dear face were on the other side, close to mine again, but for all my fancying I couldn't conjure him from air.

My fingers were stiff and curled when at last I let go the bars and faced the drive again. There was candlelight in the windows of Murkmere Hall, and house martins were twittering in and out of the eaves, busy feeding their young: tiny arrowheads swooping low under the bruised sky. For a brief moment the sight of them brought me comfort.

I told myself I was glad to leave the gates and the quarreling rooks, the loneliness beneath the dark clouds. I didn't look back. It was too late.

"What does it matter to me?" I demanded out loud. "Not a fig, that's what!" But it did matter. Jethro had abandoned me when I needed him most.

I lifted my chin and quickened my pace. The Hall was where my duty lay. I must forget Jethro, for I'd other things to think about.

There were only two days left before the ball.

XX

Porter Grouted

The storm came at last during the night, but in the vastness of Murkmere Hall the thunder was muffled. The dawn, when it came, was chill and gray; the rain teemed down.

Leah began to lament before she'd even had breakfast. "I must pick the flowers today, and now they'll all be wet."

"You can't go out in this!" I exclaimed.

"I can, and you must help me, you and Scuff and Doggett and some of the other servants too. The Hall must be decorated for the ball."

Nothing would persuade her otherwise, not even when the servant girls turned sulky and refused to budge from the house, saying they had chores to do for Mistress Crumplin.

Leah looked half-crazed that morning, her hair unbrushed, her eyes wild and desperate. In the end it was only the two of us who went out into the rain with baskets and knives, and the hems of our skirts were quickly clotted with mud and slime. Overnight, the grassy spread of the estate had returned to marsh.

Leah fretted all the while as she plowed across the wet ground. "The carriages won't make headway; the roads will be treacherous in the rain. No one will come."

"The guests will come somehow," I said as comfortingly as I could. "They won't want to miss it."

She didn't acknowledge the remark. I had let her lead me to the mere, and now we began to fill our baskets in silence. The dripping rushes and grasses were fiendish to cut; I thought uneasily that Leah was bringing the mere into the house.

As we made our way back to the house, soaked through, she turned her wet face to me and said suddenly, "Thank you for coming with me, Aggie."

"Oh, Leah," I said, overcome.

But her eyes were distracted as she looked ahead at the Hall, its gray stone façade as gloomy as the lowering sky. She'd already forgotten me.

The rain continued, all through that day and the next. The house felt damp and cold.

"Fires must be lit in all the bedchambers," said Leah. She'd not rested all day, but had inspected all the preparations with scant praise for the servants, whose faces grew sour as week-old milk.

I went up later to check that the rooms were warming. When I touched the walls, the old wallpaper still felt wet. More wood would be needed upstairs before evening, but at least Silas was overseeing that. When I looked down from a window that overlooked the drenched stable yard, I saw him with a youth who was busy chopping timber in the rain and whose sturdy outline reminded me painfully of Jethro. The youth's broad-brimmed hat was dripping; the heavy, oiled cape that Silas wore was slick with rivulets of water. There seemed no end to the rain.

In the Great Hall, Leah was worrying that the logs in the vast fireplace were too damp and green to catch properly and didn't banish the smell of age. But the tables were polished and gleaming, ready for the banquet, and I knew the tapestries had been beaten free of dust, for I'd helped in it myself.

"Tomorrow night it will smell of good food and wine in here," I whispered to cheer her, as she went to stand at the head of the receiving line.

A runner had just arrived, bringing news of the first guests, and the senior members of the household were hastily assembling to welcome them: Silas, Mistress Crumplin, and some of the footmen and keepers.

Leah's face was set and white; her hair — swept up, powdered and beribboned — seemed too big for it, like an oversized knit hat that might sink if she moved too quickly. She wore an embroidered day dress of ice-blue silk, with ruffles at the elbows, and long cream gloves hid her damaged hands.

She went to stand next to the Master, who had been wheeled to the head of the line. I saw them exchange a whisper, and he took her hand and held it. The bars across his chair had been removed so he could move his arms freely. A fur rug covered his legs, and he wore a pale-gold quilted waistcoat beneath his black silk jacket; a curled wig hid his hair.

Minutes passed, half an hour.

The rain fell steadily onto the steps outside, and the afternoon grew grayer. As they waited for their guests in the damp draft from the open door, the Master and his daughter might have been carved from wood, so still were they, hand in hand, staring at nothing.

The Master stirred at last.

"Where are these guests? The staff should go back to their duties. Silas, go out on the steps. See if you can glimpse the carriages."

Silas went out, and a second later was back again. "They've had to leave the carriages at the gates, Sir. The drive's waterlogged."

Leah came to life with a sudden hysterical giggle. The Master ignored her and she fell silent, her hand to her mouth.

"Then take out umbrellas, they may need spares. And send our manservants to help their footmen with the luggage."

Silas departed. The Master motioned Leah to wheel him out beneath the porch. And that was where the whole receiving line ended up, all of us craning to see the first guests come down the drive, for I too slipped out and stood at one side, the rain dripping from the lintel onto my painstakingly curled ringlets.

The men and women of the Ministration came slowly toward us through the rain, dark figures in their voluminous traveling garments. Their black silk umbrellas bobbed up and down as they picked their way carefully round the puddles. As the dark procession drew closer to the house, a chill crept over me. The stiff spread of the umbrellas, the curiously jerky, pecking motion as they walked, the black clothes: the Ravens of Death had come to Murkmere Hall.

I found myself clutching my amber. It was a long time since I'd done that.

Guests continued to arrive all through that long afternoon. The passages echoed with strange voices and heavy boots; the rooms held the leftover murmurs of recent conversation. There were different smells in the house: the cloying bitterness of the ladies' white face powder; drifts of rich perfumes — gardenia, jasmine, musk; brandy-laden breath and travel-stained clothes; sickly sweet hair pomade; the pungent scent of nero leaf.

I lurked in the Great Hall for as long as I could, curious to see the latest arrivals, but at last I had to take notice of Mistress Crumplin's wails for more help with the guests' teas. Later, with aching feet, I went to help Leah with the flowers.

She was still wearing her gloves, filthy from shaking so many hands, and she kept them on while she furiously twisted the long purple-flowered points of rosebay willow-herb into a garland of pale yellow grasses. The blue ribbons were dangling around her ears.

"I should be allowed to attend the dinner tonight. It's not fair!"

I tried clumsily to copy her garland. "Tomorrow you'll be guest of honor."

She shook her head so angrily that dislodged powder misted her lace collar. "I should be there tonight. I'm worried about what my guardian will say to Lord Grouted."

"But where is Lord Grouted?" I asked.

"He always arrives last. The Ministration will wait to go into dinner until he appears. He likes to keep both host and guests hungry and fearful. No wonder my guardian hates him!"

We'd supped together in the parlor and had the candles lit by the time a footman knocked on the door.

"Word's been sent that the Lord Protector comes, Miss."

Leah stood up slowly, her face ashen. She held out her hand. "Come with me, Aggie."

I took her cold hand, and together we left the parlor with its fire and candlelight and hurried down the passage to the Great Hall, where tables glittered with silver cutlery and cut glass, waiting for the dinner guests. Beyond the fire's bright circle, the tapestries hung motionless, the violent scenes they depicted obscured by shadow. The huge room was almost empty. Only the Master in his chair waited in darkness by the double doors, with Jukes and Pegg beside him.

Leah rushed to the Master and pressed her cheek to his. "You must be so fatigued, Sir."

He patted her hand. "I survive, child." He gestured at the footmen. "Bring a torch from one of the sconces. It's too dark. Light more candles."

The footmen were about to obey when the knocking came, a truly thunderous noise, as if a god at least demanded entrance. Jukes went at once to open the doors at the Master's nod, but it was only the Lord Protector's footman, resplendent in blood-red satin, sent ahead to give notice of his master's imminent arrival. I melted back into the shadows.

The outside doors remained open, and a chill breeze blew through the Hall, making the candles flutter. I saw Leah shiver. Jukes took a torch and, holding it aloft, went out to stand beneath the porch. His hand was shaking; he couldn't hold the torch still and the flame tore raggedly in the wind.

The Great Hall was suddenly filled with noise from outside: the crunch and skid of wheels over stone and mud, the crack of a whip, the frightened neighing of horses.

Leah started, but she didn't speak. There was a short pause, a heartbeat, inside the Great Hall. We stood as if frozen in an icehouse, listening to the tumult.

The Lord Protector cared nothing for potholes. Dog told me later she'd heard he'd driven his own carriage recklessly down the drive in the darkness, and as it rocked and swayed and the horses screamed in terror, he'd balanced on the carriage step and cracked the whip all the harder.

As I stood half-hidden by the tapestries, someone brushed past me.

"You shouldn't be here!" hissed Silas.

But he was too distracted, too eager to be in the receiving line himself as the Lord Protector arrived, to wait for me to go.

Boots clipped the steps. Then the doorway was filled with a dark bulk.

Porter Grouted was not a tall man; indeed you might almost have called him squat.

He had a massive head, which seemed all the larger since he was completely bald, and his pate, glistening with rain, was as smooth and brown as tanned hide. No cravat could have made his great bull neck elegant. He was not at all the aristocratic gentleman from the Capital I was expecting, and yet, as he came into the hall, shaking raindrops vigorously from his traveling cloak, he dominated the room at once.

His eyes snapped round to survey the people waiting for him. Even with his lack of height, he towered over the Master in his chair. There was a pause, too long, as they stared at one another.

"Ah, Gilbert. A long time, eh?" His accent was strong and ugly, the flat, nasal sound of the Capital.

"It's been long since last we met, yes, My Lord."

"Too long, Gilbert." The Protector held out his hand without removing his gauntlet, and the Master took it.

"We've much to talk about," said Lord Grouted. "It's too long since you came to the sessions in the Capital. Time passes, things change."

"They do indeed," said the Master dryly.

The Lord Protector turned from him to inspect Leah. "Your ward?"

Leah curtsied. She didn't look at him.

"So you come of age tomorrow, do you, Miss Leah? Well, well. I remember you as a little puking creature, tiny as a bird!" He hit his gauntlets together with a dull thud, and his teeth flashed in the candlelight. Leah bowed her head; a good thing, for I was sure her eyes would shrivel him.

"My Lord, may I present my steward, Mr. Silas Seed?" said the Master, beckoning to Silas, who was standing close by. "No man could have a better steward than Silas. He'll look after your needs while you're here."

"Mr. Seed, eh? I recall you as a youth in the Capital. It's good to meet you face-to-face again." Was I imagining it, or did Porter Grouted's tone have surprising warmth for someone he'd met so long ago?

"But where's your footman, My Lord?" asked Leah. "He must come inside, out of the rain."

Grouted let out a bark of laughter. "He keeps my fool silent. It angered me with its chatter on the journey." He barked out through the door, "Bring the fool in now."

The footman came in, his silks clinging darkly to him; the bedraggled creature he dragged on the end of a chain was equally soaked.

At first I was frightened, thinking it was a large bird; but then I saw it was a little man with bandy legs, wearing a jerkin and breeches of brightly dyed cockerel feathers. The feathers were bedraggled, like their owner. He had bare, filthy feet, and the chain was fastened round one scrawny ankle.

"I hope your dousing has curbed your tongue, Gobchick," said Lord Grouted roughly.

"But it's a dreadful evening, My Lord," protested Leah, "unfit for a dog."

"Exactly."

The tiny man scampered over to her on the end of his chain, his grotesque shadow following, and patted her feet. She didn't recoil, but put out a hand and gently touched the sodden feathers.

"'Tis not a dreadful evening at all, Missy," he said in a little, childlike voice. "Why, 'tis fine!"

"How d'you make that one out, Gobchick?" said Lord Grouted irritably, "when you've the evidence on your own shoulders?"

The little man spread wrinkled hands and beamed. "Why, 'tis the fine company here that makes the fine evening, Master."

Lord Grouted yanked the chain, and Gobchick fell over, his wet feet slipping on the floorboards. "A fine evening now, is it, fool?"

"Dinner awaits us, My Lord," said the Master, his voice tight.

"Well, lead on, man, lead on, as best you can." Lord Grouted gave a guffaw, jerking his head at the chair.

Leah's face was pinched with anger as she passed me, the Master's expressionless as he trundled after her, pushed by Silas. Only Lord Grouted noticed me standing in the shadows, and that was because Gobchick put out a hand and touched my skirts as he was dragged along.

It was a curious gesture, like a blessing. But instinctively I shrank back from the misshapen little brown fingers and must have let out a gasp, for Lord Grouted's head turned, and for a moment his eyes stared into mine. In the candlelight I saw the heavy lids had no eyelashes: they were as hairless as his head.

Then his eyes flicked away. I was worthless, not due any recognition from him, and the greatest man in the country passed on into Murkmere Hall.

Though the rain ceased during the night, the weather remained dark and dank the next day. The house sat under heavy clouds, and we had candles lit in the rooms from dawn.

A lady complained there'd been a rat in her chamber; another, of bats in the eaves outside her window and bent-legged creepies on the walls. I thought them foolish; we were used to such things, and worse, in the country.

The gentlemen stood with their backs to the fires and their coats flipped up, muttering together even before breakfast. After consuming bacon, mushrooms, kidneys, roast pork, and fried cabbage, the company went for a constitutional, parading up and down the drive between the puddles, umbrellas at the ready, ladies on the gentlemen's arms.

I stared out of the window at them and giggled, but a little fearfully, for they made an imposing sight in the gloomy day, with the rooks circling overhead.

Then they all went into Council, filing silently through into the withdrawing room, where extra chairs had been brought for them: thin-lipped, dark-clothed men and women organizing the country's business.

I could hear Lord Grouted's harsh voice as he pushed them to his will. Since the Protector's secretary had been left in the Capital, Silas slipped in like a shadow to take the minutes, and I saw how like the others he was, with his black coat, pale countenance, and lowered, secret eyes.

As the afternoon turned into evening, I went to the Great Hall to see that all was in order: the fire drawing smoothly, the tables laid for dinner.

The huge room was empty, the candles streaming in the draft. There was silent movement everywhere. In the silver bowls, which had been put in the center of every table, the flowerheads moved on the surface of the water, and in the corners the grasses rustled in their jars. I stood, breathing in the strange mixture of decay and flowers and liquid candle wax.

In front of me a tapestry bulged in the draft.

"Missy, Missy," whispered a little voice, and the fool popped out from behind it, like a jack-in-the-box.

I stepped back with a cry. He put his finger to his lips and twinkled at me over the top. His face was crinkled, like an apple left too long in the barn.

I drew the little man into the shadows behind the great chimney. He carried the chain in one hand, still fixed to the metal ankle band.

"Have you escaped, Fool?" I whispered. "You'll be beaten for it. If you come with me, I'll hide you."

He shook his head and the feathers quivered. "I 'scapes regular, but not far, not for long. My legs too weak, see? I just need the air to breathe, pretty girls to see." His eyes were merry.

I couldn't smile. "It's cruel to chain you like a beast!"

"I's bread to eat. Sometimes he'll stroke and pet me. Old Gobchick's safe if he makes his lord laugh." He peered up into my face. "Now tell me, little Missy, why you're so afeard."

"I'm not afraid."

"It's not for old Gobchick's hide, I warrant. Is it for someone else?"

I stared at him and saw his eyes gleam. But I could say nothing about Leah to this child-man.

"You know, sometimes they pretend Gobchick's one of the avia, to frighten the people. But Gobchick can't fly." He flapped his arms up and down, and a red feather floated to the floor. "See? I stays on Earth and dreams."

"I wish I could set you free, Gobchick."

He shook his head. "We'll all be free one day."

My skin prickled. "I must go. So must you. You'll be found here."

"I'll be found, Missy. Take one thing with you."

I paused, half-impatient now. "What is it?" I thought it would be a keepsake, one of his horrible garish feathers.

"A thought, that's all, from me to you." He jerked his head at a tapestry that showed a tiny group of human penitents before the Great Eagle. "That some tell it different, the story of the avia."

"Different?"

There was the creak of the door opening into the Hall from the passage; footsteps coming close and passing us. I stared at him, frightened for his safety, and he stared back, his bright eyes glazed, as if he hadn't heard, as if he were somewhere else.

"'Twas not a punishment," he whispered, "but a blessing."

I didn't have time to ask him what he meant. I left hastily, and when I looked back all I could see was the pale disc of his face, the dark hump of him squatting in the shadows, dreaming. Free.

I gathered my skirts and ran up the back stairs along the passage to Leah's room. Guests progressing sedately to their own chambers to dress for the ball moved out of my way, murmuring disapproval, but I kept my head down.

Dog was hurrying toward me from the opposite direction. "Oh, Aggie," she panted. "I couldn't come to the mistress sooner. Mistress Crumplin kept me folding napkins."

"There's still plenty of time to dress Miss Leah, Dog," I said calmly, though I didn't feel so at all. I knew what was in her mind as she stared at me fearfully; it was in mine as well. Tonight Leah would surely wear the swanskin.

It was still in the chest; I'd looked some days ago. Sick to my stomach, I'd pushed back the lid and pulled it out. A few white feathers had floated out onto the rug; there had been a square of skin still to sew. But tonight it would be finished, I was certain. Her secret treasure, perfect again.

All her nights spent repairing it — what had they been for, but this night?

The door of Leah's chamber was shut. We looked at each other for courage. Then I put out my hand and, without knocking, lifted the latch.

XXI

The Ball Begins

Leah turned from the long looking glass, a hand to her neck, as if she were almost shy of her appearance. As we came into the room, staring at her as stupidly as a couple of wild women, she gave a small smile.

She looked beautiful: that was the only word to describe her. Her gawkiness was gone; her pale shoulders and arms rising from the draped material at her breast were fine-boned and graceful. The gauzy skirt floated around her so that she seemed to move in a shining silver mist.

She had already gone beyond me in that dress; she had become someone I didn't know. "Will I do my guardian justice?" she said.

As I nodded dumbly, I could see out of the corner of my eye that the chest was still closed.

"Shall I dress your hair, Miss?" said Doggett, anxious to take some credit for her mistress's appearance.

"No more powder," Leah said, sitting down at her dressing table. "I hate the stuff."

Dog brushed her hair until it held the silver reflections of the dress in its gleaming strands. Then she dressed it simply, binding it back under the circlet of seed pearls the Master had given Leah for her birthday.

"The silver earrings now, Miss, to set off the dress? And your crystal necklace?"

"I'll wear nothing. Those women will be weighed down with jewelry. I'll not be like them."

When Doggett had gone, I pulled something from my apron pocket. "Happy birthday," I said awkwardly.

It was a bunch of pressed meadowsweet and buttercups, glued to bark and bordered with dried oak leaves. It seemed too crude now for the shining girl before me.

She looked astonished. "Thank you," she said, turning it this way and that, examining it so reverently it might have been created by a master craftsman.

"It's only a poor thing," I said.

"I've never had such a present before." Then she looked at me in the mirror with large, dark eyes. "My guardian tells me he wishes to make an announcement at dinner. What can it be, do you think?"

I stared back at her and gave a false shake of my head as if I knew nothing.

Her eyes were clouded. "I wish I didn't feel such foreboding, Aggie."

❧

Back in my own chamber I dressed hastily.

I'd lost weight in the past weeks and had had to take in the blue taffeta skirt, but I folded the black shawl into a sash to cover my clumsy stitches, and the blue beads and silk tassels looked as decorative around my waist. Another shawl, made of cream lace, covered my bodice. Then I brushed my hair until it crackled like a flame round my head, and re-twisted my ringlets.

Not as beautiful as Leah, I thought, as I stared into the glass, *but passably pretty*. I touched my amber beneath the shawl and thought of my mother. How would she feel if she knew I was about to attend Blanche's daughter's ball: proud, or apprehensive?

I could hear footsteps and voices in the passage outside. Guests were going downstairs. When they had passed I darted along to Doggett's chamber.

"Dog, are you there?"

She was tying a clean pinafore round her gray silk dress when she opened the door, and we looked each other up and down with admiring grins.

"The Lord Almighty, Aggie, you look almost a lady!"

I didn't care for the "almost," but let it pass. "And you, Dog! Let's go and watch the dancing."

"Oh, lawks, do you think we should?"

"We must support our mistress, Doggett, mustn't we? We'll stand somewhere we'll not be noticed."

So we slipped down the dark back stairs and met no one; the servants were about their duties. The whisper of my taffeta skirts over the oak made me feel powerful and mysterious; it was a grown-up sound. I held my head high and narrowed my eyes as I noticed the lady guests did, until Dog began giggling at me. Her own face was freshly scrubbed for once, her eyes and mouth agog above the starched pinny.

When we reached the ballroom it was still empty of guests: a vast, candlelit space waiting to be filled. In the golden light you couldn't see how the statues were chipped and the pillars starting to crumble. The floor glowed richly after days of polishing; the mirrors set in their ornate brass reflected the light of the candles. The place glittered brave as a bauble, and as fragile.

I pulled Dog behind a pillar at the end of the room farthest from the main doors, where we could hide behind an urn filled with rushes. Up in the gallery above our heads the musicians were tuning up. They didn't notice us standing below them: there were too many flowers woven through the wrought-iron balustrade.

"I used to watch the mistress at her dancin' classes," whispered Dog, gripping her rough hands together in excitement. "It'll be the Cavalcade first."

"What's that?" I whispered back, impressed. The only dances I knew were jigs and stick dances and swains' requests.

"It's the acknowledgment dance, when the guests greet their host."

The musicians were playing properly now, music that held a striking rhythm and was quite different from the jangling, merry music of the fairs I'd visited. It seemed to me to speak of sinister things, of darkness, power, seduction.

At the far end of the ballroom a footman opened one of the double doors and Silas came in, pushing the Master in his chair. The music hid the grinding of the wheels.

Silas maneuvered the chair up a small ramp onto a dais in the center of the floor, which had been specially constructed so that the Master could view the dancing. Gilt chairs had been placed in a half-circle up there, but there was no one present to join him yet. When Silas left him, he looked a lonely figure waiting among the empty chairs, his great hands loose on his lap.

At a signal from Silas, a footman walked the length of the floor and opened both doors wide. The candles flared, then steadied. The music grew so loud I thought the pillars might fall down around us.

And then the first pair of dancers appeared, and my heart almost stopped. Dog gave a cry and clung to me.

The first two dancers were not Leah and Lord Grouted. They were not recognizably human at all.

Each dancer had a bird's head, a black-feathered head, with a jutting beak. Stiffly, formally, they progressed up the ballroom toward the dais where the Master of Murkmere sat alone.

They had entered the room only a little way when the next couple entered, their head feathers more mottled than the first, their beaks curved and cruel. And then the next couple, their bird heads so large it seemed they might topple off.

Powdered skin and painted mouths showed beneath the beaks, and as they paraded before the Master the mouths smiled.

Dog, who had clung to me since the entrance of the first pair of birds, gasped out, "It's the avia, isn't it, Aggie?"

I'd been shocked myself at first, until I'd seen the faces. I pushed her away gently. "You know it isn't. They're masks, that's all."

But Dog looked fearfully at the macabre throng, as if she would take much convincing.

Gradually the ballroom became filled with the two swaying lines of birds. They advanced slowly, then as they reached the Master, bowed their stiff heads to each other and to him before turning to repeat the process back down the room. As pair after pair came in, it seemed the lines would never stop growing.

But then the music slowed almost to silence, the lines steadied, and down between them danced the very last pair: a girl in a shining dress gripped in the talons of an Eagle.

The bird head was so realistic that it seemed the Almighty Himself had come to furious life straight out of one of the tapestries in the Great Hall and flown into the ballroom. Then I saw the thickness of Lord Grouted's fingers on Leah's fragile shoulders, the golden glint of a signet ring.

But I couldn't control a gasp, and Dog clutched me in real terror. Together we almost fell over the urn.

"An impressive sight, isn't it?" said Silas's voice.

I tried to pull myself together, while Dog cowered back against the pillar, looking as if she didn't know which was more frightening: the Eagle dancer or the sudden, unnerving presence of the steward in all his sinister, black-silk elegance.

But he didn't bother to glance at her; his eyes took in my taffeta skirts, beaded sash, and lace shawl.

"You plan to dance, Miss Agnes? Perhaps I can tempt you to the next one? It will be open to everyone."

"Oh, n-no, Sir," I stammered, trying to hide my horror. "I don't know any grand dances."

"I'll teach you then. We'll take it slowly in a corner by ourselves before we join the other pairs."

I felt my cheeks burn. I didn't know how I could refuse without crossing him, and if I did, he might prevent me from attending the dinner where Leah needed my support.

"Sir, you must understand — the bird masks — I'd not have the courage to step out among them. It would be blasphemous."

He was diverted; he frowned. "Blasphemous?"

"Isn't it what the avia dared to do?"

His eyes narrowed, and I moistened my lips. "Sir, they desired to fly like the gods."

"You have the audacity to accuse these Ministers of blaspheming because they wear their ceremonial masks?"

"No, indeed not, Sir. But if I danced with such company myself I'd blaspheme, for the Ministration is the mouthpiece of the gods on Earth and the Lord Protector the Eagle's own anointed. Who am I to dance among them?"

Silas still frowned. The musicians struck up a different air; the new dance began. "Are you saying that I too blaspheme if I take part in the dance, since I'm not a Minister myself?"

I thought quickly. "How could I say such a thing, Sir, when you look after all our souls in this household? I'm sure the Almighty favors you for doing His work. It's right that you should take part, whereas I . . ." I spread my hands modestly, eyes cast down, "I'm only a maid from the village, Sir, and you've said yourself that my soul's in danger."

He scrutinized me, but I didn't look up. "I'm glad you're so concerned for your salvation, Agnes," he said levelly at last. "I respect your feelings."

"Thank you, Sir," I murmured.

He gave me a curt bow. "I'll see you at dinner, then." The faintest scent of flower water was left behind him.

Dog turned to me. "What did you say to make him go?" she breathed.

"He didn't realize I mocked him."

"How did you dare? You spoke of the avia to him, those terrible creatures."

"We shouldn't be afraid of them, Dog. The Almighty created their form too."

"As a punishment for their sins!" said Dog.

I thought of what the fool had said. "Not a punishment but a blessing," I whispered to myself. But I still couldn't fathom it.

I was alone now by the pillar. Dog had disappeared to her duties. Silas was sitting on the dais with the Master; I could see him bending close, solicitously, as they talked. And all the while the dancers wove their stately lines together, the rich darkness of their silks and satins catching the candlelight, the monstrous bird heads bobbing and turning.

And trapped among them somewhere, a slight, silver girl.

Why has the Almighty never punished the Ministration for daring to mimic the gods? I thought. Surely the sin of the avia was no worse?

The dancers were bowing to each other, carefully, so their heads shouldn't fall off. I felt hysterical laughter well up inside me.

But the dancing was over. Now the banquet would begin.

XXII

The Truth Is Out

First, the Ministers had to repair to their chambers to remove their masks and replace their wigs. The entry into the Great Hall that followed was almost as elaborate as the Calvacade.

I was disconcerted to find myself placed at the top table, a seat away from Leah, with a portly, elderly gentleman between us, and on my left a severe-looking stick of middle years. Lord Grouted was seated on Leah's right, the Master on the Lord Protector's other side. Before me on the table I had a glittering forest of knives and forks to find my way through, and glasses of every shape.

As I sat down, I saw to my dismay that the fool, Gobchick, had been recaptured. A footman was dragging him along on his chain, and as he scurried past me, bent to his knees, he made mournful little cheeping noises.

At first I tried to listen to Leah's conversation with Lord Grouted, but could hear little; my stout neighbor made so much noise chewing his food. Once or twice he spluttered out a question, which I answered, but he must have decided that as a mere companion I'd have no interesting conversation, for after that he spoke with the lady opposite and ignored me.

As for the stick on my left, he sucked in his sagging cheeks and pecked at his food so cautiously he must have been expecting to find maggots in it. Certainly he had no attention for the insignificant chit next to him.

It was a painful, fraught meal, and the magnificent food, which Gossop and the kitchen servants had so labored over, stuck in my throat as much as my neighbors' treatment of me. Gobchick fared even worse; he was forced to kneel behind the Lord Protector's chair like a dog. As I looked, he sat up and begged, and was thrown a piece of bread.

Each course ended with a toast proposed by one of the guests. Glasses were raised to "the long session," "short council," "the messengers" — all mysteries to me — and sometimes to the names of individuals. As the glasses clinked, I looked around at the faces masked by white makeup, the wine-stained mouths, the glittering eyes.

These weren't good people, I could feel it. After a few toasts I only pretended to drink the wine. It made me feel queasy.

❧

"Quaint," said the bony woman in puffed black satin opposite the portly gentleman, and she gestured at the silver bowls of flowers. "Quaint, yet pretty. But wildflowers don't last, do they?" She put a lace handkerchief to her nostrils and sniffed delicately.

We were waiting for the footmen to bring in the roasted oxen from the stable yard. I could hear Lord Grouted and the Master talking in low voices beneath the babble. Leah was as silent as I was; I knew she was listening too.

"This is a good turnout, Gilbert. I'm pleasantly surprised. I'd thought things might be a struggle for you, up here in the Eastern Edge — shortages and so on."

The Master smiled. "We don't think of ourselves as quite the back of beyond, you know — the front of the back, perhaps."

"Aye, but the villagers? Do they produce for you? Where do you get the stuff?" Grouted waved his thick fingers at the spread before him.

"We've had a good harvest. We produce most of our food here on the estate, thanks to Silas's management. I don't like to demand much from the villagers. They have themselves to feed."

"You always were soft, Gilbert."

"Perhaps."

"Hah! You'd live on your dreams if you could." Lord Grouted prised a knot of gristle from between his teeth, looked at it critically, then dropped it onto his plate. "The project you were working on when we last met, that contraption, you're finished with all that, ain't you?"

"Oh, I look at it from time to time, Porter," said the Master lightly.

"I don't like to hear that. We allowed you to keep your books. That was a big concession."

"And I'm more than grateful for it."

"But that contraption of yours could be conceived of as a greater blasphemy than the words your books contain."

"Hardly, I think." The Master's tone was weary. He wasn't looking well tonight, nor eating. His high color was drained, and he rubbed his arm as if it pained him.

"It's what I think that matters. Others too. Why, damn it, you've as good as made a pair of wings!"

"I hide it well enough. Only my most trusted servants have seen it."

"Do more than that, Gilbert. Get rid of the thing. Take this as advice from a friend. I'm thinking of your own good and the future of your estate, man." He leaned closer. "Do I speak plainly?"

"Thank you, My Lord," said the Master. "I'll bear your advice in mind."

When at last the steamed sponges, the jewel-colored jellies and milk blancmanges, the meringues piled with cream, the bursting summer puddings, the honey ices and fruit sorbets, and the foamy syllabubs had been consumed, it was time for the final toast.

A wheat-colored wine was poured into tiny glasses, delicate squares of sweetmeats passed around. The thin woman in black satin stood up and raised her glass. "To Lord Grouted."

Everyone in the hall rose to his feet.

Each guest had to cross hands and glasses, and drink from the glass put into his right hand by the neighbor on his left. I had no idea what to do, and had to be shown by Leah. After a great muddle on my part, the fat gentleman accepted my glass with some disdain.

When the toast was over, everyone sat down. By now, the guests' makeup had melted into greasy channels with the heat of wine and candlelight, and their wigs were uncurling. As the grotesque faces turned to the Master for the banquet speech, I felt a sudden chill.

He wasn't among friends.

"Help me stand," he said to Jukes behind him, and he placed his hands on the arms of the wheelchair and tried to heave himself up.

"Sir!" began Leah in alarm, leaping to her feet so quickly her chair fell over. A murmur swelled among the guests.

Like a shadow, Silas came swiftly from his place. "Let me, Sir," he said smoothly, and took the Master's weight on his left side. Together he and Jukes managed to support the Master, who shook with strain as if he had the ague.

Leah's eyes filled with tears. "There's no need for this, Sir."

"I must," he growled, through clenched teeth.

The murmuring died. The guests looked at one another meaningfully, a feral gleam in their eyes, and waited for the kill.

With a visible effort, the Master collected himself and began to speak. He began by thanking the guests for coming so far and for their presents to his ward. "We're both deeply honored that so many of you have managed to attend tonight, not least, of course, the Lord Protector himself."

Lord Grouted bowed from the waist, and his lizard eyes flicked around.

"It's good to see so many of my old colleagues again after my years of absence from the sessions," said the Master.

The lady opposite waved the white hand that held her liqueur glass, and bracelets clacked down her scrawny arm like manacles. "So good to see you, dear Gilbert." Her red mouth smiled at him treacherously.

The Master spoke fluently and from time to time made a little jest for his audience. Behind the Lord Protector, Gobchick cackled and clapped his hands together. In the whole gathering, I think he was the only one whose laughter was genuine.

For a moment the Master drooped between the two men who supported him. But then he lifted his head, spoke louder. "As you all will realize, this is a great occasion for me, as well as for Leah. My ward has reached her sixteenth birthday. She has come of age. The state considers her a child no longer, but an adult, owed the respect and with the responsibilities that being an adult brings.

"For Leah, the respect given her will go hand in hand with how she carries out her responsibilities, as one day she will inherit Murkmere."

People knew about the old feud. All eyes turned expectantly to Lord Grouted, waiting for his reaction. He was tapping his fingers on the table; his nails were trimmed square, like spades. Leah knelt by the Master's chair, a flush tingeing her pale cheeks.

"A long time ago the Lord Protector and I quarreled over this." The Master nodded at his guests. "I make no secret of it. Lord Grouted thought that unknown blood would defile the Ministration. We quarreled violently, and I am sorry for it and have borne my own self-inflicted punishment for many years. But now I've an announcement to make that will set things right. The time is ripe for the truth, since now Leah is sixteen she is the legal age to inherit Murkmere on my death, which may be any time."

Several guests shook their heads and protested at that. The Master smiled. "One must be realistic."

Lord Grouted examined his nails. "What is this truth you speak of, Gilbert?"

The Master lifted his head. He looked triumphant. He stared straight at Porter Grouted as if challenging him. "The truth is this, and now you'll need be concerned no longer. For Leah is indeed one of us. She has the blood of the Ministration in her veins. She is my daughter."

There was utter silence in the hall, a dangerous silence. Leah lifted her hand, touched her neck. Silas stood still as death, his knuckles white where he gripped the Master.

"Soon after my wife's death I knew the baby had survived," said the Master. "But I told no one."

Lord Grouted bore himself up from his chair, thrusting his bald head toward the Master. "Why in the name of the Eagle didn't you? It would have saved endless trouble. We need never have had our dispute for a start, man."

The Master didn't flinch. "I had my reasons. The Eastern Edge isn't like your softer south, where the occasional uprising can be quelled without difficulty. We've wildmen here, bandits and vagabonds, and you know that rebels cluster in the remoter villages and that their numbers are growing. They would seek any chance to harm us. I didn't want to lose my daughter to kidnappers, or worse."

"So now we're to welcome your daughter as one of us, no foundling at all but the true offspring of a Minister?"

"Yes, indeed."

"And we can take your word for it?"

For a moment the Master looked dumbfounded. "It's the truth, I swear it." He began to breathe heavily and I saw his hands ball into fists. "If you doubt me, I have the midwife's signed certificate of birth."

But Porter Grouted laughed. "A joke, old man, that's all. I'll not risk confronting you again." He turned to the guests with a great show of good humour. "We'll drink a toast to it. Tonight's a double celebration, ain't it now?" He raised his glass and held it in the air so that the liqueur shone like liquid gold in the candlelight. "To Leah, on her sixteenth birthday! A true daughter of Murkmere Hall!"

Silas bent to take the Master's glass from the table with his free hand, and offered it to him. I stood up; everyone but

Leah stood, waiting for the Master to take it from Silas and drink, but instead he turned to Leah kneeling beside his chair and looked into her upturned face.

"Leah?" he said softly. "Leah, my love, my dearest daughter? I believe you've known all along, haven't you?"

Leah said nothing. Her face had lost the flush of wine and was moon-pale.

There was a silence of several heartbeats' length. The Master's face took on a terrible hurt.

Then Leah rose and ran from the hall, from the guests standing open-mouthed, from the flickering candles and the shining glasses, from her father. Gobchick began to moan softly, but no one paid him any attention.

The tapestries flapped over the door, and Leah was gone.

XXIII

The Master's Message

The Master fell back into his chair. There was an agitated commotion of people around him, commiserating, comforting.

No one saw me leave but Silas. As I left my place, his black eyes met mine, defeated. He knew what I was doing, but he was trapped. At such a time it would look bad if a steward didn't stay with his Master.

I ran from the room, between the tapestries and through the door, and at the end of the passage I saw the shine of Leah's dress. She was leaning against the wall, her eyes huge and fixed.

I marched straight up and shook her. Her head flipped round; her eyes focused on me. "Leah," I said. "Leah, why did you leave?"

She shook her head; she looked desperately unhappy. I couldn't understand it. Where was the joy I'd expected?

"What is it?" I whispered. "You can tell me."

She was so deep in misery she was unaware of my question. I put my arms around her, but still she said nothing. Her shoulder blades were sharp beneath her dress. She was like a bird in my arms, a beautiful bird.

Then Jukes came around the corner on his way to the hall, carrying a silver bowl of dark green nero leaves.

Leah heard his footsteps and looked up. She pushed my arms away. "I must prepare myself for the dancing," was all she said. "I'll summon Doggett to the parlor. Go back to the Hall, Aggie."

She'd rejected me. I stood uncertainly in the passage as she slipped away, and tears pricked behind my eyes.

Then the gangling figure of Jukes came back through the door from the hall. I half-turned away from him as if I were going elsewhere, but he hurried up to me, his long face gloomier than ever. "Miss Agnes, I'm glad you're still here. The Master's asking for you."

"Me?"

"You and no one else, he says."

Bemused and apprehensive, I followed Jukes back to the Great Hall. The crowd around the Master drew back a little as I approached. The concerned, hypocritical voices fell silent.

Lord Grouted was standing back, watching. I didn't look at him. It was the Master I cared about, slumped over an arm of the wheelchair, his cheeks patchworked with red and white, his breath coming in gasps. Silas was patting his back as if he'd choked, but I knew it wasn't choking that had made him like this.

I laid my hand on the Master's. "Sir?"

"Aggie? Take me away from all this."

I stared straight at Silas and put my hands on the bar handle of the chair. Silas fell back. He said nothing; no one said anything as I wheeled the Master away.

Jukes held open the door for us and followed with a candle. I was grateful, though it wasn't needed. The sconces were bright in the passage, all the way to the Master's room. I would have run with the chair if I'd had the strength, so anxious was I to get the Master to his medicine, but it was heavy. I was out of breath by the time we arrived and Jukes had opened the door.

"I can manage now, thank you, Jukes," I said, and he bowed gravely and left as the nurse came out of the anteroom.

The Master's room was growing dim, lit only by firelight and the fading daylight. The curtains weren't yet drawn; the nurse hadn't been expecting the Master back so soon.

"He's been taken sick," I said urgently. "What can you do?"

I was glad she didn't fuss but examined his face and went swiftly to her row of bottles. She selected one, poured out a glass of a dark liquid, and handed it to me. "Too much excitement has thickened his blood. This should thin it."

I sniffed the physic doubtfully: it smelt of rotting tree bark, of ancient forests. But when I held it to the Master's lips, he drained the glass, meek as a child.

I wheeled him to the fire and propped his head with a pillow. The nurse lit some candles and poked the fire vigorously. Then she gave him another look. "He'll recover, this time."

She looked curiously at me as if she'd like to linger and find out more, but I said firmly, "I'll call you if I need you." She went then, and I checked the door was shut.

After a minute the Master looked up. The color had calmed in his cheeks and his breathing was quieter. "Has the nurse gone?" he asked in a low voice.

"She's in her room, Sir. Are you feeling better?"

"I'm well enough now. Why did she take it so, my speech?"

"I don't know, Sir."

"You went after her?"

"She said nothing, Sir."

"She made no comment, no comment at all?" His voice was pitiful.

"I'm sorry, Sir."

"I was sure she'd say something, to you." He sighed. "It must have been the shock. I should have told her privately beforehand."

"Sir." I tried to find the right words. "I'm sure Leah's happy to be your daughter, but she faces great responsibilities now. She'll not only inherit when the time comes, but she'll be one of the Ministration."

"I know that." He sounded irritable. "Why else d'you think I've taught her all I know? She'll be young, energetic — healthy." He spread his hands ruefully, indicating his legs beneath the fur rug. "She'll be full of my ideas, my learning. She'll open their eyes in Council, she'll bring about change for the better. Hah! I'll get the better of them yet!" He began to laugh, but the laughter turned into wheezing.

I leaped across to him in a great fret of fear and thumped his back. "Shall I call the nurse, Sir?"

He shook his head feebly, smiling still. "Stop, I beg you, else I'll be in my coffin — I'm half-dead already!" He subsided against the pillow. "I must hold on to my energy, I've much to do tonight."

"You're not going back?" I said, horrified.

"Of course. I must, I'm the host. Besides, I don't trust Porter Grouted, never have. And here he is, in my house. He needs watching. What plot is he hatching this very moment?" He slammed his hands on his armrests, then looked at me. "But I wanted to speak to you alone, Agnes. Can you do something for me?"

"Of course, Sir."

"I want no one to know of this. Do you give me your word?"

"Yes, Sir."

"Then go to Jukes — aye, and Pegg as well, he's another good, trustworthy man, and I'll need two of them. Tell them to come to the ballroom at midnight and find me there. They are to say they're taking me to bed."

"I'm sure the nurse will want you sooner, Sir."

"But I'll not be going to bed. I want them to take me to the watchtower and to work the lift for me."

"The tower? At that hour?"

"Quiet, Miss," he rapped out with such strength in his voice I jumped. "It must be kept secret. No one — not even Leah, not Silas — must know. Jukes and Pegg must understand this too."

"Yes, Sir, I'll tell them," I said to calm him, though I was filled with apprehension.

"Good. The nurse will bring me to the dancing shortly. Go and announce my full recovery to the company. Let them take it as they will."

And so I left him, grinning wryly to himself in the firelight. He seemed indeed to have made a miraculous recovery.

I found Jukes and Pegg in one of the pantries, setting more clean glasses on trays. I delivered the Master's message, and the three of us looked at one another.

"The Master says no one is to know," I said. "Not even Mr. Silas himself." They nodded their white wigs at me.

"Don't let the Master do anything unwise," I begged. "He's feverish and troubled tonight."

Then I went to the Great Hall, to the assembled gentlemen. The ladies had gone to their chambers to repair their makeup and put on their bird masks once more; the gentlemen would follow them shortly.

I felt very much alone as I went in through the door, pushing aside the heavy tapestry. The drowsy footman, leaning against the wall, looked as if he'd been at the liqueurs himself and leaped to move it too late.

They were clustered around the top table, chairs drawn up, wigs close together, voices low, and on the table a great muddle of decanters and empty glasses. Silas was among them and had seated himself not far from the Lord Protector.

No one saw me but the fool, still crouched behind Porter

Grouted's chair. He did a little caper, but the clinking of his chain wasn't noticed.

My feet faltered. There were too many men. But as I turned to slip away, I was seen.

"It's the wench Gilbert asked for," someone said.

Silas pushed his chair back and came striding over to me, his face flushed with wine. "What news?" His breath fumed in my face; he lowered his voice. "Why did he want you? What did he say?"

Beyond him, Lord Grouted rose to his feet. I bobbed a nervous curtsy as the Protector's hard gaze rested on me. "Come closer, lass," he said. "Tell us, how is the Master of Murkmere?"

"Better, My Lord," I said, trying to sound fearless. "He'll be rejoining you when the dancing begins."

Lord Grouted's face moved not a muscle. "Excellent," he said.

In the passage Scuff rushed up to me. "Mistress Crumplin's asking for you, Aggie. We need help in the kitchens. Can you find a parlor maid?"

"I'll come myself," I said. "Has the mistress gone through to the ballroom yet?" Most likely Leah wouldn't give me a thought, but perhaps I should let her know my whereabouts.

"She went to the Master's room," said Scuff.

"To the Master? Are you sure?"

She nodded, wide-eyed with all the excitement. "I saw her going in just now."

In the kitchens I had no time to worry about Leah or her father. Servants ran in continually, laden with trays of used glasses from the Great Hall; water bubbled in the pewter bowls hung above the fire, and everywhere washed plates were stacked in dripping piles. The air was thick with steam, perspiring bodies, the smell of leftover food. Above the hubbub Mistress Crumplin stood shouting orders, her face flushed with ale and power.

Out in the stable yard the great fire that had roasted the oxen had been subdued. Through the window I could see the glow of the dying fire against the darkening sky, as the youth in the hat damped down the last embers with a cloth.

I found myself a voluminous apron to cover my skirt and busied myself helping. A thread of music wound faintly into the room each time the door banged open. The musicians were tuning up again; soon the dancing would begin.

A flustered maid tottered in with a silver tureen, which she dumped unceremoniously on the table. "Mistress Crumplin, they want the fire in the library stoked up and a decanter of port left for them."

"Slow down, girl. I can't make head nor tail, 'deed I can't. How many's to be in there?"

"Only two," panted the girl. "The Lord Protector himself desires a private word with Mr. Silas."

I felt my heartbeats quicken.

"Well, go to, girl. Make the room ready."

"I can't, Mistress. Mr. Silas says the Great Hall must be cleared urgent now."

"I'll go to the library," I said, trying to hide my eagerness.

Mistress Crumplin eyed me suspiciously, but had no choice in the matter. I knew she was as curious as I was about this private word, but at least she stood a good chance of hearing it later from Silas himself, whereas I had none. My only chance would be somehow to hear it for myself. I was sure they would discuss the significance of the Master's speech. It was something I should hear, for Leah's sake.

I took a decanter and two port glasses from one of the butler's pantries and put them on a tray, then hurried to the library. Masked guests passed me, but I kept my head down as befitted a maid. I hoped none of them would notice the night-blue taffeta beneath my damp apron.

The library was chilly and silent. Candles still burned from before dinner, but the fire was almost out. A few logs smoldered darkly.

I put the tray down on the drum table and looked around. My eye lit on the bay of long windows, the curtains still drawn back. It was twilight now, the time when curtains should be drawn in a grand house.

I freed the heavy lengths of velvet from their bindings and let them flop down over the diamond panes. Then I poked the fire and threw on more logs.

I was brushing wood dust from my apron when I heard footsteps outside. There was just enough time to dart across the room, almost slipping on the polished boards in my haste, and slide in behind the nearest curtain.

XXIV

Evil Schemes

The curtain was thick and smelled of dust. I turned my face sideways, so I could breathe. A whisper of damp evening air came through the badly fitting panes. My heart was thumping in my ears, and my dinner curdled in my stomach.

They came in together without speaking, Lord Grouted and Silas.

I heard the chink of the chain that meant the fool, Gobchick, was being led by the Lord Protector, and the shuffle and slap of bare feet on the floorboards. There was a grunt and the stiff creaking of leather as Porter Grouted settled himself in one of the chairs, and a yelp from the fool, no doubt kicked away by his master, poor thing.

I imaged Silas standing, not sitting, his pale, handsome face framed by the collar of his black silk frockcoat. He spoke first.

"A glass of port, My Lord?" His voice was as deferential as always.

There was another grunt from Porter Grouted, a pause, then I heard his voice, flat and nasal. "That's better, now that the damned thing's off!"

There was the scratch of feathers across the leather-topped table as the great Eagle head was set down next to the decanter. I pictured Lord Grouted's naked pate, bald and round as a pebble above his black silk suit, flesh bulging in rolls around the bull neck.

"I've a mouth full of dust and fish glue. Pour me a glass, Silas. Have one yourself if you must. But you're to keep a clear head."

There was a whimpering sound. Gobchick, begging for port too, or had his chain been pulled too tight? Then a slurping sound and a belch from Grouted. "Aids the digestion, don't it, port? Nothing like it."

"Indeed, Sir."

"Now, Silas. We've much to discuss."

I held my breath. Silas's hands would be clasped together as if he were praying, his dark, glossy head bent as he listened. I heard Grouted's stubby fingers tap the table.

"So the truth is out. That wench is Gilbert's daughter and he means her to inherit his position. I feel the Ministration owes you thanks for alerting its members to the probability so long ago. You've done well to keep me informed of the girl's progress and her general state."

"Thank you, Sir."

"The remuneration's been sufficient?"

"Most generous, Sir."

"We're grateful. I asked you to find any reason why she might be unfit to inherit. Your reports have been most useful. She's clearly unstable, unsuitable for such rank." *Tap, tap* on the table with those short, squat fingers. "We know why. She's her mother's blood running in her veins."

A noisy swallow, then another, fainter, belch. Lord Grouted's voice went quieter. "Of course, it can't be proved. There were always rumors about her mother's nature, but nothing proved. But it's the excuse we need to block Leah's inheritance. Offspring of the avia cannot take on a Minister's rank and property. If she came into the Ministration, she would desecrate it. There's ancient law forbidding such a thing."

"I've watched Miss Leah closely, My Lord," said Silas. "She's no normal girl. Apart from what she may have inherited through her mother's blood, her father has educated her to hold his own blasphemous views. She could be a dangerous influence in sacred Council, My Lord."

"Then, for the future good of Murkmere the estate should pass into other hands after Gilbert's death. It's what you and I have thought for some time, ain't it so, my boy?" The Lord Protector lowered his voice further, so I could scarcely hear it.

"I've always wanted this estate to be run by one of my most loyal men, Silas, someone who can keep an eye on the Eastern Edge for me. With no heir to Murkmere, we'll have to have an election. It will be time for you to come into your own. I shall see that you do. Everyone will follow my vote, have no fear."

"My Lord, I hardly dared hope that I —"

A loud chortle from Lord Grouted, his voice rasping. "Stuff, boy! You've known it all along. Don't give me that! But I like ambitious young men who think the way I do. And you've done well. You deserve your reward."

"I can't thank you enough, My Lord. I can assure you of my greatest loyalty in Council. I could be useful to you."

"Let's drink to it." Glasses clinked.

"But what of Miss Leah, My Lord? Do you want her banished from Murkmere on her father's death, the gates locked against her? I could give orders that she's to be taken into the heart of the Wasteland and left there."

"I've other plans for Miss Leah."

"My Lord?" There was surprise and wariness in Silas's voice.

"I think we should take Miss Leah into our own keeping when the time comes. For her good, her protection, you understand. When her father dies, I think Miss Leah should become the property of the Ministration." Lord Grouted paused, and I heard him crack his knuckles one by one. "We can make good use of her."

"How, My Lord?"

"We will build her a cage. A cage large enough to hold a girl — or, indeed, to hold a bird — but small enough to be moved easily, to be transported from place to place, all over the country, wherever the need arises."

I felt sick with horror; I couldn't breathe. I heard Lord Grouted get heavily to his feet, begin to stump about the room, dragging Gobchick after him. His voice was suddenly so close by me I could hear the spittle bubble in his mouth, the harsh intake of his breath. I shrank back, as thin as I could make myself. For a moment I thought I'd faint with fear and loathing.

"What a trophy to show the people, she'll be, eh, Silas? A reminder of the punishment the Almighty sends if they don't obey me, His mouthpiece here on Earth."

"You mean we'd exhibit Leah as one of the avia?"

I heard the whack of Lord Grouted's hand on Silas's back. There was triumph in his voice. "You have it, man. The people believe the avia are the stuff of old stories, nothing more. Think of their shock when we produce a living member of that cursed race! Yes, I think we can make timely use of Leah."

The fool's chain rattled. I heard his voice suddenly, high and piping, so close he was almost under my feet. "You've forgotten one thing, Master."

"What's that, my tiny Gobchick?" Grouted's voice was good-humored, amused; he was pleased with his plan.

"There's another meaning to that story, Master. Punishment or . . ."

"Yes, little man?" Grouted's words encouraged but his tone was hard.

"Some see the Almighty's action as compassionate, Master. A fool has no knowledge of *compassion*. A difficult word to understand, for a fool." He would be shaking his head dolefully, the garish red and yellow feathers fluttering. "Aye, Master, *freedom*'s the only word a fool understands, though he knows naught of that, either. 'Twas what the Eagle gave those other fools so long ago, the freedom to choose."

"Freedom?" Porter Grouted hissed it like a blasphemy so that I shivered where I stood.

I heard Gobchick do a little shuffling dance. I saw him in my mind's eye: his thin arms held out winningly, a lopsided smile on his old-young face. "Free, free! Not like me, Master! Not like me!"

There was a roar from Lord Grouted and a frightened squeak from Gobchick. "Where is your whip, Silas?"

"Shall I fetch it, Sir?"

"Don't bother. I'll cuff him instead."

Screams from the little fool, a mad scurry and a rattle of the chain, and then all of a sudden there was a face gazing at me round-eyed, and there he was, hiding behind the other end of the curtain. We stared at each other, mouths open, for hardly more than a heartbeat, then he was yanked away by his chain.

I let out my breath very gently. I heard him slide across the floor, the dull thump of blows. Then a strangely sinister silence.

Lord Grouted, grunting with the effort of the beating, settled himself back into his chair. The decanter stopper chinked as it was lifted, and then there was the rich gurgle of port being poured out. "The other interpretation of the story is not approved." He was still breathing heavily.

Silas's voice, quickly: "Why, no, indeed, it's not, My Lord."

"Not the version I permit in schools."

"Yours is the version the people believe, My Lord." Silas's voice was soft, placatory.

"Tell me, Silas." There was a leathery *creak* as Lord Grouted leaned forward in his chair. "Do you believe the story of the avia?" A pause. "Of course you do! I see it in your face! You're a man of religion, ain't you?"

"I try to be, My Lord," said Silas stiffly.

"So do we all, but some are better at it than others." Grouted chuckled briefly, his good humor restored, but Silas didn't join in.

"You believe the girl may change shape before the people's eyes, don't you, Silas?"

"I believe it's a just punishment," said Silas earnestly, "not least for her blasphemous education. One might even put about the suggestion that it was you who punished the girl in such a way."

"Excellent, Silas, excellent! I like that." There was a pause while Lord Grouted fortified himself with port. "We must wait for Gilbert to die before any of this happens, of course. He's an ill man. It won't be long."

"You wish me to hasten his going, Sir?"

A dry laugh from Grouted. "How do you reconcile murder with all your religious stuff?"

"I believe the Almighty has chosen me as a tool to cleanse Murkmere of its blasphemous past, My Lord." Silas sounded offended. "I'd simply be giving death a helping hand. I'd do appropriate penance, of course."

"Merely joking, man. But you won't need to do anything in Gilbert's case. He's failing daily. I thought he'd go at dinner." A glass clinked back onto the tray. "You're a clever young man, Silas Seed, but I do believe you've forgotten one thing."

"You refer to the swanskin, Sir?"

"Dammit, man, how could I doubt you?" Grouted slapped his thigh in delight. "When I read your last report I thought it was the proof we needed."

"I believe the skin was her mother's, Sir."

"Whether it was or not, it doesn't matter a damn for our purpose. It's a bird's skin, ain't it? We must get hold of it."

"I can seize it tonight while Miss Leah is in the ballroom, Sir."

I heard Grouted suck noisily at his thick lips as he thought. "I don't want her to discover it gone yet. Could be awkward. I'll give you the sign tomorrow while she's playing hostess. You must be certain she doesn't suspect anything before I leave."

"She won't, Sir."

"Good, good. A young girl keeping a filthy swanskin in her bedchamber — sewing it, you say?"

"Yes, My Lord. I saw her with my own eyes."

"It's enough to damn her. She desires to change shape; she wants to be a bird! That's our proof, Silas."

"I shall get it, Sir."

"It will be good to have you running Murkmere, Silas, to know I can trust you. The Eastern Edge is too far-flung from the Capital. It's my most rebellious corner. There have been too many risings recently, too much unrest. But with you here . . ."

"I know the Almighty is with me, My Lord. I'll stamp rebellion out; I'll kill it dead."

"You dealt very nicely with that traitor packman." Grouted was amused, well pleased with his spy. He gave a rumble of laughter, hitting his thighs in satisfaction; and Silas permitted himself to join in with a polite, chilling little laugh of his own.

They were toasting each other when I heard the faint noise outside. Two guests were walking on the grass outside the window. As I stared round, they looked directly at me through the twilight: a hawk and a jay in evening dress.

I'd never thought so fast. While laughter echoed in the room on the other side of the curtain, my hands fumbled at my back. I undid my apron, slowly turned, slowly began to polish the window with the apron, giving the couple a polite smile as I did so and bobbing my head, as any maid should on seeing her superiors.

They walked on unhurriedly without a backward glance. I must have been invisible to them, protected by the dark jigsaw of the leaded panes.

And now the laughter had stopped in the room behind me. I waited, but there was no more conversation. I heard Lord Grouted heave himself up, followed by the heavy tread of his feet to the door.

Had Silas gone too? I couldn't be sure. I sensed he was still there. Did he suspect that someone was hidden behind the curtains? Was he standing in the middle of the room, his head cocked, listening? Surely he couldn't see my feet?

I kept absolutely still. The room was silent, but for the crackle of wood burning.

Suddenly he was at the pair of curtains on my left. I could hear the slither of his silk coat-skirts, the quick, excited hiss of his breath. There was the sharp rattle of brass rings as he wrenched the curtains apart. I clenched my fists and shut my eyes, and waited for him to tug at the thick velvet in front of me.

I would have been discovered, surely, if Lord Grouted hadn't shouted impatiently back into the room, "Well, are you coming with me or not? I think it's time to introduce you to the Council, eh, boy?"

And Silas was gone, almost at a run, his patent shoes clipping the floor, and the curtains still jangling next to me.

XXV

Decision

But Silas wouldn't forget his suspicion; he might come back unexpectedly.

I peered around the curtain. The room was empty, the fire still burning bright. Then I saw the huddle of feathered rags by the leather chair.

Gobchick's eyes were shut, but he was breathing. He was bound tightly to the chair by his chain, which imprisoned his arms brutally as if he were a parcel, and then was wound around the chair leg.

It was difficult to free him. He was heavier than I expected, and I had to be quiet. But finally I pulled the last length of chain from under him and looked at him helplessly. On his gaunt face there were fresh bruises, like stains of blackberry juice. I wanted to weep for him.

Then suddenly he opened a glinting eye and gave me a wink. "Little Missy!"

Relief flooded over me. "Are you much hurt, poor Gob-chick?"

He rolled over and sat up, screwing up his face. "I's had worse beatings. I feigns a little death, and then he stops. 'Tis a fool's life."

"Not anymore." I showed him the loose chain. "You saved me just now, Gobchick, you didn't tell them I was there. I want to save you. You're free."

He looked at me with his sad, old face. I thought he hadn't understood. "Go!" I cried. "Escape the house now, in the dark! They'll not see you, I'll not tell."

"But what use is freedom to me, Missy?" he said. "I'd be afeard of it. 'Tis too big stuff for an old fool."

"Please, Gobchick. You'll never be hurt again. If you go to my aunt in the village, she'll shelter you. I'll tell you how to reach her. She'll get the blacksmith to saw your chain off."

He shook his head, but a smile lit his face.

"Gobchick, please!" I stared at him, nonplussed, not understanding his slowness, desperate for his escape. My hands fell uselessly to my sides. I begged a last time, for I couldn't stay with him longer. "Please, Gobchick, go!"

He reached across and stroked my face, still smiling. "No, Missy. I cannot. 'Tis enough that you gives me the choice."

I knew then that I could not budge him for all my begging. "The story of the avia," I whispered. "Which meaning is true?"

The flames glowed on the bones of his skull, and his wrinkled cheeks were deep crevasses of shadow. "Men invent stories to tell the truth as they sees it. Both meanings is true,

Missy. It all depends on how you sees the nature of the Almighty, whether He be forgiving or no."

"But are the avia real, or invented by men?"

"You ask a fool to tell you the answer?"

"You're the cleverest fool I know, Gobchick."

"I's talked to men who've seen them."

"They've seen the avia?"

"Aye, so they said."

"Then the old story is true."

"One man might see, but another might deny. All men see things differently, little Miss."

I looked into his wise eyes. "How can I save Leah?"

"You will know."

But I didn't know. In truth, I hadn't the faintest idea what I should do.

I stood in the silent passage outside the library in a fever of worry and indecision, my hands pressed to my cheeks. Leah would have left the Master by now; she would have had to rejoin the guests in the ballroom.

What a weak-wit I was to hesitate when she was in such danger, I thought suddenly. *I must tell her the truth about her mother's nature and what the Protector and Silas were plotting. And warn her, if the Master hadn't told her already himself, that he intended to go to the tower at midnight.*

In the silence I heard a drift of music; the dancing had begun again.

I hurried along the passage, which grew hot and bright

with burning lamps as I neared the ballroom. The music grew louder, building to a series of crescendos. The doors were open, and I stood to one side so I was hidden, looking through, searching for Leah.

Beyond me masked couples swirled in the candlelight. On each crescendo the gentlemen flung the ladies from them, but just as it seemed they would fall to the floor, their partners saved them with the flick of an arm, scooping up their limp bodies, drawing them close. Then the pairs careered on, clinging to each other in hectic abandon, the bird heads too big for the frail limbs beneath.

The heat from the lamps made me feel dizzy, so that I had to cling to the doorjamb; the music thudded violently in my ears. Beneath the masks faces glistened and mouths smiled grimly. As the music drove the dancers on, their movements grew more desperate, as if they knew they were doomed, as if they knew only the strongest among them would survive the future.

And strongest of all was the Lord Protector.

I had seen Porter Grouted, and once again he was partnering Leah. Caged already by the ruthless grip of his arms, she didn't see me as he swept her past, the dreadful mask he wore dwarfing her neat head, the bill almost grazing her cheek. I'd never be able to speak to her alone.

But I could speak to the Master.

I looked over to the dais, but he wasn't there. Silas held court instead, surrounded by several members of the Ministration. My eyes searched the ballroom, but the Master was nowhere. Nor could I see Jukes and Pegg among the footmen hovering on the side with trays of drinks and delicacies.

Was it so late? Surely they hadn't left for the tower already?

I slipped up to a footman. "What's the o'clock, please?"

"When I was last in the Great Hall, lass, the clock hand was touching midnight."

"I'm much obliged," I said, and hurried back behind the ranks of footmen to the doors. I'd missed the Master. *What should I do now? Follow him into the night?*

I looked back as I left, at the dais where the Master should have been and where Silas was already producing the smiles, the conversation, and all the appropriate attentiveness of a host. Guests clustered round him, and I could see how he was charming them, nodding at their comments, bending to kiss the ladies' hands, flashing them dark, sparkling glances. They were all succumbing as I'd done. He would go far as Master of Murkmere.

But I would outwit Silas. I'd rob him of the proof he needed. I'd take the swanskin before he did.

I moved quietly away, retracing my steps past the library. It grew darker and colder and I could no longer hear the music.

Then I picked up my skirts and ran, blundering past the flickering candles in their sconces on the walls, until I reached the backstairs. I didn't look behind me. Swift as a squirrel I scurried up to the first landing. This part of the house was abandoned and quiet.

I rushed along the passage and lifted the latch on Leah's door. I saw the glowing candles first, lit ready for her return, then a white face loomed at me, and a raised poker.

"Dog, it's me," I said, as startled as she was. "What are you doing, for heaven's sake?"

"My duty," she said prissily. "Making a nice fire to warm the mistress when she comes to bed. I heard running. You frightened me — 'tis like the grave up here alone. What are you doing?"

She had been stirring up the embers of the fire, and I could feel their heat on my flushed cheeks. I thought quickly. Her face had its old, tight, wary look.

"The mistress needs a wrap," I said. "She wants some air, she says, and it's damp outside." I took a deep breath and marched to the chest.

Dog put her hand to her mouth. Her face screwed into a grimace. "Surely not . . . that?"

"It will keep her warm."

"But Aggie!" She looked as if she'd vomit.

"It's what she's asked for," I said grimly. For a second my hand trembled on the lid, then I flung it back, forcing myself to look at what lay inside.

"Give me a candle," I said.

Silently, Dog passed me the candle in the silver holder from Leah's bedside table. I put my hand in. The feathers curled round my fingertips. In disgust, I gripped a handful of the stuff, squeezing it cruelly tight between my fingers, and wrenched the whole thing out. Dog gave a cry and sank back against the bed.

"Pull yourself together," I said. "It's only feathers. They're wearing them tonight on their faces. At least our mistress doesn't do that."

"But she's not one of the Ministration yet," she breathed. "She has no right. Oh, Aggie, what will they say? It's sacrilege for her to wear such a thing."

I didn't answer. Her frightened eyes watched me as I held the swanskin from me at arm's length and, still with the silver candleholder in my other hand, left the room.

I hurried to my room, where I took down the laundry bag of rough hemp that hung on the door. A maid with a laundry bag would cause no comment. I loosened the string fastening and stuffed the swanskin inside, thankful to hide the foul thing away.

The candle guttered where I'd left it on my dressingtable and something gleamed next to it. I'd used Dog's rush sewing basket when I altered my skirt, and the long sewing scissors stuck out under the woven lid. I looked at them, and on a sudden impulse seized them up.

I took a bodice from the drawer and wrapped the scissors so the points wouldn't cut through the laundry bag, then thrust the parcel down beside the swanskin, drawing the string tight.

This time it would not be I who cut up the swanskin; the Master must do it himself.

It was as I left my chamber, clutching the laundry bag, that I realized I wasn't wearing my maid's apron. I'd left it in the library.

Such panic swept over me then that for a moment I couldn't even recall what had happened to it. I'd used it to polish the window and never put it on again. It must have dropped in a crumpled ball to the floor.

I tried to calm myself. No one would recognize it as mine even if they found it. But if Silas went back and found it himself, he'd know that someone had eavesdropped on his plans. It would be easy for him to discover from Mistress Crumplin who had taken in the port. I had to retrieve it.

While I'd been upstairs, lamps on wrought-iron tripods had been placed along the passage to the library. I felt perilously exposed in my taffeta skirts as I ventured between them, a butterfly following a trail of fire, and I soon knew the reason for them.

There was company in the library. I smelled the bitterness of nero and saw a spiral of smoke float beneath the door. Someone laughed; glasses clinked. Men and women, perhaps two couples in there, resting from the dancing.

I hadn't the boldness to go in. I wasn't dressed as a servant, and what would a companion to the Master's ward want with a crumpled apron? No doubt it had been seen already by one of the guests in there now. And then my heart sank, for suddenly I heard Silas's voice, coming clearly after a lull in the conversation.

I would have known that voice anywhere — low, melodic,

amused — followed by appreciative laughter, as if he had fashioned some witticism to entertain his new patrons.

Clutching the laundry bag, I fled, dodging a startled maid bringing a bowl of sweetmeats to the library. At the ballroom I slowed, but no one inside saw me as I slipped past, into the passage to the kitchen wing.

As I reached the side door to the vegetable garden at last, there was the sound of voices and clatter in the kitchen beyond, the familiar bang as the door was thrust open. A steamy fug rolled round the corner toward me. Someone had come out.

I lifted the latch as silently as I could, almost dropping the bag in my agitation. For a second the door stuck as if it were bolted the other side, but it was only the damp. When I pressed my knee against the wood, it gave suddenly and I almost fell out onto the path.

I let out my breath with a gasp; it seemed I had been holding myself in like an overstuffed bolster for hours. The air was cool and damp, scented with rosemary and thyme, and I could feel moisture on my cheeks and hair.

I'd left the candle behind in my room, and there was no moon to light my way. The stars between the heavy clouds were dimmed, like fish flicking through murky water. It was a long time since I'd braved the night. As I trod cautiously down the path, my old fears returned.

Most birds sleep in the night, but suddenly one may open a gleaming eye and swoop down to tear apart the disturber of the darkness. I thought of the Night Birds — ravens and crows and daws — and I shuddered, and my free hand found its way to my amber and didn't let go.

The vegetable garden wasn't silent; frightened, I listened.

Gradually I realized that the sound it held within its walls wasn't the rustle of wings or the stealthy creep of bird claws on bare earth, but the echo of music from the ballroom. I fancied I could even hear conversation carried on the air, the reassuring mumble of people talking.

I calmed myself enough to find the door in the wall, past the black lines of raspberry canes. Through it, and I was behind the stables. Between the buildings I could see the yard lit with lamps. No one was about, or so I thought, until the youth that had been tending the pyre in the center crossed the cobbles not far from me.

It gave me a start, and perhaps I moved too quickly, for he looked up, and light flickered along the brim of his hat. But he didn't call out; he hadn't seen me; I was too deep in shadow. As soon as I could I dodged behind the wall of the coach house, my shoes soundless in the damp grass.

Even against the dark sky, it was easy to see the tower on the rise. I hurried across the open ground, thankful that without moonlight I couldn't be seen. The grass had been cut recently and the ground was smooth. Even so, the hem of my beautiful skirt was soon wet through.

It wasn't long before I was in the copse at the top of the rise, with the rank green smell of nettle and fern in my nostrils, the bushes dark around me. The hollows were pools of black. Gripping the laundry bag, I stopped to catch my breath.

Then a twig snapped somewhere close. I stood absolutely still, straining my ears. My heart began a desperate rhythm. I quivered with it from head to foot. Someone had followed me. Silas?

Air moved through the undergrowth. Leaves shivered, shadows spun and flickered, dark on dark, drawing nearer. He was so close now that I could feel his damp breath on my face.

It was only the breeze, a little night breeze finding its way around the dips and hollows of the copse. The undergrowth was alive with secret movement.

A tiny creature ran out of the bracken close to where I stood trembling, a stoat perhaps; I could see only the shine of its eyes. But there would be other creatures about, not humans, but animals going about their business in the night, moving over leaves and twigs, making noises of their own.

I went on cautiously, and my hand felt for my amber again.

Then, very quickly, the ground opened out and the tower was above me. I could sense its mass rising up into the sky, and as my shoes trod smooth grass again, there it was, blocking out the clouds and stars.

What if the Master were not up there after all? The thought of negotiating those stairs to the top in enclosed darkness and then finding empty rooms — I stopped myself imagining further.

On the ground the black bones of the pulley stuck up untidily. The dark circle that enclosed the chain was stationary and silent, no grating of links to tell me the lift was still on the move. But when I looked up I could see the black shape of the lift hauled up against the top window. There was no light shining out; they must have taken their lamps to the bookroom.

So I needn't have worried. The Master was already up there.

XXVI

The Open Window

The walls of the tower were gritty and damp under my fingers. I felt my way around like a blind man, until I reached the oak door and fumbled to find the latch. It lifted smoothly, and I stepped into the ground-floor room. Either Jukes or Pegg had lit the candles in the wall brackets, but beneath the arch the stairs looked shadowy and steep.

I scrambled up to the landing, trying not to trip over my skirts; my soft slippers were soundless on the oak stairs. The black block of the lift hung against the landing window, shadowing the floorboards, and the door to the bookroom was open, the three men in the lamplight inside with their backs to me. Unnoticed in the darkness, I watched them.

My first feeling was one of relief that the Master was doing nothing more dangerous than sitting before the desk, his body humped awkwardly forward in the wheelchair, a footman standing on either side of him. He was clutching a quill pen in his hand, and the papers spread in front of him in a pool of candlelight were covered with close black handwriting. A fire had been lit, and also the candelabra on the mantel, but at night the room was cheerless with its shadowy brick walls and long black window.

The pen scratched across the yellowed parchment. The two men stood silently, exchanging a glance over the Master's bent head: Jukes, lanky-limbed; Pegg, shorter, but barrel-chested and strong. Though his strength was needed for the lift winches, I'd never warmed to Pegg. I didn't want either of them there when I gave the Master the swanskin.

The Master stopped writing and handed the pen to Jukes. "Bring up a chair. You can't write standing."

Jukes fetched a chair obediently and, having seated himself, wrote something briefly, while Pegg fetched another chair from against the wall. Then Pegg took the pen, the chair creaking as he sat down. The sheets were passed to him, and he gave them a cursory glance before he scrawled something, using much sand for blotting.

"Good," said the Master. "Thank you both for coming out at such an hour. This had to be done tonight, you understand."

He tried to collect the sheets together, but his fingers fumbled.

"Sir," I said quickly, coming into the room, "Sir, it's Agnes Cotter. I need to speak with you on an urgent matter."

The footmen rose to their feet, startled. The Master looked up from the parchment with an effort; I saw with a shock how ill he looked. The flesh of his face had sunk and his eyes, large and glistening, swam in their sockets. With difficulty he fixed them on me. "Agnes? What are you doing here? Has Leah sent you?"

"I've not seen Leah, Sir. I've brought you something." I held the laundry bag out to him.

His gaze flickered. "What is it?"

I looked at the footmen: Pegg glaring suspiciously, Jukes expressionless as ever. "Sir, I beg a word with you alone."

"It's not possible, Agnes. I must finish here before the Protector catches up with me."

"Sir," I said urgently, not caring now whether the footmen heard. "I have something in this bag, something that was your wife's and now endangers Leah. Please, let me tell you —"

"You'd best leave us," he said curtly to the footmen. "Stay close. I'll call you." As they left the room reluctantly, closing the door behind them, he rubbed his hand across his brow with the utmost weariness. "Quickly, Agnes."

I went to him, holding the bag out before me. "I've tried to destroy it once," I said in a low voice. "Now you must do it."

But I feared he no longer had the strength.

I thrust its softness at him and he took it involuntarily. I saw him turn paler still. He knew what it was. He made no move to loosen the drawstring, but sat motionless with the bag on his knees.

"Sir, this is what Leah has been keeping in her room. They know about it, Lord Grouted and Silas. I've heard them say things tonight that threaten her."

He took the bag and flung it from him with surprising

power. The wrapped scissors inside made a soft thud as it landed against the far wall. "Leah will be Mistress of Murkmere! She must be!"

I shook my head. "Sir, all these years Silas has been spying for the Protector. They mean to prevent Leah from inheriting the estate. They want to steal the swanskin as proof that she's unsuitable."

"Silas?" He interrupted me, his face working. "What are you talking about — spying?" It was as if he had taken in only one piece of what I'd said. I'd said it too fast for a sick man; I hadn't explained properly.

"Silas has been spying for Lord Grouted," I said patiently. "Silas wants to take over the estate in Leah's place, and Lord Grouted will back him."

"Silas?" he repeated, as if confused. "Silas wants this?"

"I overheard their plans only an hour ago. Sir . . ." I leaned closer, "Sir, you must decide what to do. You're still Master here. You must dismiss Silas immediately."

He reared up in his chair. "How dare you tell me what to do? You tell me lies about Silas. . . ." He fell back, put his hand to his left arm and grimaced.

"When have you known me tell lies, Sir? There's more. Let me start at the beginning. I was in the library and hid when they came in, Silas with Lord Grouted. I overheard everything."

"Has he betrayed me then?" He sounded confused, pathetic, his fire gone. "But he'll not take Murkmere. I've other plans. If Leah . . ." He looked at me, his voice tailing away as if he'd forgotten what he wanted to say next.

"Sir, if they have the swanskin, they have Leah in their power," I said desperately, willing him to grasp it. "They plan to put her in a cage with the skin and wait for her to change shape. But we can destroy it now. Without it she'll remain as she is. She can escape from them tonight."

I went over and picked up the laundry bag, offering it to him again. "I implore you, destroy it now, Sir."

He was frowning at me as if trying to focus, or perhaps he'd understood the danger at last; but he didn't take the bag.

"Please, Sir, we must hurry. I must go back and tell Leah what I heard, help her leave secretly."

He looked at me in astonishment, as if I'd gone mad. "But she is to be Mistress of Murkmere," he said, outraged. "She can't leave."

Then abruptly he called for the footmen, as if there were nothing more to say.

Jukes loomed behind me. His hand fell on my shoulder. "You must go, Miss," he said quietly. "The Master's tired, and should be in his bed. We'll tidy the business away, then Pegg and I will get the lift working."

I stood hopelessly on the landing with the bag as Jukes closed the door to the bookroom against me. I looked at the rough brick walls, the dark shapes of the lift machinery; beneath me were unreachable wood joists supporting the floor, and the struts and props that held the structure of the tower secure. I couldn't bear to destroy the swanskin again myself; the best I could do was hide it. But there was nowhere here.

A creaking sound came from inside the bookroom; a cool dampness drifted under the door, the smell of the night. They must have opened the long window. Was the Master faint? But the next moment I heard his voice, loud and hoarse, though I couldn't make out what he said.

Suddenly there was the grind of the chair's iron wheels, as if it were being moved, then the rasp of feet dragging over the floorboards with sickening slowness. I scarcely understood what I was hearing, yet suspected I did all too well.

But even as I went to open the door, there was the thud of something heavy falling as if felled by a tremendous blow, followed by absolute silence.

The two footmen were standing frozen, and between them on the floor lay the Master. His body was crumpled and seemed oddly small out of his chair, his legs twisted sideways.

I must have cried aloud, for Jukes turned an ashen face toward me.

"What have you done? Have you killed him?" I said, and felt my eyes start from my head in horror.

I knelt down and saw his face was gray, his eyes closed. His wig had fallen off and lay beside him pathetically, like a bundle of knitting wool. I put down the laundry bag and tried to straighten him.

The empty seat of the chair would be too vast for such a

little, stunted body. *How can I fit him back in?* I thought, pulling vainly at the dead limbs. *He'll roll around.*

"I tried to stop him . . . ," gasped Jukes. "I refused . . ."

My mouth was dry. "What?"

"I refused to bring out the flying machine," he whispered, and he buried his face in his hands, great grown man that he was, and started to shake.

I looked over sharply, and saw a gap of darkness between the double doors. "Who opened those doors?"

Jukes looked up, his eyes wet. "It was Pegg, before I stopped him."

Pegg started back. "Not I."

"It was indeed!" said Jukes bitterly. "You wished the Master to harm himself! Why didn't you hold him down, as I tried to do?"

Pegg looked sullen. "He was set on it, weren't he? He wanted to rejoin his wife, he said, and when we stopped his chair, he upped himself and went to walk."

Beside me the Master gave a groan.

Pegg jumped back, his cocksure manner gone. "He never lives?"

"He does," I said, and relief made my knees tremble, so that I shook like a sapling in the wind.

The Master was breathing painfully; we could all hear it. His eyes were still shut; he was unconscious.

"Go!" I said. "Don't dally here!"

"What should we do, Miss?" said Jukes weakly.

"Get help, of course," I said. "Bring the nurse and her

medicines. Tell Miss Leah to come. Fetch more men and a pallet. He must be carried back to the house." I reached up and grasped Jukes's tailcoat. "And Jukes, be careful whom you tell. Not Lord Grouted or Mr. Silas, you understand."

"But shouldn't Mr. Silas —"

"No!" I cried frantically.

"I understand, Miss," he said, subdued. "Shall Pegg stay with you?"

I shook my head, for I did not trust Pegg, now even less than before. "It will take two of you to do all that. But hurry!"

"The papers, Miss. Should we cover them?"

"Just go!"

They left, Jukes unwillingly, with a gray-faced look, first at the desk and the sheets of parchment, then at his master. They took the lamps with them, and as they went the room flickered in the light of the few candles left. I heard their boots clatter down the stairs.

I lifted the Master's head onto my lap and cradled him, so that he should be more comfortable, but I knew it would make little difference to him now. I thought briefly of the rooks of Murkmere, those harbingers of doom, but then dismissed them. Over the past months I'd grown to realize that no bird can influence man's death. Men go when their time is done, and the Master's time was sifting away as I held him.

A breeze drifted in through the open window and lifted my hair and the hair that had fallen across his forehead. A strand was tickling his closed eyelids and I smoothed it away.

His breath was dry and crackling in his chest. Behind us the double doors closed and clicked shut in the draft. I didn't think they would ever be opened again.

I'd never sat with a dying man before, but I know when men are dead, and so I knew the very moment the Master died. I sat in the silence and I felt him going from his body, going away through the open window into the sky. I had such a sense of it that I even looked to see if I could see a shape, flying.

But I could see nothing. Souls are invisible, anyway. But when I looked back at his face I saw that it looked joyful. He was happy to be going out into the sky to find his wife.

In the end he hadn't needed a flying machine.

I laid him back on the floor and put my lace shawl over him. I pulled it over his face, in case his eyelids should shrink back, and then down over as much of his body as I could, as I'd seen the Elders do with our village dead.

I'd scarcely finished when I heard the first feet climbing the stairs outside, but only one pair, and soft-soled, so I knew it must be a woman.

It was Leah. Her breathing was hard and quick as if she'd run all the way, and her chest heaved with it so that the silver dress shimmered in the candlelight. The hem was marked darkly with grass and dew. I thought stupidly that Doggett would have a hard time getting the stains out.

When she saw that my shawl covered the Master's face,

she gave one great sob that might have been a gasp, and no more. Then she sank down beside him, her eyes like stones. Her shoulders heaved as she caught her breath back.

"He went peacefully," I said. I longed to comfort her, but knew she did not want it. "I believe he wanted to go. He wanted to fly, and so he did."

"I knew it was in his mind." She rubbed at her face as if she wiped invisible tears away. "He was my father such a short time. One little evening."

"He loved you always," I said.

She said, stiffly, "And I loved him. I saw him earlier, and we made everything all right between us."

"He kept the truth about your birth secret for your protection, you know."

"But I would have understood so much more if he'd told me," she said sadly. She gestured at herself. "Why I'm like this, why I'm not like you."

"But you are like me!" I cried. "What are you saying?"

"I take after my mother, Aggie. Blanche Tunstall was one of the avia, I've heard Mistress Crumplin say so often enough. And when he was a youth Silas used to tell me stories about the Master's dead wife to frighten me. I've heard them since my childhood."

"They're only stories," I said quickly. "You are Mistress of Murkmere now. Remember the plans you made? You've so much to do, you'll forget your fancies."

She shook her head. "I can never be Mistress of Murkmere. I've known it a long time."

She pulled back the shawl and stared down. The Master didn't look frightening. He looked asleep, not dead at all, until the sense came strongly that there was no one there. She bent her head so that her own face was close to his. Her hair had slipped down, and it covered the dead face like a fine, shining web. I thought she whispered, "I'm sorry," before she pulled the shawl back up.

"I've nothing to stay for, now," she said. "I would have waited, for his sake, but now he's gone."

"But they can never prove anything about your mother," I said. "You can be Mistress of Murkmere, Leah. They won't be able to stop you. They can't prove anything without the swanskin."

She looked at me. I thought she pitied me; she spoke gently. "You don't understand, Aggie, do you?"

There were steps on the stairs far below us.

"That will be the men," I said, cursing them for coming at the wrong moment, before I'd reasoned with her.

"Men?" she said. She looked alarmed.

"I sent Jukes to bring men to help, Pegg too," I said. "But they'd have told you first, Jukes would have done that. Didn't they come into the ballroom?"

"Jukes never told me," she said. "I never saw him at all, nor Pegg. It was Gobchick's dream that brought me here. He whispered to me in secret. He said he'd seen the Master lying here, and a white bird waiting in the Wasteland. I knew then I'd be too late. But I never saw Jukes."

"Then what happened to Jukes?" I said.

The footsteps were rising closer, quick, hard, purposeful feet. Only one man. We looked at each other, then at the door.

It was Silas who came in.

We must both have looked shocked to see him, for he gave us a curt nod. "The footmen came to me. They told me what happened."

"Jukes told you?" I said, in disbelief. My heart began to pound. I edged toward the laundry bag, still lying on the floor a little way from the Master.

"You forget. The servants trust me." He stared, expressionless, at the Master's body, then at Leah crouched beside it. "I see I am too late."

"Where are the men?" she asked pathetically. "We should move my father to his room, to lie in state."

"No one's coming," said Silas shortly. "Not until I summon them myself."

"Then, I beg you, do so," she cried, twisting her hands together. "Or one of us must. It's not fitting that he stays here any longer. Aggie, will you go?"

"Gladly," I said, getting up eagerly from the floor and seizing my chance to pick up the laundry bag. Now I could take it into the dark with me and hide it safely.

"You will not go anywhere, Agnes," said Silas. "No one is leaving this room. I need to establish one or two things."

"What things?" I said fiercely. I stood, gripping the bag, and looked at the open door behind him. "You've no right to stop us leaving." It was as if he already thought himself Master of Murkmere.

"No right," he agreed smoothly. "But the means to prevent you."

And he brought out a tiny, wicked-looking pistol from a pocket inside his silk frockcoat, and pointed it straight at me. "First, you must answer some questions, Miss Agnes Cotter."

XXVII

Silas

My legs trembled so that I thought I'd fall, but I didn't let go of the bag. I'd never seen such a beautiful, deadly object. Out of the corner of my eye I saw Leah had put her hand to her mouth.

"Where did you get that pistol?" she whispered.

Silas smiled. "Your father gave it me before the ball. It's illegal — imported, of course — but your father always broke the rules. He wanted me to carry it for your protection. I suppose he thought you might be in danger once the truth about your birth was out. There's sweet irony in that, don't you think? I'm protecting you now. You wish to live, don't you?"

From the floor by her father's body, Leah nodded, speechlessly. I couldn't think. I stared at Silas like a mouse stares at a cat, and held the laundry bag against me.

"You were in the library, weren't you?" he said to me. "It's useless to deny it. Mistress Crumplin confirmed it."

"I don't deny it," I said, with a dry mouth.

"And have you told anyone what you heard?"

"I haven't had a chance," I said bitterly.

"Say nothing," said Silas. His hand holding the gun was steady, and steady too were his dark eyes staring at me with their threat.

"What are you talking about?" cried Leah, half-rising. "Put your gun away! Your master lies dead and you flourish a weapon! Where's your respect?"

"I have none," he said shortly. "Certainly none for you. I know what you are."

"What?" she cried, white-lipped.

"Daughter of the cursed." His mouth curled. "It's not meet you inherit the estate and sit with the Ministration."

Leah rose to her feet slowly. During the last few months she had grown almost to his height, and her eyes glittered sharp as daggers as she stared across at him. "The Ministration? You believe its members are better than I?"

"You'll never join them. It would be a desecration. There's proof you've inherited your mother's nature. You're avian." He kicked the Master's wig, and it slid away over the floor.

"You have to prove that," I said furiously. "Murkmere is Leah's by the law of inheritance. She's rightful Mistress here now. It's all in the will. The Master leaves everything to his daughter."

His eyes glinted dangerously. "What do you know of the will, Agnes?"

"Nothing," I said. "I've never seen it. But I know it's so. He told me."

His eyes moved from me to the desk, but the pistol still held steady. "I believe you are a liar, Agnes," he murmured. "If I'm not mistaken, it looks as if he was working on it tonight. And you were here, Agnes. Did you sign anything, witness anything? Did you?"

I shook my head, wondering how steady his trigger finger was. "He was writing, that's all I saw."

Silas moved sideways to the desk, pointing the pistol at me. The air coming through the black window lifted his sleek hair a little, ruffled the papers as he bent over them. He had no spectacles with him. He thrust aside the older, yellower sheets of parchment impatiently. It was what had been added tonight that he was interested in, and that sheet was still covered with sand. He shook the sand off onto the floor and held it out closer to the candle, squinting at it. The pistol didn't waver as he read it.

"I see Jukes's name here, and Pegg's. They've both put their signature to this." His eyes held the most intense and chilling hatred as he looked at me. "You have no knowledge of this?"

"N-no," I stammered, my heart thumping.

He put the pistol down carefully so that the muzzle was toward us, and sat down in one of the chairs pulled to the desk. "I fear Mr. Tunstall wasn't in his right mind when he wrote this tonight."

Leah gasped. "That's my father's will, his wishes for the future. What are you going to do? You can't alter it!"

"Indeed? Nothing's simpler, I fear; merely a matter of writing in my own wishes. I've had to sign for him often enough when he's been sick. I know how his hand writes. My own could do so while I slept." The look he gave Leah was venomous. "My left hand is quite practiced now, thanks to you."

He took up a quill and dipped it in the silver inkpot. Leah slumped back against the wall. "What is it you'll write?"

"That I'm to inherit, not you," he said, and his lips drew back in a smile. "I could wait for the Protector's support in my election, but I have the chance right here. I might as well take it. Then I'm blessed by both master and mentor. And I know the Almighty wants me in a position where I can carry out His will."

His anger had died away; he looked at her with revulsion and regret. "Murkmere would never prosper under you. All these years I've sent reports on your behavior to the Lord Protector. I know you're not suitable for such rank. I even know you've found the swanskin that was your mother's."

Leah's whole body tensed; there were goose bumps on her bare arms.

"So where is it?" he continued softly. "Where's the swanskin? You've been keeping it in your linen chest, haven't you? But it's gone tonight. Where is it?"

Leah had not known that. Startled, she turned to me, and I, like the guilty thing I was, put the bag swiftly behind my back, and they both saw it.

"What's in that bag, Agnes?" asked Silas slowly. His body

craned over the desk. The quill in his left hand shone with ink, but for the moment he had forgotten the will.

"Nothing for you," I said defiantly.

"You've the swanskin!"

"Aggie?" whispered Leah. She looked as if she could scarcely breathe.

I said nothing. Silas gazed at me thoughtfully, brought the quill to the parchment as if to start scratching out the Master's words. I could see the pistol resting on the green leather cover of the desk, the exquisite mother-of-pearl handle, the ridged black nose, so neat, so elegant.

"It is the swanskin," I said at last.

"I thought so," he said, with satisfaction. "Now give it to me, and you and your mistress can leave here."

"Don't, Aggie!" cried Leah.

There was a terrible silence. They were both waiting for me: Leah with bent head, as if she'd given up, as if she knew that I could only surrender it now; Silas smiling grimly, quill poised.

The fire gave a dying crackle. The breeze blew in from the long black window, stirring the papers on the desk.

I thought of Leah's life if she had the swanskin and gave up her girlhood: the coldness, the loneliness, the strangeness of living in another nature. It was what I'd been battling to protect her from almost all the time I'd been at Murkmere. If I gave the swanskin to Silas, she'd remain human; she'd find a new life away. I'd go with her, willingly.

She'd be my sister, my friend, forever. Together we could do anything.

"Come, girl," said Silas roughly. "Or do you want me to take it for myself?" He looked meaningfully at the pistol.

I opened the neck of the bag and reached my hand in. I felt the feathers soft against my fingers. He watched me, his eyes narrowed. He wasn't absolutely sure that it was in there. I sensed his uncertainty and, though it was pointless now, felt a bitter pleasure.

Then slowly I brought my hand out.

Silas couldn't see what I held, and his impatience wouldn't let him wait. He lunged over the desk, and the pistol fell to the floor, rattling away against the brick wall.

I came close to the desk, dropped the bodice that had wrapped the scissors, and pointed them straight at him. He gave a grunt of shock and jerked his chair back involuntarily, half-rising, hampered by the clutter of chairs at the desk. His own chair fell over and skidded away a little behind him. I threw the laundry bag at Leah, and he tried to dodge past me to get at her. Then he saw I was in earnest to stop him, that I was advancing on him with the scissors before me, the long blades glittering silver, sharp as swords. He thought I meant to kill him, and he gasped and lurched back again. And I came closer still to him with those murderous points, so that Leah could escape through the open door behind me.

I didn't dare look at her. I pointed the blades so they touched his throat. And he gasped again and retreated still farther, close to the window. His legs caught in the over-turned chair.

And the next thing, he was falling backward, almost grace-fully, a backward dive straight through the open window, and all I could see was the black hole of his mouth open in astonishment as he fell into the night.

I stared at the empty window blankly. It had happened so quickly, I couldn't take it in. I almost expected him to flip back up and jump nimbly into the room.

But nothing happened. There was silence outside, then an owl hooted. Behind me in the room I could hear Leah's quick, shocked breathing. I began to shudder all over, and the scissors dropped from my hand and fell to the floor with a dreadful noise. I put my hands to my eyes and I think I started to weep, though no tears came.

Leah came over to me. She put a hand on my back speech-lessly. It was a gesture of comfort, I think, though she was never one for showing affection.

I took my hands from my eyes at last. "Blow out the candles."

She nodded, and seized up a candle-snuffer. We both went about the room extinguishing the light from candelabra and lamps. It was eerie in the darkness, with the night blowing in on the Master's still body and the knowledge that Silas lay directly below us.

"I can't look," I whispered. "Is he dead, do you think?"

She hesitated a moment, then went to the window and peered out, clinging to the window frame to steady herself. There was no sound from below.

"He's lying oddly, not moving." I couldn't see her face, but her voice was emotionless.

"Then I've killed him," I said, my voice small and trembling.

"Greed killed him," she said. "Besides, he would have killed us to get the estate, if we'd defied him. You did bravely. Murkmere's well rid of him."

"But you don't want Murkmere."

"I have to leave, Aggie. I can't stay here. I can't remain as I am any longer." She paused. "Was that why you gave me the swanskin? Because you understood at last?"

"I don't understand," I said desperately. "I'll never understand. All I understand is that you must make the choice for yourself."

She came close to me and took my hands, pressing them earnestly. "All my life I've felt two people. It was as if I had a second skin, a shadowskin, that was waiting for me to grow into it. When I found the swanskin I understood."

I said nothing; I could do nothing more for her. A terrible inevitability settled on me like a weight.

"We must leave the tower now," she said. "I know Jukes better than Silas did. He's a good man, and will come here when he doesn't have word from Silas. He'll make sure my father's buried decently. Say nothing of what's happened tonight, except that Silas lost his footing and fell."

I tried to pull myself together. "We must put the room to rights. There shouldn't be any signs of a struggle."

We did our best in the dark, hastily picking up the chairs.

I picked the pistol up by the barrel cautiously and shut it away in the desk drawer.

"Come on," said Leah impatiently.

"Where are we going?" I said, but I knew.

"To the mere."

I hung back but she pulled at me. "Come."

And of course I followed her.

She didn't bend to kiss her dead father as she left. The white lace shawl lifted a little in the draft as she hurried past his body. I followed her with a heavy heart.

We left the candles burning on the stairwell; they couldn't be seen from outside. Then we slipped out into the night. The darkness was lifting a little; black clouds were blowing away like rags and exposing lighter sky. Soon it would be dawn.

We saw Silas's body, spread-eagled and unmoving, on the ground to our right as soon as we came out through the door. His face was a white blur on the black grass, his features indistinguishable. Leah put a restraining hand on my sleeve in case I wanted to see the body closer; but I couldn't touch that clammy flesh; I let her go over and feel for a pulse. When she shook her head, we didn't speak.

We ran across the open ground then, and into the copse. Leah's dress glimmered in the shadows; she clutched the bag to her breast. "Hurry!"

I sped after her, tripping over roots and nettles, my long skirts catching on brambles; but I was careless of them. My mind was dwelling fearfully on what was to come, yet I was determined to be with her till the last.

And then what would I do? How could I bear to lose her?

Inside I was crying like a baby, yet I said nothing, and Leah said nothing to me, but continued sure-footed over the dewy grass as if her life depended on it.

We came down to the mere. In the distance a white mist hid the island and the reedbeds, not the gray murk of winter but the soft, dense haze of late summer. Closer to the shore the water was silver, reflecting the sky in which the first streaks of dawn were beginning to appear.

Leah's face was filled with the same pale glow. She was part of sky and water, and I was not.

Miserably, I followed her along the path to the boathouse. She'd been here with a knife recently and cut the nettles and brambles back. Around us waterfowl woke sleepily, quacking and splashing into the water at our appearance.

She stopped at last when we had reached the boathouse and turned to face me, clasping the bag to her. We looked at each other. Our skirts were ripped, our hair hanging down around our pale faces.

"You can't come with me now, Aggie," she said. "This last part I have to do by myself."

I nodded dismally.

"I'll take the boat to the island," she said, strong and implacable.

"The rowing boat? Is it safe?"

"I've tried it out before now. It doesn't leak."

"Then what?" I said in a low, choked voice. "Where will you go?"

"To the Capital, of course," she said. "I'll live in the waterways, the canals. I'll be able to see for myself what's happening in the seat of power!" She was deliberately trying to cheer me. "People will never guess that outside their gilded water palace lurks a spy! And then I'll come back and tell you what I've discovered."

"How can you do that?" I said, and felt my anger rise at her frivolity.

"I'll come back, Aggie." She gestured at herself. "Like this. My mother changed. So will I. All I have to do is want it enough, to choose to change."

"And will you?" I said, and I felt my eyes fill with tears.

"Yes, to see you. I promise."

I began to weep. "Don't go, don't leave me behind!"

"You have something to do for me, Aggie. You must tell me if I ask too much."

"What is it?" I said, hiccupping, hating her for her coldness.

"It's not only for me, but for my father. It's in his will. You don't know he added a codicil tonight, the addition that Silas was so anxious to obliterate. When I went to see him after dinner he told me what he was going to write.

"He's left you the estate to run in my place, Aggie. 'If anything should happen to my daughter, Agnes Cotter is to run Murkmere in her stead, with the help of whomsoever she shall choose.' That's what he wrote in the will tonight. I think he knew he had to do it urgently. He knew he was dying.

"I said I was agreeable to it, and I am, most fervently. There's no one who could do it better."

Her eyes held the silver of the water; she was shining all over in the silver dress as if an energy made of light coursed through her. "He must have known I'd never take over here. He liked to convince himself otherwise, but he must have known." She turned to me impatiently, eager for my reaction. "What do you say, Aggie? Don't say nothing!"

Amazement had dried the tears on my cheeks.

"You will do it for my sake, won't you? For my father's?"

"I'll think about it," I said slowly. "I can't make the decision lightly. There's my Aunt Jennet. I've left her too long. And anyway, what about Lord Grouted? How will he react? And the members of the Ministration?"

"They can't do anything. It's legal, Aggie, it's been witnessed. You won't belong to the Ministration or sit in Council, of course. Lord Grouted may well send spies to watch you, but he won't see you as any danger to him. Murkmere's a backwater. He wanted Silas here so he could send him all around the Eastern Edge to put down rebellion. Now he'll have to send someone else."

"I'll think about it," I repeated stubbornly. "How can I do it by myself?" I thought of the loneliness, and my heart shuddered.

"What about your sweetheart?"

"Jethro?" I said. "He was never a sweetheart, and he cares nothing for me." My eyes filled again. I thought of Murkmere without Leah, and knew it was not possible.

She pressed my hand. "I must go. Please, Aggie. I can't stay while you think about it. Do what's best for yourself. I wouldn't want it otherwise."

I flung my arms around her. "I love you, Leah. Come back."

Her arms came up and she held me briefly. I wondered if she truly loved me, or if she could. But a promise was a promise.

In the boathouse I helped her release the little rowing boat and climb into it. All the time I was choking back tears. When I went back outside, down the wooden steps to the shore, the boat had slipped out into silver water that was as soft as silk.

She brought it around to where I stood. Holding the painter in her hand, she stepped out onto the shore to say goodbye. I knew I would lose her as soon as she began rowing away.

I clung to her, but she disengaged herself gently, looking over my shoulder. "Wipe your tears, Aggie," she said. "There's someone coming for you."

I turned and saw the youth in the brimmed hat striding along the path toward us. The light shone on the brim and on the face beneath, and I saw it was Jethro.

XXVIII

Shadowskin

We stood on the little beach by the boathouse and looked at each other in silence. Jethro must have seen the tear stains on my face, but he said nothing, nor made any move to comfort me. He was red and awkward, and I couldn't dismiss the hurt of so many empty fortnights.

"Why didn't you come?" I said at last.

"My father was taken sick. I couldn't leave him. It's the truth, Aggie, I swear. Then I came immediately to Murkmere to ask for a job, hoping for a glimpse of you. They offered me work in the stable yard, and I took it."

"You followed me to the copse near the tower, didn't you?"

"Aye."

"You saw Silas Seed fall to his death?" I put my hands to my face, and then he did come closer.

"He was a bad man, but men are made so by their time. He'd twisted good and evil in his mind." He took my hands away and held them tenderly. "Tell me what's been happening, Aggie."

And so I did.

Behind us, the little boat was sliding slowly away across the water, toward the misty outline of the island. When I turned to watch, it was as if I sat in it myself. I could feel it rock as I rowed, the tug of weeds on the hull, and in my nostrils was the smell of soaked wood, and white mist like wet wool.

Leah's figure was blurring; I could just see the light glint on the seed pearls she wore like a crown in her hair. I raised my hand and let it drop, and as I did so the swans came gliding out from the reeds and encircled her, drawing her away with them into the mist.

It was as if they were taking her home.

"We'll tell no one, Jethro, no one must go after her."

"If that's what she wants."

I hesitated. "Do you think she'll truly change into a swan?"

He thought for a moment, then said in his slow, considering way, "Does it matter? She's escaped. She's free of Murkmere. It's her choice."

In a choked voice I said, "But what about me? I'm bound. The Master's will imprisons me here now."

"Opportunity's no prison, Aggie. You've the chance to change things."

I thought a little, then looked up at him and smiled. "Since when did you grow so wise, Jethro Sim?"

He put his arm around me. I felt his strength, the steady beat of his heart against me, the muscles that would tend my land. My robin, my Love.

"Will you change things with me, Jethro?"

The Lord Protector ordered that Gilbert Tunstall, Master of Murkmere, and Silas Seed, his faithful steward, both be given the ceremonial burial rites due to them.

The guests, who had come for a ball, finished their visit by attending a double funeral. We stood in the rain under black silk umbrellas, a gathering of ravens surrounding two freshly dug graves.

Later Dog told me that the members of the Ministration always packed mourning clothes, for wherever they went, someone was always certain to die.

I was never questioned about Silas's death.

A tragic accident, they said, though some cast dark looks at me when they learned I'd been alone with Silas beforehand. But Jukes, and even Pegg, insisted that I'd known nothing of the Master's codicil, so why should there have been any foul play? Most agreed that Leah had somehow been involved. The girl had been unstable like her mother, and the fact that she was missing so mysteriously surely proved her guilt.

Of course Lord Grouted demanded that the estate and the Wasteland be searched for her, and all the surrounding villages and towns. But he didn't bother to send men as far as the Capital. A girl alone would never manage to travel so far safely, and then survive there.

When the search had continued for a week without success, the Lord Protector spoke to me. "We can't accept you as a member of the Ministration, but we must now acknowledge your caretakership of the estate. It's a poor place, and you can only do with it what you can." Then he gave me his blessing before he rode away.

It was an ironic gesture. He took most of the servants with him.

But Scuff and Dog stayed with me.

Leah was the closest I've ever had to a sister. I loved her, for all that she was the most provoking, unpredictable girl on this Earth. And now she's gone.

Each year I wait for the first leaf to drift down at the end of summer. It's usually the birches that turn first. I catch a small, yellow leaf in my palm. Then I know it's her birthday, as it was on the day she left; and I go down to the mere and wait for her. I listen for a girl's footfall on the dry path behind me. I imagine her hands over my eyes, her breath hot on the back of my neck.

"Dearest Aggie! I'm back!"

Two birthdays have passed, and Jethro warns me that she may not return, but I don't believe him. She was always curious — like me, Aunt Jennet would say. Sisters, indeed. She'll come back because she'll want to know what's happened to us all here at Murkmere.

And I shall tell her, with my new dignity, "We're managing well. We share the produce, from bad harvests and good, and the village and the estate support each other, as they should. Aunt Jennet runs the household and Jethro's my steward."

At this her eyes will gleam and she'll give me a poke. "You see, Aggie, you had a sweetheart all along and didn't know it!"

Shall I tell her how hard life is here? How sometimes it's too much to bear? Then, even Jethro and Aunt Jennet can't comfort me, and I long for my old carefree days back again, when I knew nothing and had no responsibility.

But love and responsibility go together. I said I'd do this for Leah and I will.

In the tower the books lie untouched, but one day I'll have time to read them.

Leah said the swanskin was her shadowskin.

Perhaps I've grown into my own shadowskin now. I'm no longer the silly, ignorant girl I was when I first came to Murkmere. Perhaps my shadowskin was always there, waiting for me to grow into it.

Jethro has always been doubtful that Leah changed shape. He thinks she rowed on in the mist, beyond the island to the dark scrub on the other side of the lake, and made her escape from Murkmere over the wall into the Wasteland.

But I know the truth.

That first evening I saw her.

❧

The bodies of the Master and Silas had been brought in earlier in the day. They lay side by side on the dais in the empty ballroom, surrounded by the musty incense of dead flowers.

I was in my bedchamber, fastening Leah's old green silk skirt around my waist and trying to feel brave. For I had to face all eyes tonight in my new position as caretaker of Murkmere. The Lord Protector, the portly gentleman, the disapproving stick, the lady with the red mouth — tonight they would pay me attention.

My window was on the latch, and I became aware of a deep throbbing sound coming from outside.

Puzzled, I went over and pushed it farther open. Above the distant cowsheds, the sheep pens, and the sodden meadows of the estate, the evening sky was streaked with dark rain clouds, as if ink had run to spoil its glow.

Then I saw the single swan, flying.

Its wings were haloed with light. They beat the air steadily, like the pulse of a heart. The swan's neck was outstretched, white against the darkening sky. On it flew, purposefully, away from Murkmere, until I lost it among the clouds.

Leah told me once that the Murkmere swans have had their wings clipped; they can't fly. When I told Jethro what I'd seen, he smiled and said it must have been a wild swan from the Wasteland.

But I don't think so. I know it was Leah.

All men see things differently.